Book Two: Awakening

The Callembria Chronicles

Book Two: Awakening

By Heather Ann Hall

The Callembria Chronicles
Book Two: Awakening

Copyright © Feb 2025 Heather Ann Hall
All rights reserved.

No part of this book may be reproduced, stored in a retrieval system, or transmitted in any form or by any means—electronic, mechanical, photocopying, recording, or otherwise—without prior written permission from the author.

This is a work of fiction. Names, characters, places, and events are products of the author's imagination or are used fictitiously. Any resemblance to actual persons, living or dead, events, or locales is entirely coincidental.

ISBN: 979-8-9922498-3-5
Cover art by AmbientPixel Designs
Independently Published
Printed in the United States of America

First Edition: February 2025

DEDICATION:

For Mom and Cyndol

ACKNOWLEDGEMENTS:

Some of you may notice that these acknowledgements are the same as Book One: Prophecy, and that is because I wrote these first two books at the same time, intending to release it as one full novel. When it came time to print, I saw that they needed to be split into two. While my book split changed, my love and gratitude for all of these people in this journey remains the same.

I would like to dedicate this book to my mother, Kathy Cadoux. She has been there since the very start and was always ready and willing to read whatever chapter I came up with next, offering ideas, asking the right questions, and generally just falling into this story with me. Thank you, Mom, from the bottom of my heart. I could not have done this without you!

I also need to dedicate this to my incredible niece, Cyndol Hall, whom I have missed over the years living so far apart. Thank you for letting me use your name in my book. It made me feel closer to you when I couldn't be in real life. And thank you to your brother, Ethan Brendmoen, as well. I hope you both like it!

I would like to thank my husband, Devin Dupuis, who sat patiently by me as I vividly hallucinated on the page while he sat next to me, playing video games or listening to me read aloud to make sure something sounded right. He was never too busy to help me, and that was the very best gift I could ask for! I love you, Favorite!

Thank you to my brother, Brandon Hall, his wife, Gilly, and their son, Cutter. Having you read my book and enjoy it like you did is the coolest possible thing that has come from writing this! I absolutely pictured you reading this to your son like they did in *The Princess Bride*. What an honor.

To my dad, Steve Hall, I love and miss you every day. I wish you could've read this. You would've really loved it. Thank you for always being so supportive of me. Until we meet again.

I would not have the best version of this book if not for the help of my exceptionally talented and amazing friend, Michelle Craddock. Thank you for catching my mistakes and teaching me how to improve. I can never thank you enough. (You should go check out her books! They are wonderful!)

To my best friend, Edna Vicente, thank you for sticking with me all these years, and for not teasing me to my face about all the things I would say about my book that made zero sense, as at the time, they were all still living in obscure connectivity in my head. Also, thank you for reading this!

A huge and heartfelt THANK YOU to all of my beta readers. Thank you for taking the time to immerse yourselves in this book and help me bring this story to life! Your feedback was very appreciated! Athena Dupen, Phil Pinheiro, Adrien Cadoux, and Dustin Hendricks.

And finally, thank you to Matt Derby for getting me a computer when mine died and I didn't have a way to keep writing. Thanks to you, I was able to finish this book!

I love you all! Thank you forever!

Dear Reader,

For almost a decade, I have lived with a magical world inside of my head that no one else could see, hear, feel, or access. On one hand, it was wonderful, having my own little world to escape to, where I could take a backseat to my own life and focus on the lives of others. So what if they weren't all human and had no idea that I existed? I knew that *they* existed, and that's all that mattered to me. I spent many years taking notes on these people, places, creatures, and things, and the crazier I felt, the more I knew I had to write this all down to share with you. So, here it is. My own little world, far, far from home, full of mystery, life, and adventure. I hope you enjoy the ride!

With Love,

Heather

Book One Recap:

The story of *The Callembria Chronicles: Book One: Prophecy* follows multiple characters as they navigate a world of magick, truth, and destiny.

Amy, a young woman from Earth, is fatally shot in a robbery and, after dying on top of her newly acquired amethyst geode, awakens on the planet Callembria as a mermaid, alone on an island with no information. After finding a portal to another part of this new world (otherwise known as a Crannie), she met the ghostly dragon-shifter, Queen Helena of Dragon Moon. Helena has tasked her with finding her grandson, Ibraxus (Brax), who has been lost for centuries, and was married secretly to Amy just before they went missing and were presumed dead. Amy was instructed to tell a magickal ruby "I love you", and that broke the first part of a centuries' old curse that kept King Ibraxus, and his friend Ifyrus, trapped in the ice of Ruskin's Snowlands Castle, away from the world that would believe them dead. There was no way for Helena or Amy to know if it had worked, so Amy was still set to go find him.

When Amy embarked on her journey to an outpost that may hold the key to Brax's whereabouts (Tripp's Tavern in Seaport), she met the wily owner, Tripp, who seemed to know exactly who she was and where she should go next: Gallanor.

As Amy was getting ready to head to her next stop, we found that Brax and Ifyrus did indeed wake up from their unnatural slumber in the ice cavern. The young Kavea had been on her own secret guard duty at the time and had been thrilled to see her frozen hero come to life as the spell broke! But before she could get much time with them, Brax dismissed her and fled on Ifyrus's back, back home to Dragon Moon to reconnect with the past he left behind and found out his wife Amaryah had returned as well. The dead Queen Helena told him where he could find her, but by the time he had arrived at Tripp's, he had just missed her. Tripp sent the men to Gallanor in hopes of catching up to Amy.

Upon entering the kingdom of Gallanor via another Crannie at Tripp's, Amy was spotted by King Ruskin's men. During her escape, she met a young boy named Colt, a pegasus-shifter who was given the quest to help Amy by Queen Miawae of Gallanor after he presented her with the very trinket King Ruskin had been searching for (he had come upon it by happenstance and had turned it over to the queen, setting him on this path to begin with). The king's men were after them, so Amy and the boy ran together and jumped off the cliffside to avoid Ruskin's men. Colt transformed midleap to catch Amy and get her out of harm's way, causing them to just miss the same dragon Amy was in pursuit of, unaware they were right on her tail. Ifyrus took a poisoned arrow to his chest and fell. Brax did what he could to help his friend, but he needed extra help. They went in search of aid.

Amy and Colt, now safely away from Ruskin's men, came upon a traveling fair where they met Ellera, a Mind Traveler who was able to see right away that Amy needed some serious help. It intrigued her. Brax and Ifyrus stumbled into Ellera's tent in a stroke of good fortune, finally connecting with Amy. Ellera knew there was nothing she could do to help the dying dragon-shifter in Brax's arms, but she knew who could: The Fae.

Amy, Brax, Ifyrus, and Colt made their way to The Fae Realm with Ellera leading the charge. When they arrived, they were welcomed by Sovereign Sai, the much-loved leader of the Fae. Sai did what they could to assist, with the help of the kingdom's much skilled healers, and were able to save Ifyrus and put Amy back to rights as best they could after a "food allergy" of sorts.

Meanwhile, Ethan, an older boy from the kingdom of Cavar, is imprisoned in the dreaded Sky Prison of Padagonya. Accused of stealing a powerful artifact (a suns necklace piece), he is tortured by the feared Mind Traveler and Dark Mage, Viego, a crony to King Ruskin, who sought to extract Ethan's memories and uncover the artifact's location. Ethan resisted, though the brutal conditions pushed him to his limits. He couldn't have known Colt would happen upon it and bring it straight to Ruskin's enemy.

Ethan's younger sister, Cyndol, refused to accept his guilt when a representative from the king came to ask if they had any knowledge of his actions. She ran away from her parents, Enid and Darrian, and spent the night on the cliff above her home. She was awakened the next morning to fire and screams as King Ruskin's men decimated her town and killed its inhabitants in their search for the missing artifact.

Cyndol almost got captured but instead chose to jump off the cliff into the sea to avoid getting taken. When she hit the water, she found she was ensconced inside a magickal bubble that protected her and whisked her off to the safety of another kingdom, far from home.

When Cyndol arrived at this new shoreline, she met a young fox (whom she quickly named Kit). They were surprised that they could talk to each other and that they had both lost their families. Kit decided to join her on her rescue mission for her brother and the two became fast friends.

Cyndol stumbled upon the kingdom of Gallanor where she met the queen, Miawae, and her suspicious granddaughter, Princess Kiara. After contact with Cyndol, Queen Miawae offered aid to Cyndol in the attempt to free her brother, and sent her Right Hand, Evony (along with a small group of magickal people) to assist. Before leaving with the rescue party, Cyndol joined Kiara for a walk in her kingdom. Kiara, after hearing Cyndol's story, questioned Cyndol about having magick. Cyndol denied having any, and Kiara decided to test that lie. She threw Cyndol off the cliffside with the intention of activating Cyndol's magickal bubble again. Luckily for Kiara, she was right (though Cyndol and Kit had a few choice things to say about her methods). Once she'd calmed down, Kiara proposed an alliance, claiming that it would be handy to have someone around who could talk to the animals. Cyndol agreed and the matter was done.

The road to The Sky Prison in Padagonya was not without its trials. When they arrived at the prison and were refused entry, Cyndol and Kit went in on their own to save Ethan. Little did they know Ethan was well on his way to saving himself. When Viego hit a particularly rough spot in Ethan's mind, it activated magick in Ethan that neither of them knew he had! His new glowing amethyst eyes were a force to be reckoned with and Ethan was able to attack his captor. Viego sent word to King Ruskin that he had found a prize worth picking, and Davina and Viego were set to remove the teen's eyes. That's when Cyndol and Kit came to rescue Ethan. After a harrowing journey away from the prison, with Davina and Ruskin's men in pursuit, Cyndol, Kit, Ethan, and the Gallanorians arrived in The Fae Realm, asking for help with Ethan's wounds, specifically the stubborn hole in Ethan's forehead that refused to close, even with use of magick.

King Ruskin, werewolf-shifter and tyrannical ruler of Callembria, is aware of Amy's return (though he knew her as his former fiancée Amaryah). Ruskin seeks to control her power and rule all Callembria, including its separate nations of Dragon Moon, The Fae Realm, the Mer Realm, and Gallanor. His ally, Princess Davina, the eldest granddaughter of Queen Miawae and King Matthias of Gallanor and a powerful Mage in her own right, was enslaved by Ruskin after she attempted to avenge her parents' murder at his hands. Her kingdom, unaware of her enslavement, shunned her, believing she had betrayed them.

While Ruskin strengthened the search for Amaryah, Ellera and Hælgah of The Fae attempted to aid Amy and Cyndol through their combined magicks. In addition to training, Sovereign Sai gifted Kit the ability to speak without the need for magickal instruments, as well as the ability to look into any mirrored surface and be able to bring forth another Kit so he would never feel alone, Colt was gifted a unicorn horn that evolved Colt's pegasus form into an alicorn, and King Ibraxus's curse to remain human was lifted.

Ikah, one of Ruskin's top generals, infiltrated Gallanor on Ruskin's orders, causing Queen Miawae and her granddaughter, Princess Kiara, to grow suspicious of her true motives. Kiara sent word via raccoon to deliver a message to Cyndol to return as soon as possible with help. She thought they may soon be under attack.

Back in The Fae Realm, having been stripped of his curse, Brax thought it would be wise to return home briefly to fetch his crown and royal ring, ready to reestablish his rule as the Dragon King. What he and Ifyrus found there was shocking: A sea of unread scrolls, written to Brax from Amy's sister, Orelle, pleading for help to save her and her daughter from the evil that was her husband, King Ruskin. Brax and Ifyrus made to return to The Fae Realm, but along the way, saw a familiar set of red curls: Kavea! When the three of them pieced together who they were to each other, "Uncle" Brax and Ifyrus took her with them to The Fae Realm. They needed reinforcements if they were going to save Orelle.

As Ruskin's men drew closer to The Fae Realm, Colt sacrificed his spot on this journey by leading them all on a merry chase as far away from The Fae as he could get them. In addition to watching out for Amy, Ruskin's army had also been instructed to watch out for the escaped Ethan. Not knowing what he looked like, the army fell for Colt's ruse and many perished in the chase. Those who didn't followed him all the way to Tripp's Tavern, a stop-over for Colt to rest before heading back to Gallanor.

Ruskin was alerted to the boy's presence in Seaport and decided it was time to join the hunt personally. While he missed Colt, he did find Tripp and had his Mage Davina torture him for information. Luckily, Tripp was able to escape, thanks to his own getaway Crannie, and Ruskin was left with nothing but anger. He turned his sights on Gallanor.

Unknown to Ruskin, during this raid on Seaport, Cyndol and Ethan's father, Darrian, had been able to track them and infiltrate the ranks, attempting to gain any information on his missing children. He knew how important they would be, and how much more important it was that he found them first.

The stage is set for war, rebellion, and the battle for Callembria's fate. Welcome to The Callembria Chronicles: Book Two: Awakening.

Table of Contents:

CHAPTER ONE: CYNDOL AND THE BEAR 1
CHAPTER TWO: KAVEA AND THE ROAD TO SAVE HER MOTHER 16
CHAPTER THREE: AMY ATTEMPTS A RESCUE 36
CHAPTER FOUR: RUSKIN'S PLAN B 51
CHAPTER FIVE: MIAWAE'S INVITATION 53
CHAPTER SIX: KAVEA'S GOODBYE 55
CHAPTER SEVEN: AMY ARRIVES IN MERCONCHAWAY 61
CHAPTER EIGHT: CYNDOL'S TASK 74
CHAPTER NINE: AMY GAINS SOME INSIGHT 81
CHAPTER TEN: KIARA SPEAKS WITH HER GRANDMOTHER 96
CHAPTER ELEVEN: AMY SCORES A WIN 101
CHAPTER TWELVE: DAVINA'S DREAD 109
CHAPTER THIRTEEN: CYNDOL GETS LOCKED IN .. 112
CHAPTER FOURTEEN: IBRAXUS ON THE BROW OF BATTLE 118
CHAPTER FIFTEEN: DAVINA'S DESTRUCTION 121
CHAPTER SIXTEEN: KAVEA'S FLIGHT 124
CHAPTER SEVENTEEN: ELLERA'S FACE-OFF 128
CHAPTER EIGHTEEN: MIAWAE'S RESOLVE 130
CHAPTER NINETEEN: DAVINA AND KIARA 136
CHAPTER TWENTY: AMY JOINS THE FRAY 138

CHAPTER TWENTY-ONE: ETHAN'S EYES 140

CHAPTER TWENTY-TWO: IBRAXUS'S SECOND WIND 143

CHAPTER TWENTY-THREE: CYNDOL'S CHARGE... 144

CHAPTER TWENTY-FOUR: ELLERA & IFYRUS 147

CHAPTER TWENTY-FIVE: CYNDOL'S ABILITY 152

CHAPTER TWENTY-SIX: IBRAXUS'S WORST FEAR 156

CHAPTER TWENTY-SEVEN: AMY GETS TAKEN 161

CHAPTER TWENTY-EIGHT: DARRIAN TAKES HIS CHANCE 163

CHAPTER TWENTY-NINE: KIARA VERSUS IKAH ... 165

CHAPTER THIRTY: KAVEA COMES TO TERMS 170

CHAPTER THIRTY-ONE: KIARA HONORS THE LOSSES 176

CHAPTER THIRTY-TWO: AMY'S NEW HOME 184

CHAPTER THIRTY-THREE: IBRAXUS LEADS THE WAY 191

CHAPTER THIRTY-FOUR: DARRIAN MAKES A DISCOVERY 193

CHAPTER THIRTY-FIVE: AMY REUNITED 200

CHAPTER THIRTY-SIX: RUSKIN THE WINNER........ 204

CHAPTER THIRTY-SEVEN: CHAOS 209

CHAPTER THIRTY-EIGHT: AMY AND THE CHAIR .. 219

CHAPTER THIRTY-NINE: RUSKIN MAKES HIS MOVE 223

CHAPTER FORTY: THE ISLAND 227

CHAPTER FORTY-ONE: AFTERMATH 274

EPILOGUE 276

CHAPTER ONE: CYNDOL AND THE BEAR

Leaving The Fae Realm felt strange now. Though they'd only been here a short time, it already felt like an extension of home.

Mostly, she was worried about Ethan. He seemed better, sort of, enough to be out of bed and moving about freely, but she was concerned about the slowly healing hole in his forehead. Thankfully, it wasn't so deep anymore that you could see inside his brain, but it was definitely still noticeable. It appeared now as a dark spot with some flimsy tissue covering. She hoped it would close up fully over time, that maybe the worst reminder would be a small scar.

Ethan finished packing up the last of the gifted supplies from Sai and loaded the bags into the wagon. The wagon was *also* gifted, along with a few horses. Sai promised to have their people return the ones Ellera had rented from Meadowtown.

Cyndol had never seen snow before. The thought of going to The Snowlands to save Kavea's mother terrified her! What would snow feel like? It was always warm in her homeland of Cavar, so she didn't own anything heavier than a light coat. This new thick one Sai had given her felt foreign in her hands. She shuddered at the thought of being cold enough to need it.

"It's not so bad, really!" Kavea said. "I've lived there my whole life, and I can tell you the snow and ice are beautiful! I've even seen foxes like yours out there, but with different colored coats."

"He's not my fox, he's my friend."

"Oh," Kavea said, her smile faltering. "I'm sorry. I didn't realize. But, hey! That's even better! That means he *chooses* to be with you, right?"

"I guess?" Cyndol shrugged. "I'm just happy he's here."

"Me, too," Kit said. "Who knew meeting you would take me on such an adventure?" He scampered off to investigate a rustling in the bushes. Both girls laughed when he leapt straight into a shrub and got his bushy orange butt stuck for a few seconds, tail twitching while he figured out how to proceed.

"What do you think he found in there?" Kavea asked.

"I'm guessing he's about to show us," Cyndol replied.

Sure enough, Kit came bounding back with something clamped in his teeth. It was the hairy back leg of a rather large bug who was, thankfully, still attached to the rest of itself. The bug had a thick, black exoskeleton with eight limbs, one of which was writhing as hard as it could while trapped in the maw of a predator.

"Kit!" Cyndol said. "Spit that out! Can't you see the poor thing is scared?"

Kit's ears did an about-face, and he hung his head in confusion, dropping the now wet bug from his jaw. He watched as it took off as fast as its legs could carry it, a trail of spittle stuck to its rear. Kit cocked his head at it, his tail flicking in interest, but he otherwise kept still, not wanting to get yelled at again.

"I'm sorry," he said, once the bug jumped back in the foliage. "I got excited."

"I know," she replied, scratching his ears. "We're almost out of here, then you can get back to hunting critters in the woods. How does that sound?"

He bared his fangs in a foxy grin and said, "Perfect!"

Kavea looked confused. "Why can't he hunt here?"

Cyndol did her best to explain. "It just seemed… *impolite*… to hunt and kill things in a place like this."

"Fine by me," Kavea said. "So, what's life like in Cavar?"

"Hot. What's life like in the Snowlands?"

"Cold."

And now they were back to awkward silence. Fortunately, that's when everyone came over to load the last of their things and head out. Cyndol couldn't wait to leave, now that everything was set in motion. She took one last look at the captivating world of the Fae and steeled herself for the trip. She wanted so badly to respond to Kiara's message as fast as possible and get back to Gallanor, but there didn't seem to be anything worse than the *implied* danger just yet. She hoped that by the time they got there, it wouldn't be too late.

***

It was almost nightfall, and Cyndol could see the second sun getting ready to set in the clear sky above. She took a look around at her traveling companions and noticed a few of them had stopped just ahead to claim a camping spot for the night.

"That'll do," Evony said. "Plenty of trees above to shelter us, and dried leaves below to alert us to approaching parties. If we go back a way off this path, we'll be less noticeable to anyone else on these roads."

Brax and Ifyrus dismounted their horses to check out the intended area, and Cyndol had to hide her smirk. She found it highly amusing that two men who could fly as easily as walk were even bothering to be on horses in the first place.

"What's so funny?" Kit whispered.

"Dragons on horseback," she whispered back.

Kit made a high-pitched chuffing noise that startled Amy so badly she almost slipped off her steed.

"Sorry!" Cyndol said as she hurriedly grabbed the reins.

Amy righted herself and fixed a strand of raven hair behind her ear. "That's okay! No problem! Just didn't know a fox could sound like a dolphin *and* a chipmunk, it's cool."

This woman spoke so strangely. Cyndol didn't quite know what to make of her, but she was definitely interesting.

"Alright, everyone, gather 'round," The Dragon King said. "We will be making camp here for the night." He pointed at Felix and Fenix and said, "You two, can you please help Ifyrus with the shelter?"

The twins followed Ifyrus into the woods to gather large branches for tents.

"Bella," he continued, "can you—?"

"Get supper started, I'm on it," she interrupted, and immediately began whistling while doing her prep work. "Come on, Kavea, you can help me! Maybe show me something you'd make in the Snowlands?"

"Evony and Amy, can you fetch blankets and pillows from the wagon and get those ready for the tents?"

The ladies agreed. Amy heaved a big grunt as she hoisted herself off her horse and limped slowly towards the cart, looking as if the riding was taking its toll. Cyndol guessed she didn't spend much time on horseback.

Brax seemed to notice Amy's discomfort and cleared his throat before saying, "On second thought, Ellera, why don't *you* help Evony with the bedding, and Amy can help Druce with the kids to make sure they have everything they need?"

Cyndol knew what that meant. *Make sure you keep an eye on Ethan.* Cyndol had been noticing the side-long glances Brax had been giving Ethan since they left the Fae Realm.

Ethan had been quieter than normal. Most of the time he had a *lot* to say, to the point of annoyance even, but ever since they rescued him at the Sky Prison, he hadn't seemed like himself. She supposed she understood, in a way. They'd both been living in a strange nightmare ever since that day he was taken, followed by the death of their parents in the village fire.

What *was* there to talk about? At least she had Kit. Her poor brother seemed to be suffering alone in this.

"It's okay, sis," Ethan said softly. "I know they're just worried. But I'll be okay. *We'll* be okay. You'll see."

He squeezed her right hand gently, but assuringly, and Cyndol gave him a weak, closed-lipped smile in return. She had her doubts, but at least she was beginning to see hope for their future again, thanks to the wonderful people helping them.

***

On the eve of the second day, as they were making camp yet again, Cyndol heard Amy say to Brax, "I thought you said it only took two days to get there?"

Brax blushed. He turned to his wife, gripped her hands in his, and said, "Forgive me. I am not used to traveling with this many people. It does slow things down a bit. Ifyrus flew ahead a few minutes ago so he could come back with a progress report, and gauge how much farther we have. I sent Kavea with him to make sure he knew where to go. They should be back soon, my love. Don't worry."

He kissed her on the forehead, and she leaned into him, their silhouettes dancing along the thick tree trunks that surrounded them, thanks to the fire Fenix had built up.

Cyndol felt a pang of grief as she thought about her folks and how much she missed them. They had often danced happily in the firelight while she and Ethan made shadow puppets on the walls.

Ethan startled her by putting his hand on her shoulder.

"Sorry!" he said when she jumped a little.

"It's okay. I was just thinking about mom and dad."

Ethan turned his touch into a full hug. They held onto each other for a minute, trying to cope with their loss and how much things had changed in such a short time.

"I'm so sorry," he whispered.

"For what?"

He retreated back to the rock behind them, hugging his knees to his chest.

"I wish I'd never picked up that stupid thing! If I hadn't, none of this would've happened, and we'd be blissfully unaware, home with our family!"

"Ethan, you don't know that—"

"Of *course* I do!" he shouted.

A few concerned heads turned their way. Druce made a step forward, ready to intervene if necessary. Cyndol shook her head at him, almost unnoticeably. He backed off but stayed alert. She turned back to her brother, and he continued.

"I just wanted to see what the shiny thing in the road was. I thought if it was nice enough, I could give it to Zachariah's daughter, maybe catch her attention. It was just a piece of a necklace! How could I know that picking it up would be the worst decision I would ever make?"

"Oh, Ethan—"

"No! It was my fault! It's *my* fault they're dead! It's all my fault! It's all my—"

Cyndol flung her arms around him, hugging him as hard as she could while he cried, trying weakly to fight her off. She could see Druce inching closer to them, as well as Amy and Brax. Everyone seemed to be on high alert now, waiting to see if they needed to subdue the tortured teen. Cyndol shook her head at them, and Kit bared his fangs in a low warning growl. They wisely kept their distance. She didn't know how long that would be good for but, for now at least, they seemed to respect her wishes.

Ethan's sobs were beginning to calm, much to Cyndol's relief, but then, between gulps of air from Ethan, she heard the crunching of leaves not too far behind them. Ethan must have heard it, too, for he took a big breath of air and held it.

It seemed that everyone heard it, as they were silent and stock-still. At first, they didn't hear anything else, and Cyndol anxiously hoped it was just an animal passing by. But then she heard the unmistakable sound of a muffled cough, and the camp broke into action.

Brax was shouting orders and Evony gathered her warriors to fight.

"Cyndol!" Kit yipped. "Use your bubble!"

"Oh! Right!"

She tried with everything she had, but she was so tired after days of travel and fear, and practice with the Fae. And now, with trying to help Ethan through their mutual despair, she just couldn't get her bubble to come out.

Druce ran over to them and threw up a protection spell, armed with a sword in one hand and a crystal dagger in the other.

A shout went up from the darkness of the tree line and more voices joined in. Men charged forward to attack.

"*IBRAXUS!*" came a violent voice at the front of the pack. "I know you're here, you winged worm! Show yourself! My whip misses your flesh!"

The man cracked the whip in the air so loudly, Cyndol could feel the air reverberating around her as if it, too, was terrified of its power.

Brax stepped forward in a protective gesture, but Cyndol could see the beads of sweat form on his brow.

"Come and get me, then, Daegan," he said before launching himself at his opponent.

The fighting began in earnest. Each side threw their rage into every swing of weapon or spell they had. The clashing of metals, crystals and voices was enough to be heard for miles. Cyndol held on fiercely to Ethan and Kit, trying as hard as she could to get her bubble to pop up, but no luck.

Druce was doing his best to protect them, but even *he* was busy fighting three different men at the moment. Cyndol's faith in his spell work was strong, but she didn't know how long he could last, especially with the amount of force the opposing side was using.

A sickening slice sounded through the cacophony, and Cyndol saw Druce's left pinky finger go sailing through the air to land unceremoniously at her feet. She held her vomit in check and looked over at Druce to see if he was okay. He was still managing to hold them off, but his face had grown extraordinarily pale since the loss of his finger.

"Give us the boy!" one of them said.

"No!" Druce shouted. "You'll have to do more than cut off a finger if you expect me to hand him over!"

"He is property of King Ruskin, and you will turn him over to me!"

"Not! A! Chance!" Druce gritted through his teeth, struggling to maintain both spell and sword at the same time. He swung his sword at the knees of one of them and managed to take one down, chopping off one leg and damaging the other. The man hit the ground screaming and passed out. Good. One down, two to go!

The demanding man took another swipe at Druce, getting his right ear this time, severing the tip. Druce got away from the sword in time to miss it taking off his head, but it threw off his concentration and broke his spell, leaving the kids vulnerable to attack.

Ethan reached for something in his pocket. Cyndol saw him produce a small obsidian knife. He palmed it, ready to use if he had to. Cyndol shuddered and tried again to summon her bubble. This time, it fizzled into place, but in and out, as if it couldn't stay intact.

"Focus!" yelled Kit from her feet. "They're coming!"

Indeed they were. Seeing that the spell had been broken, and that Druce was busy fighting the leader of their grouping, a third man, joined now by a fourth, ran at the children, ready to take Ethan into custody and presumably back to Ruskin.

"NO!" Cyndol shouted with every fiber of her being. "You can't have him!" With that, her bubble cemented itself into place. Both men smashed up against it, breaking noses and teeth in the process. Cyndol felt sickened, but triumphant. Nobody would be taking her brother tonight! Not on her watch, and never again!

She chanced a brief look outward to see how the others were faring and saw spells flying, limbs piling, and a wide variety of carnage. Still, the fight continued. Her heart hammered in her chest as she fought to keep her concentration, but she could feel her strength was waning.

"Cyndol? Are you okay?" Ethan asked.

She nodded, as she couldn't get the words out. She hoped he saw it as she was pretty sure she couldn't do it again. She could already see the bubble shimmering, threatening to pop.

"Brax!" Amy called to him while fighting off an opponent with a pan she'd borrowed from Bella. She'd already hurled her daggers into a couple of charging men. "Can't you turn into a dragon and burn them all?"

Daegan laughed as he sent his whip hurtling in Brax's direction. Daegan caught him along his right calf muscle, earning himself an angry roar from the king. "He can't! There's not enough room to turn! Too many trees."

Things were looking grim. Each time Cyndol thought she saw one of their group winning the fight, more men came from the shadows. They couldn't keep up. Druce was bleeding profusely now from several cuts, Brax was limping and bleeding as well, and there were various injuries inflicted upon the rest. Hope was dying, and Cyndol could see her bubble fizzling out more and more.

"Cyndol?" Kit squeaked.

"I— I can't... I can't hold it..."

The bubble burst, and the two men who'd been smashed against it fell. Two more came forward to grab Ethan roughly by both arms and take him away. A third tried to make a play for her as well, but Kit caught his reflection in the steel of his sword, calling his mirror-self to come forward.

In a flash of swirling amber fog, Kit Two came pouncing out and instantly went into attack mode! He viciously bit the man in the thigh, forcing him to abandon everything to hold his hands around the wound. Kit took the opportunity to do the same thing to one of the men holding Ethan, garnering a similar result. The man dropped the arm that was holding the obsidian blade and Ethan immediately jammed that into the neck of the man still holding him. The man hit the ground and grasped his neck, making ugly gurgling sounds before he lay silent.

Cyndol, Ethan, and both Kits ran over to help Druce, who was about to be beheaded by a rather large ax. The fox duo leapt forward to dispatch the man before he could drop it on their friend. Cyndol and Ethan pulled Druce to the relative safety of a nearby tree and propped him up before turning to see what was coming next.

More men were running towards them now, excited at spotting their prey within reach. Cyndol had no idea how they were going to fight this many men, especially since the rest of their group were busy fighting so many of their own.

And then, the strangest thing happened: She heard a deafening roar in the darkened woods that filled the forest around them. A silence fell over the battleground as terrified eyes turned toward the approaching sound.

The bone-chilling roar came again, closer this time. Cyndol could see readying stances across the campground, preparing to meet this new opponent.

"Breyga…" Kit whispered.

Cyndol faced him. "What?"

He looked at her with wide eyes and matching smile. "It's Blood Bear! I *knew* she was real!"

"What? Blood Bear? But I thought—"

It didn't matter what Cyndol thought when the ghostly figure of a long-dead bear came crashing through the trees! The massive bear was growling, screaming, and tearing men apart! It was a sight to behold!

"Get them, Breyga!" Kit cheered. "Avenge your children!"

And get them, she did. She tore through the mass of men as easily as swatting away flies. The adults of Cyndol's party were smart enough to flee toward the children, while Breyga sent limbs, torsos, and heads flying in every direction. The woods were painted with her rage. It was the most awful thing Cyndol had ever seen, and she knew this would haunt her dreams forever.

Ruskin's men, the ones still able to do so, fled back toward the road they came from and did not look back.

"Come back here and *fight*, you cowards!" Daegan screamed at the fleeting backs of his men. "What is one bear against an army?"

He turned around to face the oncoming bear and lifted his whip to strike. Breyga roared in his face, causing the skin that covered it to flap back so hard and fast that Cyndol thought it would strip right off to land on the ground behind him. With one lightning-quick swipe, she caught the trajectory of the whip with her left front paw, jamming it into his right shoulder, completely knocking him down. With her right front paw, she stepped on his head, crushing him instantly and ending the fight. Any remaining men ran screaming into the night, away from the bloodied corpse of their once celebrated captain.

Breyga let out a victorious roar and turned her head toward Cyndol's group, huddled around the tree Druce was propped on. Seeing no quarrel, she let out a huff and turned to leave.

"Thank you, Breyga!" Kit called after her. "I hope you get reunited with your children soon!"

Breyga turned her glassy eyes to Kit and studied him for a moment. After a quick perusal, she nodded her head and turned to leave. A fine mist swirled around her, then she was gone.

Silence filled the area, save for labored breathing from a few of the injured in their group. Cyndol couldn't help but notice how happy Kit looked.

"I knew she was real. I told you."

Cyndol scratched him and Kit Two behind the ears, trying to convince her poor hammering heart that the danger had passed.

A rustling in the trees startled them into battle stance again, ready to take down whoever popped up next.

A tall figure strolled into view and a *very* confused Ifyrus said, "So... What did we miss?"

CHAPTER TWO: KAVEA AND THE ROAD TO SAVE HER MOTHER

Kavea couldn't believe her luck! Not only was she able to find King Ibraxus, but he was her uncle, too! She was flying dragon back for the second time now, once on Brax's back on the way to the Fae Realm, and now on Ifyrus's back to show him the route to save her mother. She was beside herself with glee! Never in her wildest dreams (okay, maybe in her *wildest* dreams) did she think she could actually pull off the quest she set for herself, and now look at her. Flying in style on a dragon, heading back to camp to pick up her team!

Breathe, Kavea, she told herself. *They're not going to want to help you if you get too carried away and scare them off.*

She took a deep breath and tried to calm down. *Focus on the flight. Focus on the flight. Focus on the light. Focus on the lights. Focus on the pretty lights—*

"Wait a minute. Is our camp supposed to be lit up like that?"

She could feel Ifyrus crane his large reptilian neck underneath her as he took in the flames and auras of spellcasting below. He tensed and looked for a good spot to land that wouldn't lend damage to woods, wyvern, or woman. He headed to a small meadow nearby and Kavea instinctively held on tighter as he plunged to the ground as speedily as he dared.

They landed much softer than Kavea would have expected, but Ifyrus bucked her off so he could shift. Then he darted into the thicket, leaving her to trail behind him.

"Wait! I'm not as fast as you!" she called after him, dusting herself off and flinging her hand up to catch his attention.

Ifyrus was gone in a matter of seconds. Kavea sighed and followed as quickly as her legs could carry her.

"Just follow the sounds of disaster. No problem."

By the time she caught up to him, her wheezing had alerted the group to her presence. They turned around to face her.

"Wh— what...?" Kavea stammered, looking at the absolute carnage laid out in the camp before her. She was answered by a sea of exhausted faces. Blood, weapons, body parts, and ichor were strewn about everywhere. "Well... I'm not sleeping in *that*." She pointed at the dripping appendage hanging from the tent she was *supposed* to sleep in, then crawled into the somehow cleaner one next to it.

Brax sidled up to Ifyrus and asked, "Uh, is she a little...?"

"Strange? Oh, absolutely, yes."

Brax just nodded and turned back to helping his companions get back to rights while explaining to Ifyrus what he missed while away.

Everyone helped out with cleaning the supplies that made it through the battle, though it was mostly done by way of a magick spell that Druce had up his sleeve. As beat up as he was, he was able to manage the spell with some assistance from his Gallanorian group. The rest of the work consisted of moving their camp much farther down the road, as far away from the battle scene as they could get.

Kavea was a bit irritated at having to help, as she didn't participate in the battle, but also because she was anxious to get to sleep so tomorrow would come faster and they could go save her mother. She was on her last chore of retrieving a dagger from the chest of a deceased soldier when Amy came up behind her.

"I'll take that," she said, reaching for the bloodied weapon.

Kavea handed it over between her thumb and pointer finger with a grimace.

Amy used a handkerchief to wipe away what she could. She shoved it into its spot on her belt loop, but she didn't leave. Kavea waited for her to say something.

"So…" Amy began. "I hear you're my niece. It's nice to meet you. I'm Amy."

She thrust her hand toward her, so Kavea reached down to the other corpse and handed her the second dagger she pulled from his chest. Amy looked surprised but took the proffered piece and wiped that clean as well, sheathing it when she was done.

Amy cleared her throat and tried again. "You're Orelle's daughter? I'm told she's my sister."

Kavea raised an eyebrow. "You mean, you didn't know you had a sister?"

"You didn't know you had an aunt and uncle?" Amy fired back.

"You mean, my dead aunt and my missing uncle?"

"Touché. Sorry. That was rude. My memory... Well, it's not what you'd expect it to be. Death does that to ya, I suppose."

When Kavea didn't comment, Amy continued. "Anywho, what can you tell me about her? And about you, of course."

Kavea thought about it for a minute before saying, "Well, I read a lot. There's not much else to do where I live, I'm afraid. But I love reading about adventures around the world, and I dream of getting to go on one myself someday."

"Really? Well, it looks to me like you're on one right now."

Kavea beamed as she realized that was sort of true, and she was with the people in the story she loved the most, the one her father always tried to hide from her, but she found every time. It almost didn't feel real.

"And what of your mother, Orelle?"

Kavea's excitement began to ease as worry for her mother creeped back in.

"She treats me well but spends much of her time writing letters by the fireplace and throwing them in when they're done, especially after times when father has visited. I thought it was all nonsense until Brax came along with one of them. I was on my way to find him, you see, as I was there when the spell was broken that freed him and Ifyrus from the ice cave. I've watched over him for several years now, daydreaming about setting him free, and having him come rescue me and my mother and take us away. I wasn't even sure it was him until he woke up."

"Away to where?"

Kavea shrugged. "Anywhere but there? It's the only home I've ever known. I wasn't supposed to leave there, not ever. I was told bad things would happen to me if I left, but I knew I had to go. That's when I started searching for Brax. I thought now that he was free, he could help us, but—"

"But what?"

She let out a long breath. "I'm not sure if she *can* be helped, it's been so long. It's only gotten worse as time moves on. I'm afraid that now that we have a team coming in to help, she won't want to go. Then what do I do?"

Amy took a chance and pulled Kavea into a sympathetic hug. She could feel the tremble of the young girl's shoulders as she held her.

"No matter what state she is in when we get there, we will do everything we can to help, okay? I may not remember her, but that doesn't mean I don't care. Besides, Brax seems to remember her just fine, and you don't want to get in the way of a determined dragon! Especially when there's *two* of them!"

Kavea chuckled and pulled out of the hug. "Thank you. I needed that."

"Me, too," Amy agreed. "It's been quite the day, huh? Let's see if the boys are done with your tent and try to get a little shut eye. How does that sound?"

Kavea instantly felt the day's fatigue hitting her muscles and couldn't wait to collapse. Thinking about how big tomorrow would be made her yawn. She followed her new aunt to her tent.

***

A cold nose on her bare foot woke Kavea with a start, and she practically flew out from under her blanket.

"*Eeeeeek!*" she screamed.

An orange puff went butt-over-face on his way out the tent, calling, "Sorry!" as he sailed.

Kavea realized it was Kit coming to wake her and sent an apology through the door flap.

"It's okay!" she heard from the bush outside. "In fact, I found breakfast!" Kit emerged from the bush, licking the last bit of bug from his snout. He lolled his tongue at her, quite satisfied with himself. "We are almost ready to head out. Cyndol said that Brax said to pack what you can and be ready to leave in fifteen minutes."

With that, he promptly pounced off and left her to her own devices. Kavea yawned deeply and felt a surge of excitement. Today was the day they would save her mother! She'd heard a few tales about her father over the last couple days that explained quite a lot, and she was more scared than ever for her mother. Her father was always cordial to her. She wouldn't call it love, necessarily, but more of a toleration of sorts. But, if what he did to her mother and the world was true, she never wanted to see him again. It made her happy now that he'd stayed away for so much of her life.

She grabbed the last of her things, then helped Fenix collapse her tent. She snagged a berry muffin from Bella and joined Cyndol, Ethan, and Kit in their seats.

"Everyone here and ready to go?" Brax asked.

It seemed that all was in order, so the group began the last stretch of journey to her home.

***

At midday, they rounded the final bend that separated the forest from the Snowlands. They began the trying journey of traveling up a snowy mountainside meant to dissuade "guests". They were forced to abandon the wagon and horses and travel on foot from here. Bella and Druce planned to stay behind to guard the supplies and make sure that Druce was able to rest so he could fully recover.

Ethan took one look at the foreboding mountain, and Kavea saw him tremble.

"Uh, would it be okay if I stayed behind as well?" he asked Evony.

She looked surprised but said yes after seeing the fear in his eyes.

"He won't be there, you know," she said, "if it's Ruskin you're worried about."

Ethan winced. "I know, but... I can't go to his castle. I know he doesn't really live there anymore, but... it's still his and I— I just can't."

Cyndol's eyes widened, and she grabbed her brother's hand. "Well, then, I'm not going either!"

Ethan faced his sister and said, "Cyndol, it's okay, really. They might need you, and you have magick now that could come in handy. Besides, between Bella and her frying pan," he winked, "I don't think anyone will mess with us. I'll be fine. I promise."

Cyndol chewed her bottom lip in consternation, but saw he meant what he said. She realized he was right. They had no idea what to expect on this mission, and she didn't want to be the reason they failed. Ethan would be alright in the wagon.

"Fine," she said. "But you'd better be here when I get back! If I have to trek all over the world again to fetch you, I'm going to let you have it when I find you!"

Kit nodded in agreement and bared warning fangs for good measure.

Finally, the rescue team set off, up and over the cold mountain pass, shivering and complaining about the rapid change of weather.

About an hour into their trip, Kavea stopped everyone for a quick break.

"There's a short-cut ahead that will save us several hours. It goes under the next mountain and will lead us to the ice cavern where Uncle Brax and Ifyrus were kept."

"'Uncle Brax', how adorable," Ifyrus said.

Ellera elbowed him in the side. "It is, now shut up."

Ifyrus held his hand over his assaulted midsection and smiled.

Brax grimaced but agreed to follow. "I don't care to see ice like that again, so let's get through it as quickly as possible."

"The section you were in was destroyed when you got out, but there is another tunnel close by that will work just as well."

"Fine," Brax said. "Where's the start of it?"

Kavea pointed to an oddly shaped rock formation at the base of the largest mountain. "There. And make sure you watch where you're going. There are stalagmites and stalactites inside it that will knock you out if you're not careful. When I was a kid, I hit my head on a stalactite so hard it knocked me out cold! If my guard hadn't come looking for me, I could've died. So, you know, be careful."

With that warning hanging in the air, Kavea proceeded to make a beeline for the entrance of the tunnel. The others followed her, keeping her words in mind.

"This is beginning to feel a bit too easy," Amy said to Brax. "Does it feel too easy to you?"

He pondered that for a minute before saying, "Yes, it's starting to. I would've thought he would have more security around his castle, even if he wasn't there."

"Oh, don't worry!" Kavea threw over her shoulder. "There's plenty of traps coming up, but I know them all! Come on!"

She continued her hurried pace, forcing the others to match it if they wanted to keep up with her.

"Cyndol!" Kit said. "I need help! I'm too small and keep falling through the snow!"

She reached back to plunk him out of a hole and tucked him into the front of her coat. She fussed with his bushy tail until she gave up, then threaded it through her sleeve as far as it would go.

"Better?"

"Yes, thank you! You're so warm!"

"Remind me to thank Sai for their foresight. I've never been this cold in my life!" She sneezed, as if to punctuate her point.

Kavea laughed to herself at their complaints. She guessed that snow was just not meant for everybody. She hardly even felt the cold anymore.

"This is about as far as we flew," Ifyrus told Brax. "Kavea said if we went any farther, we could risk being spotted by the few guardsmen on detail. She reckons there are about five of them at any given time, all massive beasts just itching for a fight."

"Well, good, because so am I," Brax said with a menacing growl. "I can't believe he's kept her captive all this time! Why didn't she leave?"

"Beats me, mate, but we'll get her out of there, and make sure he can never do anything to hurt her again."

Amy began shivering, so Brax picked her up in his beefy arms and did what he could to warm her while staying on the move. She happily melted into him.

Ifyrus turned a rakish smirk to Ellera and said, "You know, if you're cold—"

Ellera halted and whipped her face around to meet his, hand up, and said, "Look, I'm going to stop you right there. I'm plenty warm, thank you very much. I do not need your assistance but, if I ever do, I will ask." She continued walking briskly and didn't look back to see if he followed.

Ifyrus smiled at Brax and said, "I think I love her."

He bounded after her like a lovesick puppy, leaving Brax and Amy to snicker in their wake.

"She doesn't stand a chance, does she?"

Brax shook his head, chuckling. "Nope."

A sudden deafening snapping sound broke them of their merriment. Brax nearly dropped Amy in surprise! Not far ahead, they saw a large metal contraption sticking up out of a snowbank with a triumphant Kavea waving happily back to them.

"It's okay!" she called. "I got it! Let's keep going!"

Evony, Fenix, and Felix came running as fast as they could from the rear.

"What in the world was *that*?" Evony said, sword at the ready.

"Kavea tripped the first trap for us," Brax said.

Evony's brow furrowed. "Out of how many?"

Brax paused to think, but realized he didn't know either.

"Kavea!" he shouted. "How many more are there?"

Now it was *her* turn to pause as she counted.

"Um… four? Or five?"

"Did you say '*UM*' four or five?!" he yelled back.

Even at this distance they could see her blush.

"It's four! Four traps! I got it! We're okay!"

The adults exchanged worried glances but followed after the teen.

"I should probably walk on my own from here," Amy said, "in case you need to, you know, go save somebody?"

"Good idea," he said, and set her down softly on the blanket of white.

Another loud noise. This time, it was more of a *boom* than a *snap* when a huge boulder came loose from its harness on a smaller mountain ahead with the intent to crush an enemy. It landed harmlessly and rolled a few times before coming to a halt.

"*Three* more!"

"I swear, I think she's having *fun*," Ifyrus said. "She's positively *glowing*!"

"She's helping!" Amy laughed. "Let her do it how she sees fit. It's not like we have any answers anyway." She jogged ahead to catch up to Ellera.

"Anything ring a bell, by chance?" Ellera asked her when she got to her side.

Amy crossed her arms over her chest to trap in what heat she could. "No, but I've come to expect that. Maybe once I see Orelle face to face?"

"Perhaps. It's definitely going to be interesting, to say the least."

"I'm glad you're here," Amy said. "I don't know what it is, but I feel like I can trust you with anything."

Ellera cackled. "Probably because I've seen inside your head and didn't run screaming!"

Amy laughed with her. "Well, there is that."

The ladies walked in silence for a moment, then Ellera asked, "So, what was it like, living on Earth? I've heard stories about it off and on for years, but they are few and far between. I didn't know how much I believed in it until I saw your memories."

Amy's face slowly became a frown as she let herself think about her life on Earth. "Honestly, it was beautiful. Not quite as beautiful as life here, just… different. For starters, we only have one sun and one moon, no Gemstone Belt. Oh! And no magick."

"You're kidding! How do you get anything done without magick? And only one sun? How does that work?"

BOOM!

"Two more!"

Amy flinched. "This kid is going to be the death of me, I just know it."

Ellera clapped a hand on her shoulder. "I wish I could say that's unlikely, but—"

BOOM!

"Okay, one more!"

Amy sighed heavily.

As the gang got closer to the entrance of the ice cavern, nerves began mounting.

Brax asked, "Uh, Kavea? Didn't you say there was one more trap left?"

Kavea faced them with a sheepish grin. "Yeah. I, uh, can't seem to find it."

He gritted his teeth. "What do you mean, you can't find it? What is it supposed to be? Perhaps we can help."

"Well, it's kind of a trap door of sorts. It *should* be right about—"

"Aaaaahhhhhh!" Cyndol screamed as she fell through the snow, tumbling face-first toward the crevasse below. Before she could react, Kit fell out of her coat and tumbled down the ice!

Everyone immediately lurched into action and tried to grab hold of Cyndol as fast as they could. Brax grabbed her ankle and hoisted her back to safety, but Kit was just out of reach, clinging to a divot in the ice as hard as he could.

"Help!" he shouted up to them. "I'm slipping!"

"Kit!" Cyndol cried. "Hang on! We're going to get you out of there!"

"Hurry!"

"I'm so sorry!" Kavea said. "I couldn't see it! I couldn't remember!"

"I'm slipping!" Kit said.

Ifyrus transformed as quickly as he could and shoved his tail down as far as he could get it. He was just shy of his target, though, and too large to fit any farther. He took a deep breath, intending to rage fire at the offending ice and melt it so he could get in there, but Brax's clear head stopped him.

"Ifyrus! Wait! You'll fry him!"

Ifyrus choked back a plume of smoke, ears thrown back in fear, but he relented and continued trying with his tail.

Cyndol was flat on her belly now, trying to direct Kit on the best way to reach him.

"I can't get it!" Kit said. "If I move, I'll lose any grip I have and fall!"

Suddenly, Amy got an idea. She flattened herself along the snowbank next to Cyndol and called down to the poor fox. "Kit! Do you see a reflective surface down there? You're literally surrounded by ice! See if you can see yourself!"

He was quiet for a moment, then, "I see it! I see me!"

"Great! You're doing great, Kit! Now, call for your double! If you can get him to Ifyrus's tail, it should be just long enough for you to grab onto him, and Ifyrus can pull you both out, okay?"

Kit made a chittering sound that Amy took as a yes. "Okay! Ready? On the count of three, call him and direct your gaze to the tip of his tail! One... two... three!"

"Kit Two, I need you!" Kit said.

Everyone held their breaths, waiting to see if this plan would work. A swirling amber fog wafted up to them from the menacing hole in this wintery nightmare. Right on cue, Kit Two popped into existence on the end of Ifyrus's tail and chirped his surprise! Luckily, he also latched on with his teeth (causing a grunt from the dragon). Kit pushed off the wall to clamp his teeth on Kit Two's tail (a foxy grunt this time). Both foxes were now swinging precariously on the end of the determined dragon.

"Pull them up, Ifyrus! *Now*!" Amy shouted.

In one swift motion, the dragon whipped his tail as hard as he could, and twin foxes flew up and out of the crevasse to land in a slushy *plop-plop*! Identical bushy butts were protruding from the snow, foxtails flicking this way and that as they worked to free themselves from their new predicament. Sighs of relief were heard all around.

Fenix and Felix each took a fox by their tail and gently pulled them out.

Brax turned a disgruntled look at Kavea, and she hung her head in shame, her bouncing scarlet curls a stark contrast to the sparkling blanket of white surrounding her.

"Go easy on her," Amy told him. "She's doing her best."

He puffed smoke from his nose but gave one abrupt nod before going to check on the Kits.

Amy hugged Kavea. "It's okay. We're all okay. Now," she said, releasing her niece, "what next?"

The poor, shaking girl took a deep breath to steady herself and turned to face the next challenge.

"Well, now that all the traps are taken care of, it should be a straight shot through this tunnel to home."

Brax and Evony joined the women.

"Where will we find the guards?" Evony asked.

"There are usually three outside, and two inside," Kavea said. "There will be one at the end of this tunnel, so we'll have to be quiet, so he doesn't hear us coming. Another one will be at the entrance to another tunnel on the other side, so we *shouldn't* see him. The third one guards the steps into the castle and will be trickier, as he's going to see us coming and be ready to fight."

Brax grunted and exchanged a pointed look with Ifyrus.

"And inside?" Brax asked.

Kavea took a second to picture it in her mind. "There will be two standing guard somewhere close to my mother. She hasn't been allowed to be fully alone for as long as I can remember."

"Were there ever guards on you?" Evony asked.

"Yes, usually just one, but I've learned to evade him when I want to be alone."

"Wouldn't he make six guards, then? Or is he somewhere in another position?"

Kavea's face reddened. "Okay, so I may have gotten him in trouble the day you two left the caverns. He is currently being 'punished' for my actions."

Ifyrus clapped Kavea on the back. "Then by *my* calculations, that's one less guard we have to worry about. Great work, youngling!" He gave her a 'Proud Uncle' type of shake, then bounced off to grab Brax around the shoulders. "Excuse us a moment."

He led Brax a few steps away from the group and said quietly, "I did not want to alarm the child, but she is sadly undercounting the number of guardsmen inside."

"Really? How do you know?"

"We saw a few outside the walls, as she stated, but I can see much farther than she can, and I counted enough for a small army through the windows."

"They must have been alerted that she went missing and bulked up the watch."

"That, or…?" He pointed a look at their young leader.

"It's a trap?"

"It's a trap."

"No… Mm mm. I refuse to believe a young girl like that would resort to all of this just to lure us into a trap!"

"You'd be surprised what children are capable of."

"That's my *niece* you're talking about there!"

"Aha! That is my point, *Your Majesty*. That there," he flicked his eyes at Kavea, who was trying desperately to pretend she wasn't listening, "is the daughter of your enemy, mate! I'm just saying, you know, be prepared. If it was just the handful of guards she claims it to be, don't you think I would've taken care of it on the recon flight and been back with Orelle already?"

Brax was forced to consider the words of his lifelong friend. He brusquely scratched his beard while he pondered the next course of action. "You may be right. We should prepare for a bigger fight."

Ifyrus clasped Brax's shoulder. "Thanks, mate. Better safe than sorry, eh?"

"Better safe than sorry," Brax said.

The dragon men rejoined the group and Brax asked Evony if she had any battle strategies that could work here. Kavea put up a fuss about how they were worried about nothing and wasting time when they could be saving her mother. Brax assured her Orelle would be saved, but they had to be smart and prepared for any situation. Kavea halted her arguments and only piped up when asked about specifics of the castle.

When they were sufficiently satisfied with their plan, Kavea led them silently through the ice caverns. Only one person bonked their head on a stalactite (Ifyrus, who turned his head when he heard Cyndol lose her footing for a moment. Both were fine).

"These kids are determined to kill me!" he'd grumbled to Brax.

Brax only chuckled and said, "Just wait until you have kids of your own."

Ifyrus paused to smile about that for a minute, causing a bit of a traffic jam for those following him.

"Hey! Pay attention!" Ellera scolded him as she scooted past to get around him. She gave him a small smack on the head to knock him back into the present and he grinned widely in return.

"Trust me, Love, you have my attention."

She scoffed and turned to Amy. "I bet he says that to all the girls."

Amy giggled and whispered to Brax, "Baby dragons?"

He smiled back. "Baby dragons."

CHAPTER THREE: AMY ATTEMPTS A RESCUE

I haven't been spelunking in years. The last time I went was up near Mount Shasta, and this was a whole different experience! For starters, I wasn't trekking through caverns of ice there like I was right now. For another, I'd had a hard hat on the last time. This time, if I slipped and fell, I'd be screwed. I tried my best to do what I could with my clumsy footing, but Brax still had to reach out to catch and steady me from time to time. Luckily, I had this big, thick coat on so there was something easy to snag when I stumbled. Reason number 463 to thank Sai again when I saw them.

Right as I was beginning to think we were lost and would be stuck in this cave forever, the group came to a quiet halt. Kavea made a motion for us to gather 'round.

Whispering, she said, "We are about to come up on the exit. There will be a guard out there for sure, so no talking beyond this point. If you absolutely have to, whispers only, got it?"

Everybody nodded, and she seemed satisfied.

"Brax and I will exit first and take care of the guard," Evony said. "The rest of you, stick close, but wait for us to wave you out. From there, it's a straight line to the castle doors."

"That's where I'll shift and take out any guards left outside," Brax said. I swear I saw a gleam of excitement in those whiskey-colored eyes.

We readied ourselves for what was coming next. Brax and Evony rounded the corner, leaving the rest of us tensed and waiting.

A minute went by, then two. My heart was racing, and I strained my ears to pick up any stray noise. Starting to worry, my eyes met Ellera's, and she grabbed my hand for comfort, giving it a quick squeeze.

It will be alright, she mouthed to me.

Thank you, I mouthed back.

A soft scrape against the ice alerted us to someone's approach, and we collectively sighed in relief when Evony waved us forward.

"Quickly, now," she said softly. "When you get to the door, stop. Let Brax and I go in first."

"And me?" Ifyrus asked.

She shook her head. "Not until we can clear a path. Keep an eye on the kids with Fenix and Felix."

He looked as if he had been slapped but knew better than to argue.

I held up my daggers and said to him, in an overly cocky way, "Don't worry. I'll protect you." I tried to spin one like I'd seen people do in movies and immediately dropped it.

His face broke into a jovial grin, and he gave me a wink. "Thanks, Love. I was worried for a moment there." He reached down to pick it up and handed it back to me as I blushed. But, you know, confidently. I'm a confident blusher.

When we got to the opening of the cavern, the first thought that hit me was that we were in a bowl of vanilla ice cream. All around us were white mountains, formed in a ring-like fashion, protecting the castle nestled in its center. A rush of icy air swirled around me, lifting my dark hair from my shoulders as if it wanted to play. It instantly froze the hairs in my nose and stole my breath. I nestled into my coat even more.

The castle itself was also white, perhaps to make it harder for someone to attack if they couldn't see what they were aiming for. Great strategy, I suppose, but we were blessed with one of its few inhabitants who knew exactly where we were going. It was smaller than I expected, for all the bluster I'd heard about its king, but still large enough to be imposing. If it weren't for the suns glistening on the powder-caked turrets, refracting bits of sparkle here and there, it would seem as chilling as the snow around it.

Looking straight up into the sky, I could see where the Gemstone Belts converged into a central point and realized why Ruskin chose to put his castle here. Probably a great focal point for power. At least, it might have been, when dragons were still around to send it down.

On Brax's gesture, we made a mad dash for the front of the castle, a large wooden double-door set into ivory-colored stone walls. So far, so good. It seemed as though Evony and Brax had gotten rid of all the guards stationed outside. Where they put them was anyone's guess. We ran as fast as the snow under our feet would let us, but our grouping, and especially Kavea's scarlet curls, worried me that we'd be spotted and charged. Fortunately, we made it to the door unscathed.

"Wait here," Brax commanded in a voice so authoritative it made me shiver.

"You okay?" Ellera asked loud enough for only me to hear.

"Yep," I said. "That was just kinda hot."

Her brows pulled together. "Hot?"

"Never mind. Just an expression where I come from. Means I liked seeing Brax take charge."

She pinned me with a knowing look and said, "Honey, he's a king. Of *course* you're into him. Plus, hello! Husband!"

I blushed again, this time in stupidity, as that *should* be sinking in by now. "So, I guess you should call me 'Your Majesty', then."

She chuckled and said, "You're absolutely right. *Amy*."

Fenix and Felix shut us up with their twin stares of irritation and the silence returned, along with a fresh batch of nerves.

As Brax was about to break down the door, Kavea stopped him. "Wait! Let me go first! They won't hurt me. I'll say I was just out exploring and got lost. Maybe they'll buy it and let me in? I'll leave the door open a crack so you can follow, take them by surprise!"

Brax, Evony, and Ifyrus exchanged worried, but considering, glances. After a minute, Brax nodded gruffly and warned her to be careful. If there were any signs that she was in trouble, she was to shout immediately, and we'd come running. Kavea nodded and slipped her key into the bolt hole. Turning it in the lock and hearing a *click*, she opened one of the doors and crept in, leaving it slightly ajar.

Now, for the hard part: Waiting.

There was nothing for a few seconds, and then, "Hey! How did you get in here?"

"I have a key to my own castle, don't I?" Kavea said.

"We have search parties out looking for you!" a rough voice scolded her.

"Must have gone right by me!"

"You didn't see them?"

"No, but here I am, safe and sound! I appreciate you going to all the trouble."

After the clunking around of shifting guards, it seemed as if this might be working. Then, "Wait a minute. Who was on guard duty at the cavern? Where's Ruprecht?"

"Ruprecht?" Kavea asked. "Uhhhh… he's right behind me. Just checking to make sure I wasn't followed, I guess. He should be along any minute now."

I didn't like where this was headed.

"Is that right?" the man said. "In that case, maybe I'll go assist him, shall I?"

"That's… really not necessary," Kavea said.

Brax tightened his grip on the door handle and got into a battle stance. The others fell in suit. I held my breath and reached for Ellera's hand again, clenching tight as a cascade of fear washed over me, knowing the inevitable was about to happen.

"Is that why you left the door ajar, Princess?"

"Of *course*, it is," she said. "Why else would I do that?"

"Mm hmm. Like I said, I'll just go lend him a hand."

The echoing of footsteps on stone was almost deafening in their approach to the door and I knew this was it. Time to battle. Dropping Ellera's hand, I folded my fingers around the matching hilts of my daggers. One last deep breath. *In... out... begin.*

The double doors flung open wide, and Brax barreled into the man's middle, lifting him bodily off the floor and sending him crashing back down to it. A sickening *crunch* alerted the rest of the guardsmen to our presence.

Kavea ran deeper into the castle, screaming for her mother as she tried to locate her. I ran as fast as I could behind her to make sure nobody tried to attack her but was knocked flat on my back by a brute running in from another room. All of the air I had so carefully taken in outside was knocked completely out of me in one quick blow. I gasped like a fish on the ornate rug under me. The man made an attempt to stomp on me with a giant booted foot, but Ellera came to my rescue with a thick pewter candlestick and cracked him in the side of the head. One more swing to the same spot and the man fell unconscious to the floor.

"Thank… you…" I wheezed, starting to get some air back in my aching lungs.

She hoisted me from the floor and shoved me down the hallway after Kavea. I spared one quick glance at the rest of my group and saw many of them were trying to make their way after us, though all were locked in battle of some kind. Even both of the Kits were biting, kicking, and clawing their way through the crowd. I could've sworn I caught a glimpse of one of Cyndol's bubbles as well.

"Go! I've got the kids!" Ellera shouted and ducked to avoid a sword sailing over her head. She yanked a dagger from the belt of a man running by and buried it in his chest.

I followed her order and took off down the hallway in the direction I'd seen Kavea go. I kept my daggers at the ready in case I met any more guards along the way.

I arrived at the end of the hall. Right or left? I took my chances going left, as a quick peek to the right looked like an empty kitchen. Kavea had described Orelle as more of a couch-sitter than a chef.

Left proved to be a good choice, as I could hear Kavea's urgent voice echoing from one of the rooms near the end of the hallway. I hauled butt as fast as I could and heard a massive roar behind me, along with several men screaming. I smiled vindictively. My man must be rocking that dragon form right now!

I could hear some of my group following my route, but I spared no more glances to verify. I focused on the sounds of Kavea and entered the room she was yelling from.

A beautiful room with a stunning fireplace stood before me. Gorgeous wood paneling with hand carved creatures were found in every corner of the room: Mermaids and werewolves, mostly, but I saw a few Fae folk as well. I wasn't surprised at the lack of dragons, seeing as how the Master of the House wasn't their biggest fan.

And there, there in front of the fireplace in a large wingback chair, sat a frail looking woman with tired greying curls, age and despair siphoning out the red that shone so clearly in Kavea's. She turned a gaunt face to me as I shuffled clumsily into the room, once again losing my breath as her eyes met mine.

"Amaryah...?"

"Orelle." Memories of her slammed into me with the force of a freight train. My knees buckled, sending me crashing to the floor. Kavea burst into action and tried to catch my head before it hit the ground. She got to me just in time.

Memories of my childhood with Orelle flooded my brain. Memories of swimming happily in the sea, playing hide-and-seek among the reefs, throwing starfish at each other. Memories of giggling over cute boys we liked. Memories of treasure hunting and contests to see who could find the shiniest object. All of them, pouring in faster than I could make sense of them all, but enough for me to recognize my sister. I felt an abundance of love, fear, and sadness all at once. Tears streamed from my eyes, and I couldn't stop them if I tried.

Kavea didn't understand. She thought I'd hurt myself and ran to grab a pillow to prop me up on. I waved her away and stumbled awkwardly to my feet, needing to reach my sister and hold her in my arms again.

"Orelle." I made it to the chair and grabbed it to steady myself. I looked down at her, sitting so small in this behemoth of a chair, and I hated Ruskin for what he turned her into! She looked up at me with a mix of awe and misery, wanting to believe her dead sister had returned, but afraid it was just another lie.

"I'm so sorry I left you," I said, tears making it hard to see her face clearly. I didn't care. I flung my arms around her and sobbed. She flinched but hugged me back when Kavea assured her this was real.

"Amaryah, you've returned, but—how? I thought you were dead!"

"I was, I was! But I'm here now, and it's a very long story, one I can't wait to tell you all about but, right now, we have to *move*! We're breaking you out of here!" I tried to pull her out of the chair, but she finally showed some strength and yanked her arm back.

"No! You can't! *I* can't! I mustn't!"

I paused, confused. "What? You want to stay here? In this fancy prison?"

She looked as if I'd slapped her. "Of *course* not! But he— ah—" she glanced at her daughter. "I'm so sorry. He put a spell on me. I cannot leave here. Ever."

My blood ran colder than this icy hellscape. Nobody prepared for this.

"I thought he'd done it to Kavea as well, but when she escaped, I thought, maybe…" A tear fell. "Maybe she was immune? I wasn't, but perhaps she could be free of this place?"

My heart shattered. I pulled her up into a fierce hug and promised her we would find a way to fix this. I let go and ran to the doorway, calling for Ellera.

"On my way!" I heard from down the hall. A few grunts and crashes later, Ellera appeared in the doorframe. "How can I help?"

"Ellera, this is my sister Orelle. Orelle? This is my friend Ellera. She's going to help you."

"Wait, what?" Ellera said.

"I need you to do that magicky finger trick thingy and see if you see any spell work there. She says Ruskin trapped her with a spell and she can never leave here."

"That wretched little—!"

"I know!" I said. "Can you help her?"

She sized up a worried Orelle, then shoved her sleeves up her arms.

"I will give it my best shot."

Sounds of battle reverberated down the hallway, sending shivers down my spine.

"Can you do it quickly?"

"Not leaving me much of a choice, are you?"

"I'll apologize later! Please, *hurry*!"

Ellera sprang into action, thrusting both her hands up to my sister's temples (to Orelle's credit, she didn't resist). I saw Ellera's eyes do their crackling blue light routine, searching for whatever mayhem Ruskin and his Mages left behind. I made a mental note to *extra* throttle him when I got the chance.

Sounds of battle continued, and my anxiety was through the roof.

"Almost there… almost…"

I bit the inside of my cheek to keep from screaming and tightened the grip on my daggers. Kavea was sloppily shoving things into a bag for her mother.

Another dragon roar, followed by more screams and sword-clashing.

"Almost… got it! HA!" Ellera cheered at finding the spell, then laughed gleefully at its destruction in her hands. "Take *that*, Viego, you complete and utter bastard!"

"That was your brother's handiwork?" I asked.

"Yep! And guess whose neck I'm breaking when I see him next?"

"You and me, both! Is it done? Is she good to go?"

She nodded and pulled her hands from Orelle's face.

"Good! Then let's fly, ladies!"

I grabbed Orelle's hand and yanked her down the hallway toward the front door. Kavea and Ellera were right on our heels.

"They're coming in from a Crannie!" Ifyrus yelled at us as we approached. "Every time we knock them down, more show up!"

"Well, we've got what we came for!" I said. "Now let's get the hell out of here!"

"You got it!" he said. "Brax! Evony! They're coming! Let's move!"

The Dragon King in all his glory was flicking men left and right, hurling guards into walls, furniture, or straight out the front doors. It was quite the sight to behold. Evony was crouched over Fenix and Felix, unconscious and bleeding on the floor.

"Somebody help me get them out of here!" she yelled to the group. Ifyrus and Ellera rushed forward to help lift them up and drag them out, but a new swath of guards poured in, overwhelming us again.

I fired off my first dagger straight into the chest of a man about to run Evony through, felling him where he stood. She sent me a nod of thanks and went back to defending her fallen comrades. My second dagger, now switched to my right hand, swung at anybody that got near us. Orelle shrank into herself, but stuck behind me as best she could, Kavea helping to guide her by the arm and kick out at the guards lunging towards her.

Another one somehow got past Brax's flame and headed straight for us, so I flung my dagger at him, finding purchase in his stomach and stopping his rapid approach. *Damn! Now I don't have any weapons! That was stupid!* I looked frantically for something I could use to defend myself with and locked onto a heavy candlestick.

We were next to Ellera and Ifyrus now, still working on getting the twins out of harm's way, when a guard took a chance at Ifyrus. Seeing that he didn't notice his opponent, I ran forward to stop the attack.

"Face, meet *ELBOW*!" I said while smashing into the side of his head with brute force. Ifyrus finally looked backward and saw that I'd just saved his life.

"Your *Majesty*!" he chuckled. "I'm impressed! Who'd have thought those thin little bird bones of yours could come in handy?"

"Shut up and help me!" Ellera scolded him.

"Right! Helping!" The pair of them dragged their charges through the doors and laid them against the castle wall to wait for the others.

Two quick, consecutive *thumps* pulled my attention to the wall on my left in time to see both Kits sliding down it. My stomach boiled with rage, and I delivered their punter a mighty *whack* with my gripped candlestick. He slumped to the floor as I leapt over him to the downed foxes, scooping them up and depositing them onto a torn purple couch before jumping back into the fray.

"Brax! Evony!" I shouted. "Let's *go*! We've got them! Now!"

Brax gave a deafening roar, and Ruskin's men covered their ears, some dropping to their knees in agony. Brax didn't even bother to shift, just burst through the double doors, breaking them off their hinges and leaving a trail of splintered calamity behind him. Ifyrus and Ellera loaded up the twins on Brax's back, then Ifyrus effortlessly pulled up Orelle and Kavea, settling them in as well.

"There's no saddle, so hold on to this rope as tight as you can!" he instructed, producing a rope that he lashed about Brax's neck and snaked down his back to make sure everyone had a hold of it.

Cyndol ran out next, Kits One and Two shoved hastily down the front of her coat. Evony was right behind her, sending blow after blow to the steady stream of enemies flowing freely from what was left of the entryway.

"Next batch on Ifyrus!" Ellera called to the remaining members of our group.

Ifyrus shifted so fast that if I'd've blinked, I'd've missed it. Ellera produced a rope-tie for his back, and everyone scrambled up as quickly as they could. Brax sent bursts of flames in rapid succession now, knowing everyone was safely out of the way. Charred guards fell one after the other until they realized they were losing to the Dragon King. After that, arrows began to fly.

"Watch out!" I screamed, remembering my own dance with those arrows.

I needn't have feared, though, as the last of us grabbed hold of the rope. Both dragons sent flames so large at the castle that everything was instantly singed in sickening black and smoky gray. The smell of barbequed flesh made my stomach twist. Then the dragons kicked off, shooting us lightning fast into the sky and away from this nightmare.

Safe. We were safe.

I threw up.

CHAPTER FOUR: RUSKIN'S PLAN B

Every single one of his guards was going to die. Again. He would find his necromancer and bring them all back from the dead, just to kill them all over again! How could they fail so *spectacularly*?! How could they let his wife and daughter escape with them?! He smashed his clawed fist on the tavern table and split it straight down the middle.

"*My* wife! *My* child!" he bellowed, pounding his chest in a show of possessiveness.

Davina laughed sardonically under her breath. "Maybe they'll come for me next?"

Ruskin whipped his attention to her. "What was that, *Mage*?"

Her eyes shot to the floor. "Nothing, Majesty."

He stood stock-still for a moment, staring in fury, before smacking both hands on the split table behind him to propel him into Davina's downturned face. She winced but stayed put. Like a good girl.

"You… are *mine*," he said. "You stay as long as I want you to stay." He curled his taloned fingers slowly and sharply around her shoulder. "Besides, no one's coming for *you*. Why ever would they?" He let go in a slick twist, neatly slicing the top layer of skin on Davina's shoulder as he sauntered away. Again, she stayed put.

"My apologies. They wouldn't."

"That's right. They wouldn't. And why is that?"

Her lip trembled. "Because my family abandoned me, and no one is coming to save me. I am yours."

Ruskin paused to stare at her face for a moment. "Well said, Pet." He walked over to the curtain behind the bar. Over his shoulder, he said, "Grab your things. We're heading home for reinforcements. Then, you'll be so happy, we're headed to Gallanor."

CHAPTER FIVE: MIAWAE'S INVITATION

"Message for you, My Queen," Avery said, stepping quietly into Miawae's field of vision. She was standing at the guardrails of Lookout Point, located above the kingdom's largest waterfall. She was staring out at the cerulean ocean as if expecting to find something.

"Who is it from, Avery?"

He cleared his throat and shifted uncomfortably, something he is not prone to doing.

"It is from King Ruskin, Majesty."

"Is it? How utterly… *expected*."

"Majesty?"

Miawae turned to face her advisor. "So? What does it say?"

Avery unrolled the scroll and scrunched his face in worry.

"It reads:

"To the Lesser Sitting 'King and Queen' of Gallanor,

"It has come to my attention that a boy has escaped from my custody and is believed to have traveled to your realm. Whether this is to your knowledge or not is irrelevant. I demand his return at once. You have three days to surrender him. Should you choose not to relinquish him to my authority, then you are cordially invited to attend a war, commencing posthaste.

"Warmest regards,

"High King Ruskin"

Avery rerolled the scroll and presented it to his queen.

Miawae took it with grace, tucking it into the pocket of her billowing rose petal skirt. "Thank you, Avery. I will tell my husband."

Silence stretched on and Avery's worry built higher.

"Majesty, may I ask, do you know where this boy is?"

Miawae continued to stare out at the sea and said, "Oh, yes. I'm afraid I do. Though it won't do Ruskin any good. He's of no use to him now. What he is after is information and an artifact. I am in possession of both."

"So what do we do?"

Miawae let out a long breath and turned to her friend. "Prepare for war."

CHAPTER SIX: KAVEA'S GOODBYE

Normal breathing returning after their narrow escape, Kavea felt the stirrings of hope, *real* hope, for the first time in ages. She just knew Brax was the answer to her problems. Apparently, her mother did as well. He had finally come through for them and she couldn't be happier. They were free! Free from that castle and free from her father! Thankfully, they had also gotten to Bella, Druce, and Ethan rather quickly on the rush out of there and told them to meet them at Tripp's in Seaport. They would convene there and decide the next steps.

"Time to find a spot to land!" Amy shouted to Brax and Ifyrus. "I can see Tripp's from here!"

Brax grunted and shot a plume of smoke from his nostrils as he began his descent to an open patch of ground. Kavea clutched tighter to both the rope and her mother while they braced for landing. She marveled at how effortless this hulking beast made it seem! Ifyrus, right behind them, landed just as gracefully.

The passengers started to unload themselves and find their land legs again. Kavea patted her uncle on his winged shoulder and said, "Thank you. You're my hero."

He shifted back and she threw her arms around him in a bone crushing hug. He grunted again, this time in surprise at how strong this child was! He awkwardly patted her on the back and said, "You're welcome. It was a team effort. We just wanted you both safe."

Amy stepped forward and pointed at the sea. "This looks like the area I swam into when I first got here. I remember seeing some kind of city below, somewhere over in that general direction." She wiggled her fingers in a haphazard fashion over the spot she was referencing.

"Yes," Brax replied, "This is where I used to meet you. Your home is a few miles in that direction. Well, your home before we were stationed together on our island."

Evony gracefully vaulted off of Ifyrus and came over to join the conversation. "You have all been away from here for far too long. Much has changed. Ruskin and his allies are banned from the water. If caught by the Mer People, it is a death sentence. Now, Orelle and Amy, as you are both Mer royalty, you would have safe passage, especially if you are returning to your family. However, Kavea, I'm sorry, but as you are also the daughter of Ruskin, I'm afraid your presence would cause quite a stir. It might be a while before you're accepted into that side of your family. It would be safer to come back to Gallanor with the rest of us. Your mother is welcome as my guest as soon as she is healthy enough to do so. You have my word."

Kavea's heart broke all over again, but she knew that Evony was right. She would not jeopardize any chance her mother had of regaining the health and happiness her father had stripped away from her for all these years, even if that meant they had to be apart to do it.

She put on a brave face, took a deep breath, and grabbed her mother's frail hands, clutching them as tight as she dared. "It's okay, Mother. I am in good hands with these people. They will take care of me, I promise. I'll be okay, and so will you. It'll be good for you to get back in the water. Then, when you're healthy enough, you can meet me in Gallanor and tell me all about it."

Orelle's eyes began to well with tears as she stared at her daughter, the most alert she'd looked in ages. "Thank you," she whispered shakily. "Thank you for saving me. You are *my* hero." Her tears fell in earnest now as she gripped her child's shoulders. "I have been absent for so long. I am so sorry. And yet, you somehow still have the kindest and bravest heart of anyone I've ever met. I am immensely proud of you." She reached up for her face now, holding her with a strength she hadn't shown in years. She then pulled her close to kiss her cheek, hugged her fiercely, and let go. "I will see you soon, my love. Be careful."

With that, Orelle turned away and made off toward the beach to wait for Amy.

Kavea took a deep breath and let it out slowly. This was going to be rough. But her mother needed this, and she would be reunited with her soon. She couldn't wait to see her mother happy again, so she would do everything she could.

Brax, clearly uncomfortable, cleared his throat and followed Orelle down to the waterside to exchange a whispered word with her. After a moment, she hugged him and he returned it, gingerly, as if afraid he might break her. Then he turned abruptly toward the others and made his way back over.

"So, what's the plan?" he asked Amy.

She sighed. "Well, I'm the only other Mermaid here, so unless you guys have some fancy magick for joining us under the water, I think you'll just have to wait here for me. I'll be returning her to our family, or whoever is left, I suppose. I wish I knew who all I'd be seeing, or literally what to expect from any of this, but I will be happy knowing she is somewhere safe, where she never has to see that vile creature again."

The group nodded in agreement, feeling terrible for the poor woman.

At that moment, Bella came around the bend with Druce and Ethan in the wagon.

"Damn! That was fast!" Amy exclaimed, shocked by how quickly they made it there. "What, did you teleport here or something?"

"Teleport?" Druce repeated. "We met a traveling sorcerer on the road and bought a one-time Crannie, if that's what you mean?"

Amy's mouth fell open. "You mean to tell me you can just *buy* a Crannie and pop up wherever you want? Just… whenever?"

Druce exchanged amused glances with the others from Gallanor. "Well, it's not like it's common or anything. That power is quite rare."

"Oh, well, as long as it's rare." She rolled her eyes. "Well, whatever it is, I'm glad you're here. I was worried about you guys."

Evony said, "And, to that point, so must our king and queen be. We have been away far too long as it is, and I think it's time we hasten ourselves home. Any who wish to join us are welcome. Since our princess sent word to Cyndol that there were dark tidings on the wind, I have been terribly worried. Our kingdom may have need of us, so the sooner we return, the better."

"Of course." Brax said. "We wouldn't think of keeping you further. Your help in all of this was instrumental. We couldn't have done it without you. Especially your help with the children. Thank you. If you ever need to call on me or what's left of my kingdom, all you have to do is ask and I'll be there."

The pair shook hands firmly, an understanding forging between the two, then Evony faced the group again. "Cyndol, Ethan, you are welcome to come back with us until you can find suitable lodgings for yourselves. I don't know if you have other family to reach out to, but you can stay with us, if you like. We also have a great team of healers that can help you, Ethan. And Cyndol, our princess seems to have taken an interest in you, our queen as well, so what do you say? Will you join us?"

Cyndol and Ethan put their heads together to discuss. Kit wriggled his face in there to insert himself in the conversation, obviously going wherever Cyndol was going.

When they came to a decision, Cyndol said, "Thank you, we will. I made a promise to Kiara, and I intend to keep it as best I can."

"What about you, Ellera?" Amy asked. "Are you going with them, staying with us, or heading your own way?"

The stunning woman sauntered around the group, sizing up her options, and stopped at Bella. "I think I'm going to miss you the most. You, and your glorious morning muffins."

Bella belly-laughed and said, "Oh, pish-posh! You'll be fine! Besides, I'll whip some up for you anytime you like. Just come visit me sometime, eh?"

"You got it," Ellera winked at her before joining Ifyrus at his side. "I think I'll just see where this road takes me for a while. Besides, Amy needs some female energy to balance out all this dragon."

Amy laughed. "You're probably right!"

"I'll just wait here with the boys until you get back, if that works for you?"

"Of course!" Amy said. "And thank you. I appreciate it, really."

So, the group said their goodbyes and the Gallanorians loaded themselves in or around the wagon to head home.

Kavea took one last look at her mother, sitting quietly by the water's edge, and sent her a silent wish of healing.

"Until we meet again, Mother. I'll miss you."

CHAPTER SEVEN: AMY ARRIVES IN MERCONCHAWAY

Brax pulled me into his arms and whispered, "I don't want to let you go."

I returned the embrace. "I know. I don't want to let you go either, but I have to do this. I have to help my sister."

"I know," he said, his beard tickling my ear. "I just can't wait to get our lives back and to feel safe with you in our home again."

"We'll have that, I know we will," I promised. I could see life with him being happy and comfortable and I found myself longing for that. I *thump thump thumped* his muscular shoulder with my thumb, and he mirrored the gesture. *I love you*. Our secret code.

"Please be safe."

"I'll be back before you know it," I said. "Besides, Ruskin and his men can't follow us down there, so it's actually the safest I can be."

"You make a valid point," he said. "But please hurry, I miss you already."

I gazed sweetly at him. "Charmer."

He pulled my face closer to kiss me deeply and I hungrily obliged.

"Do you guys want to stop by your room at Tripp's, or...?" Ifyrus asked. "Because it's right there, mate. It is *right there*." He gestured dramatically at the tavern.

We pulled apart, a fiery shade of scarlet licking its way up my face.

"Fine!" I shouted. "Goodbye, all of you! I'll see you soon. Stay out of trouble!"

We said our farewells and they made their way to Tripp's. I walked back down the path to the water's edge to join my sister, patiently waiting for me. It was still bizarre having a sister I didn't know about. But, then again, why should things start making sense *now*? Nothing else had since I left Earth. Why should this be any different?

Orelle was staring out at the water with a faraway look in her eye.

"Orelle?" I said softly, startling her anyway. "Are you ready?"

She reached for my hand. "It's been a long time. I might need some help."

I chuckled. "Me, too."

A ghost of a smile teased her face, then retreated just as quickly as it came.

I took both her hands and led her into the shallow end of the water, lightly lapping at our feet. Orelle came along hesitantly, looking as if any sudden noise or movement could scare her away.

"It's okay," I said. "I've got you."

The look of terror behind her eyes was a stake in my heart and my insides clenched with anger. Anger for her, anger for how her life was taken from her, anger at Ruskin for damning my sister to centuries of torture and heartbreak. This poor, fragile woman was a shadow of the girl I knew and loved. I would do whatever I could to fix it.

"Are you ready?" I asked.

When she nodded, I pulled her out farther, both of us in water up to our shoulders now. A bit farther, and we were almost completely under. I shifted, still holding one hand, barely tugging her, trying to show her we could do this. I closed my eyes briefly and let my tail pop up above the water line to wave at her, something I recalled doing to make her laugh when we were kids. My eyes opened again, and I saw her face take on a hint of recognition. She let out a singular laugh in spite of herself.

"Your turn," I said.

Orelle closed her eyes, and I saw the water change around her. There were ripples and swirls as she slowly brought forth her own tail, iridescent and beautiful, a full range of rainbow colors so unlike my own mix of greens and teals. Light sparkled around her as it took the first layer of pain and fear away. She was magnificent.

"Orelle," I said, in awe, "there you are."

She beamed at me, and, for the first time, I really got a glimpse of my sister, the way she once was.

It was a start.

***

A string of jewel-toned bubbles danced merrily towards the surface from the scattered rocks in the sand. The kelp and creatures carried about harmoniously with them. A wave of orange and fuchsia twirled around me, beckoning me to play. I remembered how much I used to love that. How strange… it felt like it was just yesterday that I was doing this. Is this more of my memory coming back? I could almost swear that that's where we—

"That's where you used to hide from Father," Orelle said, pointing. "Oh, he'd get so mad at you for taking off like you did! I used to hear him screaming around the palace, 'Where did my daughter swim off to *now*?'"

I suppressed a grin, marveling at the fact I could hear her just fine underwater as clearly as if she were standing next to me on land. "Was that a common phrase?"

Orelle chuckled. "Well, you *were* a bit of a handful. You don't remember this?"

My mirth faded. "A little, here and there. If you'd've asked me before I saw you, I would've said it was all a blank slate. But it's slowly starting to come back to me. I remember hiding here from Father, though it's vague. Why was I hiding from him?"

"Oh, you know, typical growing pains, butting heads and the like."

"And I hid because, what, temper tantrums?"

"When you were younger, yes. I'd find you here, playing amongst the flotsam, jetsam, and hydrophytes. There was even a small cave, right—"

"There!" I pointed excitedly at it. "Yes!"

In my excitement, I darted over to it, eager to see if my memory of it would prove to be accurate. Sure enough, when I peered inside, the same twinkling gemstones that were embedded in the walls were still there, as if no time had passed at all. Amazing.

I swam back over to Orelle, and we continued onward.

The trip itself was not so long to our childhood home. What took a while was the stopping and reminiscing. On Earth, I would've called it a "Walk down Memory Lane". But here, it felt so much deeper than that. It felt like returning. I guess it was fitting, then, as that's exactly what we were doing.

A flurry of fins to my right caught my eye, and I saw an older Merman stop his fishing to watch our path.

"Amaryah? Orelle? But—" he furthered his look of confusion. "How can that be?"

He dropped his tools, letting them sink to the sandy floor below, and jetted off quickly.

"What was *that* all about?" I asked.

"If I had to guess, I'd say he just went to sound the alarm. We may have a convoy to escort us the rest of the way."

"Is that a good thing or a bad thing?"

She grimaced. "I guess we'll find out soon enough. Here they come."

She pointed over my shoulder. I turned around to check and, sure enough, a pod of Merpeople were headed straight for us. My nerves shot from my heart to my stomach, and I wondered idly, *If I threw up, would everyone see it float in front of my face? Eww.*

Willing the yuck away, I called, "Ahoy, there!" *What, was I a pirate now? Yikes.*

A woman with hair as dark as mine came forward first, wearing what I could only describe as lightweight battle armor. I wonder what it was made of.

Flicking her purple-black tail at us in warning, she asked, "Who are you? And why have you come to our kingdom?"

I swallowed my bile. "I am Amy, and this is my sister Orelle. We've come to look for our family."

Orelle said, "Please take us to King Volmar."

The woman turned to her companions and exchanged some words I couldn't make out. When they were through, she faced us again and said, "Show me your eyes."

I sighed, which just came out as a flurry of bubbles. "Let me guess, you're looking for purple?"

The woman remained silent, waiting for compliance. I closed my eyes, hoping I was doing this right, and when I felt the familiar sting from Tripp's, I opened them.

The pod collectively gasped. I had to refrain from laughing at how dramatic it felt.

"It's her!"

"She's returned!"

"They *both* have!"

Suddenly, they swarmed around us, excitement stirring them on. Orelle and I were quickly grabbed on either side of our arms as we were hurriedly pulled along.

"Easy, buddy! I can swim on my own, you know!"

Instantly, my arms were dropped, as were hers. One of them said, "Apologies, Highnesses. We just want to see you safely home. Your father will be very pleased to see you."

"Fine, then," I said. "Just show us the way. I promise we will follow,"

"Of course, Highness."

With that, we had our own personal escort through the rest of the short journey. The Merpeople chatted happily about what the current events were down there, but I was only half listening, mostly because I didn't know who or what they were talking about most of the time, but also because I was distracted by the stunning colors and creatures we passed along the way. I wished we had the time to stop and explore our old stomping grounds. I made a promise to myself to do just that the first chance I had.

Waving wistfully at a curious dolphin, I followed behind the Merpeople until they stopped in front of a large rock cavern. I was not prepared to see what was inside of it. Instead of the usual sight you would see in a standard cave, I was greeted by what looked to be a bustling city, alive with Merpeople and sea creatures alike. It lay half underwater, half above water. The enormous cavern looked as if it could house at least a hundred ships, and it blew my mind how something this large could stay hidden under the sea for so long without Ruskin finding it.

As my eyes took in all the people and sea buildings, Orelle chuckled next to me and said, "Almost takes your breath away, doesn't it?"

I nodded with my mouth open, then said, "I've been dreaming about this for so many years, I'd almost convinced myself that I'd made it all up."

My eyes met hers and I could see a tragically wistful haze shine over them.

"I'm so sorry for everything you've gone through," I said. "I truly am."

She reached out to squeeze my hand. "I feel the same for you. Your homecoming was sorely needed. I'm happy you're here with me."

"Me, too."

"Are you coming, Highnesses?" asked one of the Merpod.

"Right behind you," I said.

We tailed the group (pun intended) until we reached what I surmised to be an entry port of sorts. Those who were able to shift and get their land legs came up from the water at a specific landing. This was, of course, surrounded by guards, as we were now in the royal city of Merconchaway, according to the sign posted at the landing site.

"Merconchaway?" I stumbled over the word.

"Because the castle looks like a conch," Orelle said.

"Huh."

When my gaze finally landed on the castle in the distance, I could absolutely see why it was named so. Even from this far away, I could see it spiraling up from the water to touch the top of the cavern. It was enormous and gleamed in opalescent pinks and whites. It was resplendent and, most assuredly, conch shaped.

Orelle caught me ogling the castle and laughed. "Wait till you see the inside."

We finally got to the landing deck and took our turns shifting back to human, then exited the water to the cavern's stone pathway. Not for the first time, I spared a thankful thought to whatever power allowed me to keep my clothes and supplies safe and unwet. I'm going to have to ask someone to explain that to me one day.

"Your Highnesses," boomed a deep voice to our left, "please follow me. I will escort you to your father. He is waiting."

Orelle and I exchanged surprised glances and fell in behind a handful of guards.

Relaxing my face, I leaned in toward Orelle's ear and whispered, "I wonder how many alarms we set off by coming here?"

"Ones loud enough to catch Father's attention, at least."

"I'm happily surprised to hear he's still alive."

"I'm less surprised, but still very glad. I should like to apologize for the way we left things. I can only hope he will respond kindly."

"I take it you didn't have his approval to marry Ruskin?"

She scoffed. "Oh no, I had it. It was *me* who wasn't quite onboard. I left him with an earful."

I sensed this wasn't the time or place to delve into *that* particular tale, so I let the subject drop for now.

We followed along behind the gaggle of guards, ever closer to what my sister informed me was called Conch Castle. I could feel my nerves mounting and I started to shake. Orelle took my hand and gave it a squeeze.

"Me, too," she said quietly.

I gave her a grateful smile and squeezed back. "We've got this."

She nodded and let my hand drop as we took in the sights around us. Above the water line were the vaulted walls and ceiling of the cavern, mostly dark grey stone with interspersed divots full of glittering gemstones and multicolored coral. When I peered to my left, I could see gently swaying plants below the surface of the water. Schools of brightly colored fish, mermaids, and other sea creatures were making their way to and fro. The whole scene breathed life like I had never seen on Earth, and pinpricks of memory tickled my brain.

Orelle chuckled. "Are you remembering?"

I nodded and turned my gaze to the approaching castle.

Without warning, a trio of trumpeters came out onto the balcony above the entryway and blasted a few notes loud enough to wake the dead. I jumped a foot in the air, much to the mirth of my sister.

"His Royal Majesty, King Volmar, welcomes home his daughters, Princess Orelle and Princess Amaryah!"

The crowd erupted in a mix of cheers, applause, and audible gasps of surprise. That would keep the rumor mill busy for a while, I thought.

I turned to Orelle to ask if this was a common greeting and found her composure had changed and taken on an air of authority. She curtsied and confidently replied in a loud voice, "Thank His Majesty for his kind regards and inform him we humbly await his audience."

Stupidly, I fumbled my way through a curtsy and said nothing, not knowing what else to add. But it seemed to satisfy the speaker as the guards led us through the entryway and into the castle proper.

Conch Castle was precisely what it seemed from the outside: A giant conch shell that had been upgraded inside to accommodate life. The walls were shimmering shades of pearl and pink, adorned with tapestries of golden filigree and portraits of the royal bloodline. I found my own portrait and was shocked by how connected I felt to her— er, I mean, *me*.

"This way, please," a guard said, turning on his fancy heel.

He led us deeper into the castle, winding this way and that, passing more people and royal adornments the farther along we went, until we reached a spiral staircase.

"The king awaits you in his upper chambers."

He gestured with one hand, clicked his heels together, and left us to ascend alone.

"Well," I said, "I guess that's the end of the guided tour. Are you ready?"

Orelle was quiet for a moment, staring at the top of the stairs with a faraway look in her eyes, and I could see she was beginning to tremble.

"We can turn around right now, if you like. I can come back another time," I said gently, reaching for her hand again.

She didn't respond at first but, after a moment, she took a deep breath and steeled her shoulders, pulling on an air of practiced confidence, and let go of my hand.

"No. Father awaits us, and it has already been too long. Let's go."

Up the stairs we went, each step causing my anxiety to climb higher, my pulse jumping as if I'd slammed a Starbucks triple espresso. I had no idea what to expect.

Finally, we breached the top. There was no door at the landing, just a large room that had a domed ceiling, coming to a point at the far side, like you would see in a typical conch shell. Underneath that point was a throne, and in that throne hunched an aging king. His salt and pepper locks cascaded past his shoulders, hanging loosely about his royal blue and gold filigree coat. His beard was full and bushy, matching the greys and whites of his hair, looking as though it'd been a while since he'd seen a comb.

Silence filled the empty room. Neither Orelle nor I spoke or moved forward.

After several eternal seconds went by, the commanding voice of my father said, "Come."

It sent a shiver of recognition down my spine. The voice I'd heard my entire life on this planet once again rang in my ears. The voice of unchallenged authority in all matters, the voice that reprimanded me when I misbehaved, the voice that fought with my own when he found out about Brax, coursing through my brain and piercing my soul.

I seethed and stepped forward.

What greeted me was not what I expected. I sincerely thought I would meet the stern gaze of the kingdom's patriarch, ready to vocally (and quite possibly physically) lash out at me. But, instead, I saw the wizened features of a tearful man, powerful even in his frailty, trying badly to hold his composure lest he show a sign of weakness.

"My daughters," he choked on a sob, "you've come home to me."

CHAPTER EIGHT: CYNDOL'S TASK

Though she hadn't known her very long, Cyndol already felt saddened at the loss of Amy on their journey. She felt a sort of kinship with the strange woman and was disappointed they would not be traveling together to Gallanor.

Luckily, the rest of the trek was a streak of inactivity. No signs of Ruskin's men, no injuries or ailments to add to the mix, just peace and quiet and a clear path through.

Once Cyndol caught sight of the massive twin redwood tree entrance to Gallanor, a wave of relief dropped from her shoulders. She hadn't realized just how tense she'd been, and now that she was somewhere she felt safe, she could breathe. Ethan squeezed her hand, and she knew he felt it, too.

As they arrived at the main gate, Cyndol noticed Princess Kiara was standing impatiently with her guardsmen, literally tapping her foot in irritation.

"Well," her young highness said, "it's about time!"

She practically yanked Cyndol off the wagon so she could drag her into a walk and talk. Kit obediently followed.

Cyndol stumbled but caught her balance before she tumbled into the bushes.

"I'm sorry we took so long," she said. "We came as soon as we could. We had to go on a rescue mission."

Kiara stopped dead in her tracks. "Who needed saving?"

Cyndol gulped. "Kavea and her mother, Orelle. Ruskin's daughter and wife."

Kiara paled and stood stock-still.

"I'm sorry, you what now?"

Now it was *Cyndol's* turn to pale. She took another rough gulp and said, "We saved Ruskin's wife and daughter."

The beautiful princess looked like she was either going to throttle her or pummel her, but before she could decide which punishment was best suited, Evony came to the rescue.

"Your Highness," she said. "I can assure you, the mission was just. I will explain it all to you and your grandparents, if you will follow me to their chambers?"

Kiara was livid, but wisely kept her ire in check and followed her queen's advisor.

Cyndol breathed a sigh of relief and pet Kit's furry head to calm her nerves.

"I thought she was going to kill you!" he said.

"So did I!" Cyndol said.

"Uh," came the hesitant voice of her brother behind her.

"Oh!" she gasped. "Ethan, I'm so sorry! You've never been here before. Let me show you around a bit, then we can go find something to eat."

He gave her a weak thumbs up and the children went off to sightsee.

***

After an hour's worth of exploring, Cyndol could see Ethan was having a hard time keeping up. His movements became slower, his responses distracted. They opted to stop for a late lunch at Madame Mason's Meals and Heals, a combination potion shop and restaurant.

The building itself was like most of the structures in this realm: Wooden, appearing seamless in its connection to the living trees it shared its space with. It also boasted stained glass windows with an avalanche of flowers and ivy dancing along the outside walls, some even on the inside. It smelled of a mix of flowers, spices, and fresh roasted meats. Large batches of dried herbs hung from various spots along the ceiling. Mouths watering, they all agreed they could spend forever in this place.

"*Please seat yourselves*," Cyndol read off the sign in the inner doorway. "You got it, Sign."

The children spotted a plush burgundy booth by a window and promptly fell into it. Kit smashed his nose against the translucent stained pane, becoming highly entertained at seeing the world through a rose-colored glass.

A beaming middle-aged woman bounced over to their table.

"Hello, and welcome to my shop! I'm Madame Mason, and it's lovely to have you here today! You're the talk of the town!"

Cyndol's face reddened, not sure how she felt about being the center of attention. She glanced at Ethan, but he was staring intently at the middle of the table.

"What can I get for you?" Madame Mason asked, eager to be of service.

"Um," Cyndol said, "surprise us, I guess?"

Kit made a huffing sound and Cyndol added, "And a side of whatever meat you have handy, for my—uh… for Kit."

The polite proprietor smiled and said, "Two daily specials and a side of venison, coming right up!"

Kit's eyeballs almost popped out of his head! "I can have *deer*?"

Madame Mason's smile faltered as she realized the fox could talk. She quickly excused herself to fetch their food. Cyndol chuckled as the woman beat feet out of there.

***

Halfway through their delicious meal, the pale green front door to Madame Mason's opened with a flourish, and Evony, Felix, and Fenix walked through.

"Cyndol," Evony said. "The queen requests your presence at the Royal House."

Cyndol glanced down longingly at her half-eaten bowl of stew, a crust of brown bread still clutched in her hand.

Evony smirked. "You may finish your meal first but be quick about it. We will await you outside and escort you there."

With that, the kids and fox slurped down the remaining contents of their lunch and joined the guards outside.

Luckily, being fairly close by, it only took a few minutes to reach their destination. Cyndol, Ethan, and Kit once again rode in the wagon, as they were too tired from their journey to go on foot.

The Royal House seemed quieter than usual, almost as if it was holding its breath. Cyndol chided herself for the odd thought and tried to push down her growing sense of unease. Whatever this was, she didn't think it was *good* news. Why else was she being summoned by the queen's guard?

Ethan shuddered as they passed through the doors at the top of the steps, and Cyndol worried that he might not be as healed as they thought when they left the Fae Realm.

"Are you okay?" she whispered to him.

He kept walking. "Just a headache. I'm fine."

Princess Kiara's was the first face she saw. She looked less mad than before but still held an edge Cyndol didn't quite know how to read.

"Thank you for coming," Queen Miawae said. "Please, have a seat."

Instantly, Cyndol felt calmer. She barely knew this woman, but she knew she was safe in her presence. She allowed her shoulders to fall a bit and relaxed into the proffered couch cushions with ease. Kit jumped up and settled on her lap after turning around a few times to find just the right spot. Ethan sat awkwardly next to them and kept his eyes on the floor.

"Are you alright, Ethan?" Miawae asked.

"I'm fine," he said. "Just tired."

"I'll try to keep this brief so that you may have the chance to rest. You've all been through quite the adventure, and you'll need your strength for what's to come."

The hair on the back of Cyndol's neck prickled and she sat up straighter. "What do you mean?"

The queen sighed heavily, and a forced smile crossed her face. "War is coming. Here, to Gallanor. I have Seen it, and I'm afraid there is no stopping it."

Cyndol's heart hammered in her chest and her breath caught in her too-tight throat. "What do we do?"

Kiara stepped forward and said, "I need you to use your ability to speak to animals to pass along the warning to all in our kingdom. Those who wish to hide or flee may do so with no repercussions from the Crown. However, those who wish to stay and fight will be under *my* command, and yours, if you are willing. At least, as far as speaking to the animals goes."

Cyndol didn't know what to say. She'd never been in charge of anything more than making sure her chores were done! Now one of the biggest kingdoms in the world needed her to help with a *war*?

She gulped and nodded her head, finding she didn't have the words to speak.

"Very well," Miawae said, "then you and Kit will leave at daybreak to get started on your mission. As for Ethan," she turned to face the boy whose face had not lifted from the handwoven rug on the floor. "I would like for you to join Druce in the House of Healers to see if he can check that the Fae magick is still holding strong."

Ethan nodded in the affirmative but offered nothing else.

With instructions for Cyndol to join Kiara and her guard at dawn, Miawae sent the kids off to their temporary lodging to get some sleep before the chaos.

As the door to their room was closing, Cyndol caught sight of Ethan scratching his head.

CHAPTER NINE: AMY GAINS SOME INSIGHT

"My daughters, you've come home to me." My father reached out the feeble right hand of a once muscled arm, tears flowing down pale cheeks.

I couldn't move an inch. My feet felt glued to the floor as my heart hammered painfully in my chest. I had the sudden urge to fight or flee, but my inner stubbornness pushed it back down enough for me to take a deep breath.

Orelle paused only a moment before flinging herself forward to land bodily in his lap. She threw her frail arms around him, hugging him as tightly as she dared. He huffed a pained gasp as her weight knocked a bit of wind out of him, but in their eagerness to reunite, it was easily forgiven. He hugged her in return and closed his eyes in relief.

I remained motionless. Memories of this man began to flood back to me. Memories of being chastised and threatened, in this very room, even, with words like, "Over my dead body!", "You will marry who *I* tell you to marry!", and "You stupid, selfish girl! You will do what is best for *my* people, *my* kingdom, or you will find yourself cast out of it!" Anger bubbling, I just stood there, hate and love for this man warring within me.

Orelle noticed that I hadn't moved and pried herself from Father's arms.

"Amy?" she asked. "Are you alright?"

I gritted my teeth and glared. A long moment passed, but I held my ground.

"It's alright," came a voice behind me. "He's on *your* side now."

As if a blanket of warmth had been placed on my soul, the comforting timbre of Tripp's voice calmed the raging beast inside me. My shoulders loosened and I turned around to see a hesitant smile cross his face.

"Tripp," I breathed. "What are you doing here?"

His hand came up to scratch his head. "Well, now, you see, I was in a spot o' trouble—"

"He's come back because Ruskin chased him out," Father said, a slight bite to his tone. "He's on the move. Tripp is conveniently choosing to help us. As much as a human *can*, anyway."

"A magickal one, lest you forget!" Tripp winked at me and said, "Your pa always knew how to hold a grudge."

Orelle gave the king a scolding tap on his arm. "Father! That's your best friend you're talking to! Be nice!"

Best friend? I hit Tripp with a quizzical look.

"You don't recall that either, huh?" He chuckled in resignation, then focused his attention on my father. "Can we do somethin' about this memory o' hers, please? It's gettin' in the way o' things."

Fury burned through me, and I put a hand up to stop further conversation.

"If anybody else wants to mess with my head, I'm going to need some answers first!"

"As will I!" Father said. "For instance, where is Enid?"

"Now who in the hell is *Enid*?!"

Orelle's face fell. She whipped her head to face our dad, jumping off of him, but sticking close. "She's not here?"

"I thought she left with *you* when you married that psychotic werewolf king! I thought all of my daughters abandoned me!"

"Wait, I have *another* sister?" Just when I thought things couldn't get more complicated.

Tripp stepped in and laid his hand on my arm in a calming manner. I felt some of the fight drain out of me, and then I was just tired.

"Can we please just sit down somewhere and talk? I have so many questions," I said, putting pressure on my temples. I felt a headache forming and it was beginning to throb. I just wanted to rest and have everything make sense again. Not for the first time, I missed my quiet little life back in Sebastopol.

"Volmar," Tripp called, "if you don't mind, may we adjourn to the dinin' room? We can get your girls somethin' to eat and have ourselves a chat."

Father sighed wearily but waved his left hand in a dismissive gesture. His guards appeared out of nowhere to usher us towards a door I hadn't noticed before. It blended in nicely with the walls, and I suspect the reason I hadn't seen it was because it was designed that way.

We walked down a short hallway to the first door on the right, opening up to a petite room, likely tucked away behind the throne room. The table itself looked to be a single polished piece of driftwood that I might see in any sea town back home, but it had a stunning shine to it that I had never seen produced on Earth. It was propped up on four equal heighted stalagmites with matching chairs around the perimeter.

"For a mermaid castle, I'm surprised it's not under water," I said, looking around the room.

"The lower half *is*," Tripp told me. "You know, for those of the gill persuasion."

"Got it."

We sat down around the table, each eager to find pieces of what we'd been missing. Orelle looked happy for the first time, truly happy, and my heart thumped happily for her. *Oh! Enid!*

"So, tell me about Enid," I said. "Are there more siblings I don't know about? And where's Mom?"

The happiness I'd seen on Orelle's face a moment ago disappeared as quickly as it came, and I could have kicked myself for doing that to her. I didn't want her to suffer any more than she already had.

"Gone," Father said, limping in to take his seat at the head of the table.

"Gone?"

Orelle sniffed, and I reached my hand out instinctively to protect her.

"Dead."

My own breath caught this time. "How? And when?"

A silent tear slipped down Orelle's sunken face, and I gritted my teeth harder.

"It was an accident—" she said.

"Accident, my ass! That dragon *killed* your mother in cold blood!" Volmar thundered, smashing his fist so hard on the table that it left an impressive dent behind. I had no idea he had that kind of strength left in him!

"Father, please," Orelle begged, cupping his hand in hers. "Please."

He softened, but it was a struggle. I watched as his face parried a myriad of emotions. Finally, he took a deep breath and steeled himself in kingly fashion.

"A few years before you... *died*... your mother was on a mission on land, en route to Gallanor to meet with the queen. There was trouble brewing at the time in several places, and your mother was trying to meet with the queen to devise a plan of peaceful action. She never made it. She and her guardsmen were attacked by a dragon. The dragon claimed your mother was part of an uprising and murdered the lot of them. Good King Ibraxus II opted *not* to kill him, as would have been just, but let him live out his days in a jail cell on Dragon Moon. Then he just... carried on, as if everything was fine. I never forgave him for that."

Understanding dawned on me. "That's why you didn't want me to marry Brax."

He shook his head slowly, not meeting my eyes, instead focusing on the memory of his fury and pain.

"Oh, Father, I'm so sorry," I said. "So why was I engaged to Ruskin?"

He sighed, pulling out of his dark memories. "I thought you would be better suited for a land dweller, and his father was king. And, if I'm being honest with myself, I wanted more power. I thought if you married him, it would give us more access to power on land, not just the sea. In my greed and foolishness, I didn't think to find out what kind of man he truly was. I had no idea what a monster he'd become, or I never would have allowed him near my family. His father was a decent man, if you can believe it. I'd had many dealings with him in the past and had never suspected his son would run so afoul.

"When you ran off with that accursed dragon prince— oh, I was furious. Then, when you died, well, Ruskin blamed it all on the dragon. I'm ashamed to say, I believed him. So, when he came around asking for a different daughter, I agreed and gave him Orelle." He choked on a sob and turned sad eyes to his other daughter. "I'm so very sorry, sweetheart. I wish I'd never done that. If I'd known the truth…"

She began to cry as well and got up from her chair to hug him. I wiped a tear from my own eye.

"I have a daughter of my own. Her name is Kavea. I'd love for you to meet her. I was afraid to bring her, being Ruskin's child. I didn't know if she would be welcome."

He wiped his eyes roughly with the back of his hand. "I think I'd like that. Assuming she takes after you and not her father."

She chuckled and said, "She's nothing like him, thankfully. In fact, I think you'd quite like her. She has a big heart and an even bigger thirst for knowledge."

"Where is she now?"

"I sent her to Gallanor with the Queen's Guard, along with a couple other children. They'll be safe there."

Tripp cleared his throat and asked, "What other children?"

"A brother and sister," I said. "Ethan and Cyndol. Said they're from Cavar. You know, there was something so familiar about her, but I can't put my finger on it. It's been bothering me ever since we met. But she's just a kid, so I wouldn't have known her from the last time I was here, right?"

It was Tripp's turn to pale, and I watched as the blood left his cheeks.

"Well, funny you should mention…"

"No, no, no, wait! Let me guess. Umm, she's my long-lost daughter and next in line for the throne!" I laughed at my own joke and looked at the faces around me. No one else was laughing. Not even a little. The hair on my arms stood up. "Tripp, I wasn't serious. You can laugh, you know. It's just a joke… right? Right?"

Tripp hastily grabbed a flagon of alc on the table next to him, slugging back an impressive amount before it caused a coughing fit. I pounded him on the back harder than I intended to and he finally caught his breath enough to wave me off.

"Enough!" *Cough.* "I got it! Thank you."

I sat back down, but never took my eyes off him, making sure he'd feel the weight of my stare.

He gulped and said, "So, you are actually pretty right on the money."

"Explain."

We all leaned in closer, not knowing this story. *Glad I wasn't the only one this time.*

Tripp sighed and gave in. "So, you know that you and Ibraxus were on guard duty on that island together, right? Well, I was there, too. I'd been there since your daddies were, back when *their* daddies were, and even longer still. I'm a lot older than I look. Well, I never had children of my own, and my kingdom fell lon' ago, but I stayed on as I had no heir and no throne, ever guardin' that island. Your father and me, we became close, best friends, even. But then came time for him to assume the role of king, and same with Brax's father.

"Eventually, you two came in and I sort of felt like you were the kid I never had. You treated me like your favorite uncle, and we became a family by choice. When the two of you fell in love, I was the only one who understood and rooted for you. In fact, I officiated your secret weddin' on the island."

"A fact of which I still don't approve!" yelled my father.

"Note taken," Tripp yelled back. Attention back to me, he continued. "Not lon' after, you shared with me that you suspected you were with child, but I was the first person you were tellin'. I was elated, by the way. But you knew there would be some push back and you weren't sure what to do."

He paused to take a deep breath and another swig of his ale before the next part. "Well, Ruskin found out his bride-to-be had wedded the dragon prince, and somehow found out how to get to the island. My guess is it was gleaned through magickal means, likely his father's Mage. Anyway, he snuck his way onto the island and the alarms started to go off. You, me, and Brax took our positions to fight, not knowin' who was headed our way, so when we saw that it was Ruskin, we stupidly stood down, thinkin' we could work it out without a battle. How stupid we were." Another sip. "Ruskin told the world Brax killed you in a battle for your hand, but it didn't go exactly like that. Ruskin confronted you two and demanded he release you into his custody to be married back on land immediately. See, while your father craved the idea of power on land, Ruskin set his sights on the sea. He may have convinced himself that he loved you, in his own way, but mostly he loved himself, and he loved power even more."

I risked a glance at Orelle, having to sit through this story about her husband and my heart broke all over again. Any signs of happiness had retreated. All I saw now was a hollow woman sitting across from me. I tried to reach for her hand, but she slipped it under the table and into her lap. I sighed and focused my attention back on Tripp.

"The men decided to fight for your hand. Brax to keep it, and Ruskin to steal it. He couldn't accept defeat, so he attacked first. We didn't know he'd brought a Mage alon' with him who'd been hidin' in the bushes. The first bolt of magick came from behind a tree and hit Brax squarely in the chest. He roared and transformed into his dragon self. He blew a flame towards the Mage, but the Mage managed to escape. You shifted and jumped into the water to speed over to him, grabbing him by his ankle to pull him under. He was able to fend you off but caught my fist in his face when he turned to flee. I knocked him out cold and went to help Brax, who was now fendin' off Ruskin. Ruskin's claws were out, and his face elongated with razor sharp teeth. None of us knew he was a werewolf back then, so he had the upper hand in shock value. Brax was momentarily thrown off and took a handful of claws to his belly. In his defense, you ran forward to stop Ruskin from further attack. You tackled him to the ground and pulled him, kickin' and screamin' under the water. You almost killed 'im, too, but he bucked you off, swipin' at you as well. Luckily, he missed, and you were able to follow him back out onto the ground and position yourself in front of Brax. Brax took another chance at sendin' fire his way and singed the hair on his left ear. The Mage unfortunately came to at that moment and rushed to his master's aid, throwin' a curse at Brax that devoured him completely, stealin' his dragon shiftin' powers and causin' him to resume human form. We both freaked out, and while I fired off at the Mage with some of my own magick, Ruskin tried to attack Brax while he was down, and you stupidly got in front of him, takin' the brunt of it all. Brax's scream— well, let's just say I'll hear that rattlin' around in my head till the end of my days." He shuddered. "I looked up in time to see you fall, and the Mage took the opportunity to hit him with one more curse before I snapped his neck. I was too late. Brax was immobilized. That's when I noticed Ifyrus had come to join the fray and was hit by a ricochet of the curse, downing him as well. I still don't know what happened next, but I assume there was another intruder, because I remember standin' in front of Ruskin one minute, ready to fight him to the death, then I woke up next to your body, and everyone else was gone."

He took the last swig of his ale.

"I saw the light of your soul leave your body, too far above me to be of any help, and I crumpled to the ground, defeated. But then... I saw it. There was a second light, one that was only startin' to leave your body, a smaller, lighter soul than yours had been, and I remembered your secret. I fumbled for a potions container I'd had in my coat pocket and caught it before it could get too far. As soon as it was in my jar, I heard a whisper, just a small one, mind you, but she called to me. She wasn't ready to leave just yet, and I knew what I had to do. First, I ran to your home on the island, knowing I didn't have a lot of time to get this right. I found the amethyst geode that was your weddin' gift from your pa—"

"I did *not* gift her those! You *stole* them out from under my nose!" Volmar said, finger pointing accusatorially at the wily barman.

"You told me they were set aside for Amaryah's weddin', so that's when she got them! Who gives a griffin's hynie if it wasn't exactly to who you thought it'd be?"

Father glared daggers at his friend but allowed him to continue.

"Anyway, like I was sayin', I went to grab the geode, and, thinkin' fast, I cast a spell that sent the geode alon' with your departin' soul. I'd lon' heard tales of reincarnation to another place, and I wanted to make sure you could find your way home someday. You and that geode set are inherently connected. I see that it worked, by the way, or you wouldn't be here right now, so... you know... you're welcome.

"Then, after sendin' it off after you, I Crannied myself to the Mer Kingdom and found your sister, Enid. I told her what'd happened and warned her of Ruskin's thirst for power. I was afraid he'd make a play for her next. I tried to find Orelle as well, but," he turned to Orelle, "I'm sorry. I couldn't find you."

He faced me again, tears in his eyes as he relived the chaos. "Enid swore to me she would hide somewhere far from Ruskin's reach and keep the little soul safe. I recalled how you'd told me before the weddin' that you always loved the name Cyndol, so I told her to call it that. She fled to a nice beach town far from here and married a man named Darrian in Cavar. Together, they had a son named Ethan. He shares your eyes, by the way.

"A few more years went by, and a terrible quake hit the land, causin' the whole place to shake. The soul jar fell and broke. Enid thought all was lost until she woke up nine months pregnant the very next day. A week later, Cyndol was born. They had a Mage friend who'd spelled Ethan's eyes when he was born, so they did the same for Cyndol. This was to hide both the purple color and the Mer lineage, lest Ruskin find out and come lookin'. From what I've been hearin' lately, both children have managed to get on his radar anyway."

I was completely dumbfounded. Was his tale true? It rang true in my heart but reconciling that with my brain was going to take a minute.

"Does somebody else want to talk now? I'm a bit parched." He tried to take another sip of ale but found his flagon empty. One of Father's servants appeared out of nowhere and refilled it for him. Tripp took a grateful gulp and sat back in his chair to rest.

"So. I have a daughter," I said.

Tripp nodded.

"Who I just sent to Gallanor."

He nodded again.

"And where is Ruskin?"

"On his way to Gallanor, if my sources are correct," Volmar said.

"Damn," I swore. "I'm going to kill him." I got up loudly, flinging my cup against the wall, not caring if it broke. I strode to the door, fully intending to make my way to Gallanor as quickly as possible. I cursed myself and my dumb luck, and cursed the bastard who took my life, my husband, my memories, and who was now after my child.

"Wait." I paused in the doorway, turning to Tripp and my father. "What does he want with Cyndol?"

Father said, "Power. Always power. Her brother supposedly stole an artifact and was in Ruskin's care—"

"Yeah, I know that part. But what does he want with my daughter?" I interrupted, sick of this.

"She's your daughter. He wants to rule. She's technically in line for both Sea and Sky. You guessed that yourself just a few moments ago, joking as you might have been. If he has her, he can control it all. He can even have *you* at that point. Why *wouldn't* he want her?"

My blood boiled under my skin, and I felt the last vestiges of green melt from my eyes. I was full amethyst now, and this wolf was going to die.

"I'm going to Gallanor. Who's coming with me?"

"I can send you all the help you need, daughter, but I'm afraid I cannot come with you, not until Ruskin is dead."

"Why not?!" I asked. "After all of this?"

"Because, my darling, I was cursed as well. If I leave Merconchaway, my life and my power, along with all Mer magick, will die. My soul is connected to the Callembrian Core, directly under this castle. One of Ruskin's Mages saw to that once he returned from your battle. I haven't left here in two hundred years. So, you see, I *want* to go with you, to fight by your side, to see this evil struck down in front of my very eyes for all he has taken from me, from us. But I cannot. I will send you all that I can, and I will spend the rest of my days doing all that I can to help. From here."

I gave him a curt nod. That would have to be enough. I left to gather my army.

CHAPTER TEN: KIARA SPEAKS WITH HER GRANDMOTHER

"So," Kiara said, "Ruskin is on his way here."

Ikah seethed from behind the bars of her cell, clenching and unclenching her talon-esque nails along the hardened stone posts. "That's *King* Ruskin, you filthy peasant, and you will show him the respect he deserves!"

Kiara chuckled. "Oh, I'll show him the respect he deserves, alright! Don't lose any sleep over *that*."

Ikah's ebony eyes caught a sparkle of sunlight coming through the grates of the dungeon, giving the eerie impression that one could get lost in the depths of her soul. Kiara shuddered.

"What can you tell me about his army?" she asked. "How many are with him? When and where will they attack? Is there any way to stop this before people get killed?"

Ikah made a dramatic showing of buttoning her lips closed and sat back on her cot, looking deliciously satisfied with her noncompliance.

"You're never going to leave Gallanor," Kiara promised her captive. "Be it death or imprisonment, you will never step foot outside of these walls."

"I look forward to proving you wrong, *Princesssss…*"

Kiara glowered at Ikah's simpering face and left the woman to rot. She turned on her heel and made her way back outside to the fresh air of midday, drinking in the shining suns and the light breeze that tickled her face.

Evony was waiting outside for her.

"Your Highness," she said. "Your grandmother would like a word with you."

"Of course," Kiara replied. "Lead the way."

Evony escorted the princess to the queen, who was enjoying a fresh purple apple and surveying her forestry kingdom from Lookout Point. Miawae bit down on the succulent fruit and the juice dribbled down her chin. Her grandmother looked as if this was the most blissful anyone could possibly be, and Kiara suddenly wished not to disturb her.

Evony cleared her throat so as not to startle the queen. Miawae took one more moment, then focused her faraway gaze front and center.

"You wished to see me, grandmother?" Kiara asked.

Miawae wiped her face gently with a linen napkin. "I did, yes. I wished to see if you had managed to get any answers from our 'guest'."

Kiara bit her lip in frustration, knowing she had nothing helpful to report. "I have not. She seems to delight in being majestically unhelpful, and unless I threaten her with torture, which I'm sure she would probably enjoy, I don't see her being very forthcoming in information."

Her sovereign smiled softly and said, "Do not fret, darling. I did not expect her to be. But I had to give you a fair shot at trying." She paused, then said, "You know, all of this will be yours someday, and dealing with folk, both desirable to have around and not, will be a skill you must develop. What do you think we should do with her, then, if she is refusing to cooperate?"

Kiara furrowed her brow in distaste, not liking the idea of Ikah's fate being up to her. Logically, she knew her grandmother was right, she *would* be in charge someday and would have to know what to do in situations like these. But, as for this one in particular? How do you tell your loving grandmother that you'd rather just be done with her and kill her off before she had the chance to harm anyone or escape? She bit her lip, stalling for the right words.

Miawae saw her granddaughter's thoughts as if they were written on her face. "Not everything in life will fit neatly into a box, I'm afraid. Every choice we make bears its own consequences. You will draw your own line in the sand for those which you are able to live with, and those you simply cannot."

Kiara paused for a moment, then asked, "Are you going to kill her?"

Miawae took another bite of her apple, once again turning to face the view of her beautiful realm. She never did answer.

"Your Majesty!" Avery and Bella approached Evony, Kiara, and Miawae, Bella huffing and puffing up the small incline to their perch at Lookout Point.

"We bring news on several fronts," Avery continued when he had the attention of the queen. "Firstly, we have received another missive from King Ruskin."

"Please read it," Miawae said.

Avery cleared his throat and read:

"To the throned thieves of Gallanor~

"It is time to make a decision. Surrender the boy and any and all artifacts on his person, or the Army of the Great Emperor Ruskin will descend upon you. This will be your final warning.

"Warmest regards,

"Emperor Ruskin"

"Emperor now, hmm?" Miawae scoffed. "Over my dead body."

Kiara was afraid of that. "What would happen if we gave him what he wants?"

Miawae turned sad eyes on her heir. "The very worst. Ruskin will use the information and the artifact to unknowingly open a rift in our world, one that creates a portal from this world to the next. Not only will he kill us and the boy anyway, but he will end up destroying the world he so desperately wishes to rule over in the process. He wants power, but he will end up with more than he bargained for."

The small group was silent a moment, thinking some very dark thoughts.

Miawae pulled herself from bleak musings and refocused her attention. "I'm sorry, you said there was more?"

"Yes, Majesty," Bella said. "I've received word through the grapevine that Cyndol and Kit are making good progress in speaking to the animals and some of the harder to reach shifters.

Druce went with them to speed things up a bit and make sure they found everyone, but if all continues to go well, most or all will have been alerted by nightfall. I'm told they will be bringing back those who wish to fight. I'll have a feast prepared for dinner when they return."

"That's very kind of you," Miawae said. "Thank you, Bella. I'm sure it will be much appreciated. Is there more?"

"Yes, Majesty," Avery continued. "King Matthias is readying our fighters and asks that you come by to lend an encouraging word before battle. He believes any insight from you could be helpful in the fight ahead."

"Of course," the queen replied. "Please tell him I will be there shortly."

"Yes, Majesty," he said, then left with Bella in tow.

Kiara met her grandmother's tired eyes, and they gave each other a tight-lipped smile. Miawae took one last, longing look at the breeze kicking up over the water and sighed. She brought her lips to Kiara's cheek for a quick kiss, then pulled her into a side hug before traveling back down the slope with her.

"You will be a fine ruler someday," the queen said to the princess. "I just know it."

CHAPTER ELEVEN: AMY SCORES A WIN

I have a daughter. I have a daughter. I have a daughter.

The words did not seem real. And, yet... something clicked inside me that deemed the sentence true. I guess if Brax and I were lovers in my past life, then *married* for a short time, dying pregnant wasn't too big a stretch, especially considering every other weird thing I'd been through since coming back here.

I'll kill him twice *for this!* I wanted to rage. *How dare he fight us, how dare he kill me and spell my husband and his friend, how dare he rule with force and fear, and HOW DARE HE GO AFTER MY DAUGHTER?! I will kill him THRICE!*

"Where the hell am I?" I stopped short in the hallway, I was wandering down and flapped my arms at my sides, completely lost. "I can't believe they just let me take off like that! I don't know where I'm *going*!"

I looked around myself, trying to get my bearings, but all I saw was more pink- and pearl-colored walls with fabulous sea-themed decorations. Shells, gemstones, and artwork of prominent mermaids past. Fantastic. This helps me zero percent.

Tired now, I let out a long breath and leaned against a rounded wall, letting my poor, aching body melt into the concavity of the conch.

CLICK!

"Crap." The wall gave way and I landed bodily on the floor. Figures. Another secret panel.

"You know, I used to love these damn things. They look like such fun in the movies," I said from the floor, talking aloud to myself yet again. Or so I thought.

"Took you long enough," Tripp said.

I yipped and scrambled back to my feet. "What?"

"What, *what*?" he asked, face scrunching.

"What *this*!" I screamed. "What *any* of this? Where are we? And how'd you get here first?"

He laughed then. "Highness, you've been goin' in circles for almost an hour. I was gettin' ready to come find y'a, but I wanted to make sure you had enough time to cool off first."

"How kind of you."

"So? Have you?"

I shrugged with my whole body, surrendering myself to whatever this was about to be. "Sure. Lay it on me. What's next?"

He made a wide sweeping gesture to a beautiful pewter statue behind him that stood about five feet tall, modeled to look like a beautiful mermaid queen. She stood silently in front of a rock wall with no adornments.

"Your mother," he said, searching my eyes for hints of recognition.

My breath caught in my throat as I moved forward, suddenly aching to touch her hair. I let my fingers slide from her flowing curls down to her petite shoulders. I felt a tickle of electricity, like static shock, dance across my fingertips. I jerked back, afraid.

"She can't hurt you," Tripp said softly. "In fact, that voltage you feel is the connection to the Mer Core. It sits behind these walls, only accessible by one of your bloodline. It's the main source of all the magick in Callembria that doesn't fall from the Gemstone Belts. Some say it's even stronger than that."

"That's why Ruskin is after my daughter," I said.

"That would be my guess, Princess."

"Show me."

"You got it." He gestured for me to stand directly in front of the statue of my mother and look straight into her eyes. "Now, in order to access the Core, you need to allow the amethyst eyes to connect."

I noticed then that despite the statue being completely grey, her eyes were indeed very purple. The closer my face got to hers, the brighter they shone, as if they expected me. A shiver of anticipation went up my spine. I took a deep breath and let it out slowly, bringing my full gaze to hers, locking in completely.

A loud rumbling startled me, and I jumped back as if burned. Tripp delighted at my reaction as the rock wall gave way to reveal a large, open cavern with vaulted ceilings and a giant glowing orb in the center. The orb was several shades of purple and white, its blazing electric amethyst energy writhing and coiling around itself like a living, breathing thing. It was half in the water, half not, just as Merconchaway Castle was. I was utterly transfixed.

"Princess?" Tripp said. "You alright?"

I couldn't take my eyes off the beauty swirling before me.

"I—I have to touch it..."

Without waiting for a response, I walked to the natural rock guardrail and jumped straight into the water, called by the Core. The shock of icy water should have taken my breath away but, instead, it felt warm and inviting. It caressed me in ways that felt familiar, comforting. I had to get closer.

I felt myself shift without even thinking, and I propelled myself closer to the Core, faster now, desperate to get there. The closer I got, the more I swear I heard music. It was reminiscent of both wind chimes and waves crashing against the shore, gorgeous and haunting in equal measure. *Almost there...*

Within reach of it now, the water around me began to bubble merrily, pulling me into a mini whirlpool until I was at the bottom-most point of the Core. And it did indeed come to a point. I couldn't help myself. I had to touch it.

I reached out my right hand, slowly, terrified, but compelled to connect. The second my fingers touched the tip, I felt a jolt of molten fire streak through my brain, singeing through every last bit of spell work that had been placed there. My world exploded in a frenzy of memory.

Father, teaching me how to swim when I was a toddler. I could swim before I could walk.

Mother, singing with me on journeys to help our kingdom in the sea. I had her same ebony locks and amethyst eyes. In fact, I could almost be her carbon copy, if it weren't for my father's smile.

Orelle and Enid, laughing and swirling around everyone, playing with seahorses in the water and sea otters on land. They would chase each other and the marine life for hours. Everyone loved and doted on them, me included.

Tripp, throughout my life, always there, like an unofficial uncle. Helpful on The Island, and helpful as a friend, whenever we needed him. He was Father's best friend, but also ours.

Then there was the day my mother died. The whole kingdom fell into despair and disarray. Father did the best he could, but he fell apart in her absence. I watched as he succumbed to his pain, time and time again.

Following that came the day I met and fell in love with Lord Ibraxus of Dragon Moon. It was our first day stationed on The Island. His pomposity was only outweighed by his humor and charm. He fell in love with me the same day for my intelligence and quick wit. He claimed I was the only woman who could match him joke for joke, and Tripp had to agree.

I remembered meeting Ruskin for the first time, too. He was arrogant, vile, but glaringly handsome, despite his chillingly pale turquoise eyes. Our fathers were so eager for us to wed that they announced it before asking me first. When I went to talk to Father after the announcement had been made throughout the kingdoms, he only assured me that all would be well, and we'd soon be more powerful than anyone in the sea had ever been. After losing Mother, power was the only thing left that he cared about. He obsessed over it. It even eclipsed his judgment with his daughters. He pushed us away and it broke us. Orelle was always trying to win back his favor, while Enid was content to be done with him. In my own fury over the Ruskin situation, I was happy to be on duty, spending my days with Brax and Tripp.

I remembered my wedding day, and all the secret, romantic days leading up to it. Tripp was our biggest supporter, as well as the officiant, as he'd said. We moved in together on The Island in the small home I'd been staying in since drifting further away from my father. It made sense, being stationed here anyway. Brax was shucking his duty of learning how to take over kingship on Dragon Moon from his father, but King Ibraxus II was a far more understanding man and wanted to give us time alone after being wed. He was one of the few who knew.

When Father found out we'd wed, he went to apologize to Ruskin's father, King Rousard, not knowing the depths to which this betrayal would hit. It pained King Rousard, but it infuriated Ruskin, who went off in search of us. He hired his father's most questionable Mage and made him divine where we were. He set out to attack.

The attack went down just as Tripp had said. I even recalled the feeling of being hit with the magick bolt. I'd known it was meant for Brax, but was too afraid that it would kill him. I tried to push him out of the way, thinking I had enough time. I was wrong. Too late, I remembered the child inside me, the one I had just found out about a week prior. In an instant, I knew what I had done.

I broke away from the Core, absolutely shattered. I screamed into the cooling saltwater with every fiber of my being. *How could I have done that?! How did I misjudge that so badly?! How could I risk my daughter's life like that, even as I was trying to save the life of her father?!*

An icy calm encased my body, and one thought burbled to the top: Ruskin has to die, and I would be the one to do it.

I left the water in a fury, land legs back, kicking me into high gear to my old bedroom. I knew the way now.

I front-kicked open an aged wooden door and saw that my room was exactly as I'd left it. Perfect. No spiders down here, just dust. That was fine. What I needed was in a cupboard anyway. I hastily flung open the lavender armoire door and shoved my hand into a cubby hole, pulling back another star ruby to match the one I'd carried with me since arriving on Dragon Moon. These were a set spelled to communicate through time and space and had a specific connection to Brax and me. We might need them in the near future.

I also loaded up on weaponry: More bejeweled daggers and sharpened starfish husks. I would have laughed, calling them ninja stars, but my fury decimated any humor I might have found.

Tripp knocked hesitantly on my splintered bedroom door.

"Princess?" he asked. "You alright?"

I flung my head around and said, "Get a message to Brax at your tavern. Tell him and the others to go on without me. I'll meet them in Gallanor."

"As you wish, Highness," he replied, bowing with a smirk and exiting the room.

Good. Now to call on my father's army.

CHAPTER TWELVE: DAVINA'S DREAD

This was it. The day she had been dreading. Today was the day she would go home again.

Home. The place where she longed to be, but lived in fear of, thanks to her perceived betrayal. She couldn't blame them, after all. She had done terrible things since making the poor decision to exact revenge on the werewolf king by herself. Hubris is an awful thing.

Ruskin had done his best to break her, with the help of the loathsome Viego, but she had been getting stronger and stronger in her stay with them. She was slowly breaking down the spell Viego had placed within her, the one that controlled her allegiance to Ruskin. She wasn't out of the woods yet, however. For now, she had to continue to do as he bade, committing each of the atrocities he demanded of her. She hated herself and the king with every fiber of her being.

Her new chambermaid, Ida, interrupted her musings.

"Heading out today, mi'lady?"

Davina sighed heavily. "Yes, I'm afraid so."

"Afraid, Lady?" she asked, whilst fluffing fresh sheets for the lavish canopy bed. She never turned to face her, keeping focused on her task, but Davina could tell she was very much interested in her answer.

"Perhaps I misspoke," Davina said. "I couldn't *be* more pleased to return to my former home and collect what is rightfully the property of our glorious Emperor Ruskin."

Ida said nothing in return, but simply nodded while tucking in the fresh linens.

"Do you not agree?"

"Of course, ma'am," Ida replied.

"Hmm," Davina said. "You missed a wrinkle."

While Ida set about smoothing the perfect sheets, Davina strode out to meet the departing army.

The army consisted of hundreds of men from various backgrounds. Some had magickal powers while others did not, just an unhealthy love of killing and brutality. Some humans were just here for the riches promised them. Other groups were fellow shifters like Ruskin himself: Werewolves, were coyotes, beasts of that nature. There were troops of trolls and centaurs, dark elves and wild creatures that gave Davina nightmares just to look at them. The list went on. Davina could hardly keep track of them all, nor did she much care to.

She wished she had her grandmother's power of Sight more than ever so she could See what was about to happen in Gallanor. Just imagining the horrors that were about to go down terrified her. She hid her shiver as best she could, lest Ruskin see and demand to know what she found so repulsive.

"The necklace piece is in Gallanor," Ruskin said to his army. "Ikah sent word that she found it in the clutches of the self-proclaimed king and queen. I aim to get it back at any cost!"

The crowd cheered and stomped, smashing weapons in rhythm on the ground, bloodthirsty and ready to fight for their leader.

"Onward! And take no prisoners!" Ruskin screamed, sending his horse forward with a kick to its hindquarters.

The rest followed suit while Davina entered the carriage that had been waiting for her. She took a deep breath and closed the door. Once alone, she let a single tear fall. She didn't need her grandmother's power to see this was going to end badly.

CHAPTER THIRTEEN: CYNDOL GETS LOCKED IN

King Brax and Ifyrus had been in a meeting with King Matthias and Queen Miawae since late morning. Cyndol guessed it was to strategize. Kit had brought word this morning that a bird had seen Ruskin's army on the move and brought the information straight to Gallanor. Cyndol had relayed the info to Evony, who took it straight to her queen. They'd been shut up in that first-floor room ever since. "The Battle Room", Evony had called it. *Fitting,* Cyndol thought, *as it was adorned in weaponry and shields.*

Cyndol was nervously pacing around the Overlook, chewing her bottom lip and fidgeting with her hands. She jumped about a foot when Kiara placed a hand on her shoulder.

"Follow me," she said in a tone that brooked no nonsense.

Cyndol, heart stuck in her throat, did as she was told, and followed the princess without commentary. Kit was still out in his last assigned section of the kingdom, spreading the news.

Kiara led her back home to the Tree Palace, up the outer winding pastel-colored stairway to the third floor.

"I haven't been up to the third floor yet," Cyndol said. "Is this where you live?"

Without looking back, she said, "Yes. You are to stay in my room where it is safe."

"What?" Cyndol cried, balking on a pretty lavender stair. "But— I need to be out there to fight!"

Kiara did stop this time, bringing the full weight of her station with her.

"You will do as you are told, *child*. We cannot risk you getting into the hands of the enemy. My grandmother assures me you are *too* important, and I will *not* go against her wishes."

Cyndol puffed up her chest and stood her ground. "No."

"No?"

"No."

The two stood there on the steps, staring each other down, each wordlessly daring the other to make the first move.

"*There* you are!" Kit's voice came from below. "Be right there!" He bounded up the steps, sometimes two or three at a time, until he reached Cyndol's feet. "I'm s'posed to tell you to hurry up and hunker down! The army's approaching the outer walls."

"Well?" Kiara gestured to the top of the stairs. "After you."

Kit leapt happily up the remaining steps, taunting Cyndol about beating her there, especially since she had gotten there first. Cyndol let out an irritated breath and followed him up with a low growl. Kiara simpered and brought up the rear.

At the very top of the steps. Miawae's guard, Avery, was waiting for them. He greeted them briefly and opened the door, ushering them all inside with a stern look at the surrounding area before closing it behind them.

"Her Majesty has instructed me to keep you young ones here. I believe your brother and Kavea will be here shortly, as will young Master Colt."

"Master Colt?" Cyndol asked.

Avery's face cracked enough to allow for a wry smile. "He's been... promoted."

Cyndol couldn't help but smile back. "Good for him."

"Indeed." Battle face back in place, he continued. "I am to guard this door with my life. There will be more guards on duty, of course, but should you need anything, I am right outside this bedroom door. Once you children are all safely inside, do not open this door for anyone but me or the royal family, got it?"

Kit and Cyndol both nodded.

"Good. With that, I will start my duty. And do not worry, you are safe here."

Not certain he could promise such a thing, Cyndol nodded again and went to sit on the large four poster bed that hung from the ceiling. Kit jumped up and snuggled against her, lending warmth and comfort.

"Stay here," Kiara said. "There is more I need to see to. The others should be here any minute. Do what you can to keep everyone calm and, I cannot stress this enough, *stay in this room*."

"Yes, Princess," Cyndol promised, lying. She knew full well that if she was needed, she would flee. So would the others, she was sure. But telling the princess that would not do her any favors, so she played along.

Kiara narrowed her eyes at her but left it at that. Upon closing the door, Cyndol heard a soft *click* and knew they'd been locked inside.

"Wait," Kit stood up on the bed. "Did she just—?"

"Lock us in?" Cyndol finished. "Yup."

"So, we're staying here?"

"Nope," she promised again, this time meaning it. "We've already lost one family each, I don't intend to lose another one."

"What are you going to do?"

Cyndol chewed her lip again. "I'm not sure just yet."

A few minutes later, a knock was heard at the door.

"It's just me with the rest of the group," Avery said.

He opened the door and let in Ethan, Colt, and Kavea, none of whom looked entirely thrilled to be sequestered away.

"Remember," he said, "don't open this door to anyone but me or the royal family."

He closed the door and locked it again, causing Cyndol to clench her fists and start plotting an escape.

"Don't you think we should stay here, though?" asked Kavea, once Cyndol had voiced her frustrations to the newcomers.

"What good are we to anyone if we stay here?"

"You *have* powers, though! Not all of us do," Kavea said. Noticing the disappointment on Cyndol's face, Kavea tried again. "I understand that you want to protect these people, I really do. I know how much help they've been, and I know about your losses. But trust me when I say, we will just get in their way. Adults have a way of making things… well… creatively messy, and brutal in ways you never want to see."

The children all blanched, suddenly realizing whose daughter was talking.

"If Ruskin is really your dad, do you know how to beat him?" Colt asked.

Kavea sighed. "Not really. I never saw him all that much. He didn't seem to care that I was there. When I did see him, though, he was brutal to everyone around him, and he basically destroyed my mother. I will never forgive him for that. Not ever."

"He killed your mother?" Colt squeaked.

"No! No, no, don't worry. She's alive. We rescued her! Amy brought her back to the Mer Realm to be with her family, where she will be safe from him forever."

"Do you miss her?" Cyndol asked, missing her own parents.

"Every minute," she replied.

The children went quiet now, none knowing what to do next. Ethan sat in a soft scarlet chair by the window, staring out of it, and absently scratching his head scar.

"It's looking better," Cyndol said. "I bet it'll be fully healed in no time."

Ethan shrugged without looking at her.

Several minutes went by with idle chatter, all but Ethan recounting their parts in the story. Kit and Cyndol took turns filling in the blanks for him, though Kit seemed to enjoy the retelling more than she did. He was becoming quite the chatterbox now that he could actually talk to everyone. Colt especially didn't seem to mind and jumped in wherever he could.

Suddenly, a loud boom echoed throughout the palace. The room shook and the bed swayed back and forth. The kids who were on it clutched the posts for dear life! Kit's claws dug deep into the headboard.

An eerie keening of laughter rose up from the floors below, raising the hair on each child present.

"Oh no," Kavea whispered. "Ikah."

CHAPTER FOURTEEN: IBRAXUS ON THE BROW OF BATTLE

Brax held his breath at the Gates of Gallanor. He could see Ruskin's troops lined up along the closest tree line, chomping at the bit for a fight. He turned back to look at the people and creatures that had volunteered from Gallanor, along with the usual Gallanorian warriors. A sense of fear shot through him like a shockwave.

Be brave! he told himself. He felt his knees start to shake. *Braver!* He let out a growl and a puff of smoke from his nose. *Better.*

He knew they wouldn't win this fight. How could they? Ruskin had more fighters, Dark Mages, and was as insane for power as they came. What did *he* have? A couple dragons, a few Mages, a Seer, and a decent contingent of trained warriors that would likely die trying to protect the rest of them. So many more of them were the untrained masses just there trying to save what they had. It broke his heart to see how many farmers, shopkeepers, and everyday folk were clutching whatever they could use as a weapon.

At least the children were safe. He couldn't imagine them being out here on this field of fear. They must be scared enough as it is, away from all of this. He hoped with all of his might that the guards would be enough to protect them, and that

Ruskin wouldn't care about them if he won. Maybe he would just take his prize and go?

Brax spared a thought for his wife. He was glad she was in the Mer Realm and far from this war right now. Perhaps she was swimming about with family in a beautiful oceanscape right now, marveling at the sea creatures and playing in the coral caverns like she used to? It was a pretty thought. And one that was ruined by the next sound he heard.

"Give us the boy!" Ruskin said. "And have him bring me the necklace piece!"

Brax's knees began to shake all over again.

"I will gladly turn this group of miscreants around and be on my merry way if you deliver these things to me *right* now." He took a moment to gloat atop his gigantic black steed. "I don't see the gates opening up. Shall I take that as a 'No'?"

Brax kept his eye on the werewolf and held his left arm back to make sure everyone stayed put. He didn't want to make the first move, just in case anything could still be avoided. He gripped his hand over the hilt of the sword slung against his right hip. He heard the tightening of leather as he did so, and it brought him a modicum of comfort. He knew he could call on his dragon powers at any point, but he needed something for tight quarters. Being a dragon wasn't always conducive to that.

"You alright, mate?" Ifyrus whispered. "You want me to blast him right here? I could do it, you know. My flame length was revered, once upon a time."

Brax chuckled, grateful to have his best friend at his side, a man he always considered his brother. He shook his head and clapped him once on the shoulder. "Thank you, but no, tempting as it sounds."

"Are you sure? Char-broiled bad guy at the blink of an eye." He winked to show he was only half kidding.

The two dragon-men looked at each other for a long moment, knowing this was it. The fight had come.

"If you two are quite done admiring each other, I'd like to start killing you all," Ruskin said.

King Ibraxus III, Lord of Dragon Moon, and husband of Princess Amaryah Amethyst of The Sea, prepare to fight for your life, your kingdom, and your world!

He took a deep breath, turned to face his troops, and shouted, "Prepare for battle!"

Ruskin raised his razor-clawed hand in the air and screamed, *"CHARGE!"*

CHAPTER FIFTEEN: DAVINA'S DESTRUCTION

Davina heard the sounds of war starting from her hiding place along the Gallanorian Tree Wall. Ruskin had instructed her to find a weak spot that she might be able to sneak into without being detected. Unfortunately, she knew exactly the right spot to do so. She'd found it once, many years ago, when trying to sneak out to meet a boy she liked from a neighboring kingdom that her parents had forbidden her to see. Being the precocious youngster she was, she'd used her powers to enlarge a small hole in the Tree Wall, then shrank it back down upon completion of her task. She'd never told anyone about it and was definitely regretting it now.

She couldn't ignore the mission Ruskin sent her on, especially since he had Viego go back into her head before the battle began "to make sure all was still working". She had hurriedly thrown up a magickal block around his original spell that mirrored his handiwork, just barely hiding the fact that it had been tampered with. Luckily, Viego was either too stupid or too lazy to notice, and she passed his test with flying colors.

Davina continued with her task to free Ikah from her grandparents' dungeon. Once she was through the Tree Wall, she made her way quickly and quietly through the trees, doing everything she could to not be caught. It seemed as though all eyes were on the front gate, as Ruskin suspected they would be, so she was able to slip past without detection.

When she caught sight of the palace, her breath caught, and all she wanted to do was fling herself at her grandmother's feet to beg for mercy and forgiveness. She was fighting so hard with herself, but Viego's original spell still held dominion in her head. *For now.*

Compelled to keep moving, Davina slunk past the last set of trees that bordered the palace, then threw a spell in front of the guards at the first-floor door. A small fire erupted at their feet and the two guards stationed there did everything they could to stamp it out. While they were distracted, she bolted behind them and slunk in through the door, closing it swiftly behind her, unseen.

Making her way to the cell, her eyes began to blur as her emotions fought with her actions. Not for the first time, she wished Ruskin had just killed her the night she came to him. She wanted to be doing *anything* but this.

Seeing the door to the dungeon, she grabbed a rock from her pocket that she'd snagged on the road and focused all her energy on it. Before her eyes, the rock melted into the shape of a key, just the right size to fit in the lock. Inserting it, she heard the telltale *click* as it gave way with her twist.

The door opened and she heard the muffled chuckle of the woman she despised.

"Come to fetch me home, Princess?" Ikah asked from her prone position on the small bed.

"Your Master requests your presence. Stand back."

Ikah slid off her perch and backed up as far as she could, clearly enjoying the prison break.

Davina pulled out a diamond rod with a sulfur inlay and sent a wave of dark magick into it. She then rapped it with all her might against the thick stone bars of the cell and jumped out of the way right as the rod ignited and caused an explosion.

BOOM!

Dust and debris filled the room as the small dungeon took on the quake. Davina coughed and squinted through the ash to see if her plan had worked.

A chill went up her spine at the satisfied laughing of Ruskin's favorite pet.

"Thank you, dear. It was quite cramped in there. Now, shall we wreak some havoc?"

Ikah reached out to help Davina to her feet with her snaked hand and Davina bit back her revulsion. *What have I done?*

CHAPTER SIXTEEN: KAVEA'S FLIGHT

Kavea's hands sprang to her ears as an explosion rocked the room. Despite muffling the sound as best she could, she could still hear the unmistakable laughter of that vile woman her father had brought home before. He'd paraded her in front of her mother like she meant nothing to him, fawning over Ikah instead. Just the thought of her made Kavea's skin crawl.

"Oh no," she whispered. "Ikah."

"Who?" Cyndol asked.

"A toy of my father's."

The group wore looks of shock on their faces that matched her own. Nobody moved, they barely breathed, waiting for whatever came next.

Less than a minute went by before someone outside called, "Fire in the palace!"

The children exchanged looks of sheer terror now.

"Fire?" Kit whined.

"Now we *have* to get out of here!" Cyndol said. Kavea wholeheartedly agreed.

They leapt up from wherever they'd been perched to start collecting anything they could before attempting to flee. Cyndol and Ethan grabbed the heaviest chair and swung it at the room's only window, shattering glass. They let the chair fly out and land, crushing an opponent running by. The scream from below cut through the cacophony, and Kavea wished she could drown it all out.

"How are we getting down there?" she asked, panic rising.

"Don't worry!" Cyndol replied. "I can bubble us down, or Colt can fly you down. Either way, you've got about thirty seconds to decide!"

Just then, sounds of a fight outside their door were heard as someone was slammed against it.

"Avery?" Kit said. "You okay, buddy?"

One more slam and the door gave way, Avery's body now a heap on the floor.

Standing above him with flames at her back, was Ikah.

"We have to go, *now*!" Cyndol shouted, grasping Kit to her chest and bubbling herself with Ethan. "Colt, help Kavea!" They hopped up to the windowsill and flung themselves out.

Kavea's heart leapt to her throat as Ikah approached, moving strangely and too quick for comfort.

"Aha! Daughter of our Lord and Savior. Your return to your father will greatly aid in my standing. Come here and let me reunite you."

Kavea barely had time to thwart Ikah's snake arms that lunged at her. Kavea squeaked and swung the closest heavy object she could: Her Earth book. It acted as a shield of sorts and managed to block Ikah's viper swipe. However, it did succeed in snapping the book in twain, so Kavea was forced to abandon it. It broke her soul to do so, but she had no choice.

Colt went into pegasus mode and used his mighty hooves to knock Ikah back a few steps.

Kavea swiped her rucksack up from the back of the chair, grabbed it in both hands, and dumped all remaining contents unceremoniously to the floor. She would use it as a makeshift hang-glider. Without wasting time thinking about it, she clambered up to the busted window and hurled herself out of it, narrowly missing another swing from that monster in the room.

Kavea screamed all the way to the ground, shaking now in every possible body part, wishing with all her might to not crash too hard when she hit the ground. Her sack was barely helping, and the ground was approaching much faster than she'd like.

Right as she was about to smash into a rather large tree, a streak of chestnut rushed under her. Colt was there, yelling at her to hang on tight! Snagging her before she collided with it, Colt used his hooves to absorb the impact of the tree. He used that as a jumping off point to propel them in a different direction.

Kavea tried to regain proper breathing. She gripped Colt's mane with all her might, doing her best not to cry or vomit. She saw that Cyndol, Kit and Ethan had made it to the ground but were set upon by her father's army and were almost under attack!

The harpy cry of Ikah was heard as she screeched out the busted window, spewing all sorts of ugly words and curses in their direction. The flames were right behind her, and she disappeared within them. Kavea hoped she would never come out.

"Colt! Kavea!" Ellera waved frantically at them from behind another tree. Kavea saw the others were already joining her, trying to get out of the way of battle swords and flying spells. "Hurry up!"

Kavea and Colt quickly made their way to them, Colt kicking at enemies left and right. Kavea hadn't seen him do so, but at some point, his horn came out and he used it to knock a sword away from connecting with Ethan's head. Gallanorians were coming in at all angles now, doing their best to fight off the villains in their midst.

Once together, Ellera motioned for them to follow her on a path to a safer area.

"Miawae sent me to find you! You should be safer here!"

She led them into Madame Mason's and told them to wait there, out of sight.

"There is plenty here to eat and drink, and you may help yourselves. But, please, whatever you do, stay hidden!" With that, she left the children and ran back outside.

Cyndol *tsked* angrily and Kavea knew she would not stay put. She just hoped it wouldn't cause them any grief.

CHAPTER SEVENTEEN: ELLERA'S FACE-OFF

After leaving the kids at Madame Mason's, Ellera went back outside to find her friends and jump into battle, fists flying! However, when she got about five steps past the door, she saw a woman all in black, slinking in her direction, a crazed gleam in her eye and a toothy smile that didn't fit her face. Farther down on her chest, Ellera saw a fragment of a suns necklace hanging from a thin, golden chain.

"You must be Ikah," Ellera said.

Ikah licked her teeth with an elongated tongue. "And you must be my supper."

She made a move to creep closer, when another woman appeared by her side.

"Ikah!" she yelled over the sounds of battle.

Ikah flinched and turned to face the newcomer.

"That one is not to be killed just yet. We can use her as bait. Once we have her, the others will come running. I am sure of it."

"As you wish, Davina-dear, but once that is done, I will swallow her whole."

Davina shuddered but nodded. Ellera assumed this was the long-lost princess of Gallanor she'd heard so much about. After seeing her agree to her specific demise, she decided she was, most definitely, not a fan.

Ellera gathered up all of her Mind Traveler magick and was getting ready to strike, but Davina was too fast. She hit her with a bolt of energy that knocked her completely off her feet to land roughly in the shrubbery behind her. She tried to get back up to return the blow, but Davina hit her again. The world went black.

CHAPTER EIGHTEEN: MIAWAE'S RESOLVE

The time had come. This was the vision she had Seen when meeting Cyndol. Two dragons flew above her perch at Overlook Point, letting out streams of fire here and there, trying their best not to burn down the whole kingdom in the process of war. Miawae knew Gallanor would take some damage, that was war for you, but she fervently hoped it would be minimal.

With one last look at her beloved mountains, sea, and forest, she took a deep breath and clasped her husband's hand.

"It's time, Matthias."

He gave one curt nod and released a shaky breath of his own.

"And it has to go this way?" he asked.

"It does," she replied.

He nodded again and kissed the tops of his wife's loving hands.

"Well, then. Here we go."

They climbed on their steeds with practiced grace and made their way toward the fight.

Man and beast littered forest floors. Some alive, some not, some could be said to be somewhere in between.

Matthias and Miawae made their way confidently past the battle, not a soul disturbing their arrival. Magick spells and poisoned arrows flew past them, but they continued their steady march to the self-appointed Emperor.

They came to a stop in front of Ruskin, who sat smugly atop his inky equine, basking in the decimation of their beautiful realm.

"Bow to me," he demanded.

"No," Miawae said.

"Then why are you here? Shouldn't you be fighting with the rest of your lost causes?"

Miawae steeled her nerves and disembarked her horse. She gave it a loving pet on the neck before facing the maniacal monarch.

"We are here to ask you to stop. Turn back. We will give you one chance to flee this place and never return. It is the only chance you will get. I have Seen your future. Trust me when I say that this is your best option."

Ruskin stared incredulously at her for one brief moment, then actually began laughing! A true, guttural belly-laugh, one that caused his claws to clutch his middle to contain his mirth.

"You expect me to, what, just... turn around and go home? Because you had a dream? How absurd. You must think me daft, or you must be unwell, Highness. Retreat, indeed. Ha!"

The king continued to chuckle, and the men surrounding him smirked as well, as if this was the funniest thing they'd heard all day.

"One chance, Ruskin, one chance to spare your life."

The simpering king's face fell and took on an insulted pallor. "My name... is *Emperor Ruskin*, you ancient hag! I will take this kingdom from you and *raze* it to the ground if I so see fit!"

The wolf in front of her continued to wage threat after threat, but Miawae let him get it all out.

"Davina!" he cried at the end of his tantrum. "Come forth and dispatch your kin!"

Her lovely granddaughter, the once would-be heir to the throne of Gallanor, stepped forward from the looming shadows and slowly brought her eyes up to meet her own. Miawae, never knowing the truth about Davina's choice in staying with Ruskin, finally caught the wisp of sincerity in that gaze.

I never wished to be here. This is not my choice.

As if Davina had whispered it into her ear, Miawae heard the truth all the same.

"I forgive you, child," she said, a single tear in her eye.

"Give us the boy and the necklace!" Ruskin screamed at the royals.

"No!" Matthias shouted stubbornly. "We will *not*! This is *my* kingdom! *My* family you have stolen and murdered for your own gains! And there is no way in this world, or any other, that we would give you anything you ask for! Now, begone from my realm, or face destruction!"

Miawae could see Brax flying closer now, having spotted the face-to-face going on on the ground below. She could see the moment he took a breath to fire at Ruskin, such a beautiful open shot. Ruskin saw it, too, and shrieked at Davina to block it.

Davina's face took on a myriad of emotions, ranging from anger, to fear, to absolute acquiescence, and Miawae could see the moment the spell took hold and forced her to do his bidding. She scrunched her face tight, rolled her hands in a lightning-fast ball, a move Miawae had seen her do a thousand times before, and launched her spell at the dragon fire, catching it before impact and sending a swath of energy back onto Brax. Not only did it blast him out of his position in the sky, but it took the very top off of the nearby mountain, hurling him through it, tumbling this way and that with the rock and debris.

Miawae held her breath for just a moment, knowing he'd survive, but needing confirmation. Then again, her visions were never wrong. She let out her breath when she saw him land on another mountainside a bit farther away. She could tell he'd been hurt, but he was upright and walking now as a man. Good enough.

Davina stood panting, clearly having overtaxed herself with this mammoth feat. Having her granddaughter weakened in this way was the only way she'd survive this. She felt sorry that it had to cost her and the Dragon King some damage along the way, but the ends justified the means.

"Well?" Ruskin snarled at her. "What are you waiting for?! Kill them!"

Davina gasped and said, "I can't."

"You can, and you will, or I will kill them *and* you together!"

"Please, no," she said. Miawae wanted so badly to hold Davina in her arms one last time.

The war continued to rage around them. Voices were heard as they caught sight of what was going on. More and more people were making their way to the king and queen's sides. They were not going to make it.

"*Kill them now*!" he yelled at her. "Viego!"

"Yes, Majesty?" the half-faced man said.

"I have asked the princess to kill her former king and queen, but she is having trouble listening. Fix that."

"Of course, Emperor Ruskin."

As if she were watching a horrific puppet show, she saw the light behind Davina's eyes go dim as her arms rose up and took aim at her and Matthias.

"I love you," she said to her husband.

"And I love you," Matthias returned.

"Davina! Wait! *Nooooo*!" came the earnest cry of Kiara running up behind them.

Too late. They were all too late.

The blast from Davina's hands hit them square in their chests, and they hit the ground with hardened thumps.

Kiara bolted to her side as quickly as she could, gathering her grandmother and pulling her into her arms, refusing to let go.

"No! No, no, no, no, no, no, no…" Kiara said, holding Miawae's face in her hand now, willing the life to stay in her body.

Miawae had one last breath left in her, and she knew this was it. She had to make sure Kiara knew.

"Tell Cyndol… to find me… in Atla—" She hoped it was enough.

CHAPTER NINETEEN: DAVINA AND KIARA

"No…" Davina whispered, falling to her knees. Her grandparents had dropped like stones at her blast and had not gotten back up. She knew they would not. *Ruskin* knew they would not. In her shock and anguish, she began to shake, a horrible, life-shattering shake that fizzled and popped in her boiling bloodstream.

"Grandmother! Grandfather! No!" her sister was shouting over and over, trying her best to get one of them to show signs of life. Davina knew she would find none.

And then? Cold. She felt utterly, and all encompassingly, cold.

"Very good, Pet," Ruskin said. "You may live to see another day after all."

Davina broke.

So did Kiara.

Her sister was on her before she could blink. The violent rage Davina felt thrust upon her was nothing short of what she deserved. Any attempt at fighting back was met with Kiara's Seer power, blocking each and every hit before it could land. Davina had never stood a chance against her sister. Ruskin chose the wrong woman. Kiara was always the strongest.

"*How could you do this*?!" she wailed at her, arms flying and feet kicking out. "*How could you kill them? I will never forgive you for this! I will kill you for this!*"

The sisters fought, no one coming to help, no parental figures left to quell the combatants, just vengeance.

And then, "Kiara! Don't!" Druce. Druce was running up the field, much as Kiara had done moments before. But much like before, there was no stopping the madness. The will must be done.

Kiara snatched up a broken tree branch and jammed it into Davina's stomach. Her once sweet sister's face loomed above her, tears, spittle, and dirt marring the beauty underneath. She twisted the branch, making sure Davina stayed down.

"Thank you..." she whispered, feeling the last of Viego's power break from her, like snapping a carrot in half. She crumpled to the ground and lay there, unmoving.

And then Druce was there, cradling her in his arms, waving crystal wands and talismans, nattering on with words that sounded like gibberish to her ear.

Ruskin made a noise of disgust and spat at her. "Useless to me now" and "Leave her" was all she managed to hear. He gathered up his men to find his target, now that the royals were defeated.

Kiara made no move to help her. Davina couldn't blame her. She might have done the same in her position. Druce began to lift her up to assist her to the House of Healing, but she wasn't sure she would make it. She let out a shallow breath and closed her eyes.

CHAPTER TWENTY: AMY JOINS THE FRAY

I could hear sounds of battle, even from my vantage point under the water. My army was at my back, and we were ready to roll. I had one last thankful thought that Orelle was safe at home with Father and Tripp. I motioned my guards forward.

We swam silently through the River of Gallé that connected to the Gallron Sea. Nobody was watching the water, being too concerned with the magickal war being waged above. I'm sure two massive, fire-breathing dragons helped distract them! The thought of those two melting Ruskin in his boots made me smile, albeit a twisted one.

I waved a hand at… oh, shoot, Tommo? I made a mental note to learn names faster once this was all said and done. Things were moving too quickly for me to get them all right. To be fair, I had a pretty large contingent of Merpeople with me and we were short on time.

Tommo swam to my side, and I said, "According to the map Tripp showed me, this is the best place to launch our attack. Is everyone ready?"

Tommo said, "Yes, Highness. We are a 'go' at your command."

"Perfect. In that case," I looked above me to make sure we timed this right. Seeing a few of Ruskin's men ambling closer to the water, I yelled, "Go!"

At my word, utter insanity broke out as my army leapt out of the deep river, landing on solid ground with legs and weapons aplenty, swiping left and right at anyone wearing Ruskin's black and crimson colors. So nice of them to mark themselves clearly! And was that a "Wilhelm" scream I just heard? Outstanding.

"Foes from below!" someone shouted, and I grinned in anticipation.

I put my own legs back in place and unsheathed my trusty daggers. They gleamed in this light, almost as if they came to life and were ready to bury themselves in the enemy. I felt a tickling sensation inside me as bloodlust took hold.

"Oh, *Ruuuuuuusssssskkkiinnnn*!" I yelled to the world. "I'd like for you to meet my friends!" A different werewolf launched itself at me, and I promptly introduced it to Kitty. (I had named my daggers Kitty and Connie, after my rather strong-willed grandmothers back on Earth.) The wolfman collapsed at my feet as I yanked Kitty back from his stomach, then stepped over him, on to the next.

CHAPTER TWENTY-ONE: ETHAN'S EYES

This was all too much. All of it. From the day he'd spotted that stupid necklace, his life had been an endless nightmare. He'd been kidnapped and tortured, his village burned down with friends and family still in it, and he will likely have a visible scar on his forehead for the rest of his life. Now, trapped in a wellness tavern with the other kids while war raged on around them... it just kept digging the damage deeper.

Cyndol and Kit had their faces pressed against the frosted glass windows, trying their best to see outside without being spotted. Ethan wasn't sure how effective that was, but as no one had tried to come in yet, maybe it worked better than he thought.

Suddenly, Cyndol cried out, and it wrenched Ethan's heart to hear it. It wasn't a sound he'd heard from her since her beloved cat died when she was seven. He knew this wouldn't be welcome news.

"What's wrong?" Kavea asked.

Cyndol pulled Kit into her arms and began sobbing into his fur. Kit allowed it, as he appeared to be crying now as well.

Colt bounded over to where she'd been standing and looked outside the window.

"No... *Noooooo!*" he yelled. "Miawae!"

"What happened?" Ethan asked, not wanting the answer.

Colt went full alicorn mode, kicking tables and chairs across the room in his fury.

Finally, Kavea peeked out and saw the problem. "Oh," she whispered. "He killed them. He killed King Matthias and Queen Miawae."

Cyndol's sobs ebbed just enough for her to spit out, "No, it's worse. It's so much worse!" She sniffled, hiccupped, and continued, "He made Davina do it. That horrible woman we saw at The Sky Prison— she was their granddaughter! How *could* she?"

Ethan remembered her as well. He'd seen her a few times during his stay at that Nightmare Inn, and he had no interest in ever seeing her again… unless it was to shove her off a cliff.

"Does this mean we lost?" Kit asked.

Nobody seemed to have a good answer for that, so nobody spoke a word.

Ethan continued to pick at his head, as it was throbbing something fierce. He could almost swear he heard Viego's voice whispering to him in the cavern of his mind. He tried to ignore it, blame it on Ruskin and his army being right outside, or on the stress of everything he'd been through, but… this felt different. This felt as if it was coming from *inside* of him and he didn't know what to do. He decided to keep it to himself for now, as he figured if *he* didn't know the answer, being the oldest one here, nobody else would have a good answer, either.

"Ethan," Kavea said, "your eyes."

"What about them?"

"They're glowing purple!"

Of course they were. Just what he needed.

Before anyone could react, a sudden pounding on the front door made them all jump a few feet off the ground!

"Children! Open up! It's me, Ifyrus!"

They breathed a collective sigh of relief and let the dragon in.

"Have you seen Ellera?" he asked.

"Not since she left us here a while ago," Kavea replied. "Why?"

Ifyrus puffed smoke from his nose in agitation. "I can't find her. She was supposed to meet me at Overlook Point, but she never arrived."

From outside, a rowdy group began making their way closer, shouts of spells and successful hits rang in their ears. Growls from the various shifters and clangings of swords clashing were impossible to avoid.

Ifyrus poked his head out the door and slammed it shut again.

"Right. We have to go. Now!" He gathered up the group and tried looking for a back door. "Do any of you know how to get out of here without using the front door?"

Ethan sighed. "Stand back. I've got this." He summoned up all of his pent-up rage and fear and focused his eyes with all his might at the back wall of the restaurant. With a touch of surprise, even to himself, he blasted a hole with his plum-colored peepers big enough for them to make their way through.

CHAPTER TWENTY-TWO: IBRAXUS'S SECOND WIND

Brax was still reeling from being tossed through a mountaintop and rolling in the rubble. He stood up shakily and dusted himself off as best he could, swaying a bit as he did so. He took a look around, but his vision was blurry at best. When he was able to see more clearly, he focused his attention to where he'd been attacked and saw a sickening sight: The bodies of the king and queen being hauled away from the fray.

"No…" he breathed. "NO! *RUSKIN*!"

Brax went to shift back to dragon form, but discovered his left arm was badly damaged. It hung uselessly at his side now, bleeding and covered in bits of debris. He did what he could to get out the little pieces while trying to find a way off that small mountain top. When he'd made it to the side along the River of Gallé, something caught his eye from below that made him exhale a sigh of relief: *Amy*.

He wanted to shout to her, but saw she was not alone. She'd come back with an army of her own. His beautiful wife, resplendent in her warrior glory, fighting side-by-side with her people. His heart swelled, and he doubled his pace down the rocky cliffside, only slipping a few times.

CHAPTER TWENTY-THREE: CYNDOL'S CHARGE

Ifyrus led the children out through the hole in Madame Mason's that Ethan had created, and they ran to a cropping of trees not far from where they were exiting. Ifyrus held his hand back at them, indicating they should pause and wait for direction. Cyndol was getting tired of adults telling them what to do, but she was also terrified of the battle around her and desperately wanted to protect her remaining loved ones. So, she continued to listen... for now.

Ifyrus looked around for a safe space to hide them. After a moment, his gaze landed on another living treehouse, and he ushered them inside.

"Quickly now, before we're spotted!" he said.

They scrambled to get in before a cry could alert anyone to their presence. So far, everyone seemed too caught up in battle to notice a few kids running around with a human dragon. Cyndol knew their luck was bound to run out sometime and her anxiety cranked up a few notches.

"Stay here," Ifyrus said. "I need to find Ellera. I'll be back to check on you shortly."

With that, he left the five of them in this small foyer to tend to their own devices.

"Can't say I love being carted around like this," Kavea said.

"Better safe here than out there," Ethan countered.

Colt was pacing back and forth, working himself up. "Just let me at them! I'll gore them all! They killed our king and queen!"

Cyndol laid a hand on his shoulder. "I know how you feel. They've taken so much from all of us but, I promise you, Ruskin and his followers will pay dearly for it in return."

"But, *how*?" he asked.

Cyndol chewed her bottom lip. "I don't know, but I trust our friends. I trust Brax and Amy and Evony and the rest."

Colt didn't say anything to that, just nodded noncommittally and continued to pace around the small home.

Ethan took a chance at peeking out the little window and saw a bone-chilling sight— the necklace piece that had started this whole fiasco in the first place was about to be handed off to Ruskin by the woman that attacked them in the palace.

"She's got it!" he yelled. "She's about to give it to him! That can't happen!"

"What?" Cyndol asked. "What does she have?"

"The necklace piece! She's giving it to Ruskin!"

Cyndol burst through the door without a thought to her safety and ran directly toward the king and his crony.

"Cyndol! No!" Ethan said, chasing after her.

"You can't have it!" Cyndol shouted as Ikah gleefully handed the necklace piece to Ruskin. He snatched it and held it up to match the Little Sun's placement in the sky. The look of victory that passed over his face was sickening, and the hearts of those left fighting against him sunk at the sight of it. He lifted the chain from around his neck and happily connected the missing piece to it.

"Ahhh," he said. "At last."

It was then that he turned his gaze toward Cyndol, her brother in tow behind her.

"And look, Ikah! They've brought me a gift as well!"

Cyndol's blood boiled. *No! He can't take Ethan from her! Not again!*

"You... can't... *have him*!" she screamed at the top of her lungs. Her fury erupted in a flash of fire, and any ounce of fear that held her back was gone. She summoned her bubble with hardly a thought, and her eyes began to glow with amethyst ire.

"Oh, I see," Ruskin said. "It's *you*. It's been you all along. How marvelous." He threw a command over his shoulder to his closest guards. "Seize her. And the boy."

CHAPTER TWENTY-FOUR: ELLERA & IFYRUS

Ifyrus was searching every possible place he could to find Ellera. After several unsuccessful searches, he was about to give up and take to the skies again, perhaps to look on the ground elsewhere. But then, he heard a muffled sound...

Somebody? Anybody? Help me!

"Ellera?" he asked aloud, though the plea had been inside his head.

Ifyrus? came her voice, slightly clearer this time.

"Yes! It's me! Where are you? I can't find you!" He began throwing doors open in earnest, finding nothing but terrified families. He threw out apologies for disturbing them and slammed the doors shut.

I think I'm in the palace dungeon. I'm chained and can't move! Please help me!

"I thought the palace was on fire?" he said.

I think they've put it out. I don't see smoke anymore, but I can't be sure.

"Be right there, love!" he said.

Ifyrus shifted back to dragon to fly there as fast as possible. Many poison-tipped arrows flew his way, but he managed to dodge them this time. He even lurched downward to snag a few men in his maw, crunching them and flinging their corpses haphazardly about the battlefield. He hoped they smashed into more of Ruskin's men, killing two birds with one stone.

He had the remains of the smoking palace in his sights now and landed harder than usual, due to his haste. He shifted back and ran inside, making his way to the bottommost subsection.

"Ellera?" he called out. "Ellera?"

"Mmmph phmere!" she tried to reply.

"Oh!" he said, spotting her chained to a chair in the middle of what was left of the room. "There you are! Are there any guards nearby?"

She bobbed her head as best she could to indicate he should turn around now.

A sword came slashing down toward his head and almost took it clean off. Ifyrus ducked in time and sent his fist flying, connecting with the man's stomach. It doubled him over and Ifyrus hit him again with an uppercut, lifting him off his feet. The man was knocked out cold as he slid down the wall that stopped his trajectory.

"Was that it?" Ifyrus laughed. "One measly guard? That's insulting."

Just then, a small horde of guards began to attack as they piled into the room. Claws, teeth, swords and magick flung this way and that. Ifyrus, in turn, gleefully blocked, kicked, punched and bit anything that came within arm's reach, taking the enemy out one by one. The only one left was a Mage who was readying another spell to fling at him.

Ellera grit her teeth and called upon her Mind Traveler powers, sending a psychic tendril to attach to the man's temple.

He froze as his eyes clouded over, jaw going slack as he dropped his hands, standing in place to stare at nothing.

"Wow... creepy," Ifyrus said, doing a circle around the man to make sure he was well and truly stuck. "But effective. Thanks, Love." He punched the man square in the face, knocking him out as well.

"Is that all, do you think?"

Ellera tried to nod, and Ifyrus immediately went to free her.

"These must be spelled or something," he said. "I can't seem to break them." He kept tugging with all his strength, to no avail.

"Kmmphs!" she tried through her gag.

"What?"

She closed her eyes in frustration and tried again.

Keys!

"Oh! Right! Where are they, darling?"

Her eyes and toes tried desperately to point to where the keys to free her rested, but her idiot companion couldn't grasp her limited movements.

"What? Where? I don't see them," he said.

She rolled her eyes so far back into her skull that she could see into her childhood. If her legs were free, she would've kicked him. She thrust her raging eyes and toes to the right as hard as she could around the restraints.

RIGHT!

"Oh!" The idea finally seemed to click, and he ran over to the corresponding wall, snagging the keys from the hook with a flick of his fingers. He smiled cockily at her.

She relaxed her face back into whatever this gag let her manage and tried to slow her thundering heart. This *man-dragon* was so infuriating sometimes!

Ifyrus sauntered over and squatted down next to her, so they were at eye level.

"So… If I set you free, will you promise to let me take you to dinner somewhere?"

Ellera's blood pressure spiked once more as he got too close to her face with that smirk of his. She thought she was going to pass out— from anger or from his closeness, she couldn't be sure. She gave one last muffled grumph and did the best she could to nod.

Ifyrus grinned in satisfaction and made a show of unlocking her restraints.

"You know, you might want to keep these—" he saw the look of outrage flare in her eyes and decided to stop teasing her. "You're right, I'm sorry, you're right. I'll be a perfect gentleman." He wriggled her face free from the gag and gave her nose a cutesy *boop*.

Lightning crashed in Ellera's eyes as they flinched away from his nasal tap.

"Perfect gentleman, my left butt cheek! You'd have to go a long way to be a perfect *anything*, let alone a man, err, dragon, man-dragon—I don't even know what to *call* you!"

He whipped around with an exaggerated hurt face and said, "I'm both, of course. *Rude*," and gave a dramatic toss of his hair.

Like she thought. *Infuriating*!

"Just shut up and get me out of here. We have to go find the others."

"You got it! Once we're out of here, jump on my back and we can go find them."

Ellera agreed, and they fled the crumbling palace.

CHAPTER TWENTY-FIVE: CYNDOL'S ABILITY

"What are you doing? Get them!" Ruskin shouted at his nearby soldiers.

They leapt into action and made a move to snatch the kids, but when one determined were coyote tried to grab them, he instantly met the shield of Cyndol's bubble, and it shattered his furry fist.

"*Ahwoooooooo!*" he howled, jumping back and holding the remains of his busted hand with his good one.

Cyndol smiled victoriously. "Anybody else want to try me?"

"Shut up, Cyndol! You'll get us killed!" Ethan said. He made a move to pull her back toward the relative safety of the buildings, but they both saw that Ruskin had set his sights on them now. He would stop at nothing to have them.

Ruskin laughed joyously. "You know, I don't really *need* you anymore, seeing as how I only wanted you for this," he held up the necklace, showing it off. "However, you have been a pain in my neck since your grubby little mitts first touched my prize, so I think I'll just go ahead and kill you anyway."

Before the kids could respond, a whistling noise sounded through the air. Ruskin turned his head in time to see a large wooden staff headed straight for his heart. It succeeded in knocking him off of his high horse and Kiara came charging through the woods at them. She was hurling bits of debris at lightning-fast speeds, this way and that, taking out crony after crony. Her primal screams echoed through Cyndol's entire body, and she watched in awe as she took on the battlefield alone.

"That's for my grandmother!" She hurled another stick. "That's for my grandfather!" More rocks and debris. "And my mother! And my father! And even my awful, conniving, *murderous* evil sister!" She let loose a flurry of power that looked like a cloud of violet violence, and it knocked out the fresh wave of men coming at them from the tree line.

"Cyndol!" Ethan said, "let's get out of here! Now!"

He took a step to run to safety and somehow escaped the bubble in his haste.

"*Mine!*" Viego said. He snapped his right arm and turned it into a horrible tentacle, attaching it instantly to the hole in Ethan's head.

Ethan screamed in anguish, dropping to his knees in the dirt.

Viego cackled madly as Ruskin righted himself back on his horse, pleased with his servant's capture.

"Get him to the cage," Ruskin said, "then grab the girl."

"Yes, your Eminence," the Mind Traveler replied. He dragged the boy from the ground to the rather nasty-looking cage on the back of a nearby cart.

It was then that Colt came flying into the fray, kicking and gouging anyone that got in his way.

"Colt!" Cyndol yelled up to his spot in the air, "get Ethan!"

Colt made a beeline for the boy. His horn was pointed straight at Viego, intending to gore the evil Mind Traveler where he stood. Viego threw a spell that hit him square in the chest, knocking the wind from his lungs and forcing him to the ground.

Colt gasped, trying desperately to regain his breath.

"Let him go!" Cyndol demanded. "Let them *both* go or—!"

"Or *what*, you impudent child? You're going to hit me with your precious little bubble?" Ruskin asked.

Cyndol was shaking now, out of fear for Ethan, fear for Colt, and fear for herself. She glanced in one direction and saw Ethan getting hurled into a cage by Viego. In the other direction, Colt was transforming back into human to try to get his breath back but failing. She didn't know what to do.

Kiara took a chance and plowed directly into Viego with every ounce of strength she had. He'd already locked the cage on Ethan, but it forced him to lose his concentration on the flailing alicorn. Colt took a giant gulp of air.

"Viego! Back on your feet, you miserable wretch!" Ruskin screamed.

Viego was grappling with Kiara on the ground, both fighting with all their might. Kiara was a few seconds ahead of the creature, until he used his *own* psychic powers to blast her off of him. She smashed into a nearby tree, knocking her unconscious.

"*Kiara!*" Cyndol shouted, trembling in terror now with how badly they were losing. She feared this was the end. Something like a burning feeling streaked through her shoulder blades, then suddenly, she was ten feet off the ground.

Ruskin's eyes grew as large as saucers, and for once, it was *he* who looked afraid.

"How…?" he whispered.

Cyndol didn't know how she'd suddenly sprouted dragon wings, but she didn't have time to care. She used this moment to throw all of her rage at this monster while he was caught off guard. She took a deep breath, trusting her instincts, and let loose a stream of fire.

CHAPTER TWENTY-SIX: IBRAXUS'S WORST FEAR

Finally, off the mountainside, Brax managed to catch up to Amy and her army.

Amy caught sight of her injured husband and said, "Brax! You're bleeding!"

She ran over to him, punching a charging troll in the kneecap to down him on her way past, and continued without stopping until she reached him. The guardswoman behind her finished him off.

"What happened?" she asked, searching him all over for any further damage.

He chuckled, gently brushing her off, and pulled her into a crushing bear hug.

"Oh, how I've missed you," he said. "I've been so worried!"

"Mmmph!" she replied, pushing at his chest so he would free her.

"Oh! Sorry," he said, letting go enough so she could breathe.

"What happened?" she repeated.

Brax saw a figure approaching them, about to swing a blade into Amy's back. Despite his busted arm, he spun them both around, holding onto his wife as tightly as he could, then dropped low, using her body in a swinging fashion to trip their foe. He stomped and crushed the man beneath his booted foot.

"That Dark Mage of Ruskin's blew me through a mountaintop, that's what happened!"

"Davina did this to you?"

"Yes, but don't worry, my love, I fully intend to return the favor!"

Suddenly, Ifyrus and Ellera flew by overhead, and Ellera called down to them, "Hi, guys! We're off to attack Ruskin! He's in the village near where we left the kids, and we plan to get to them before he does! Want to come along?"

Amy blanched and faced her husband. "Brax, there's something important I have to tell you…"

"Can it wait? I don't trust him with the children and, if he's that close, I don't want to take any chances."

"Of course, but—"

"Ifyrus!" Brax shouted up to his friend. "I could sure use some dragon magick right about now! I've been injured and can't fly! Think you can fix me up so we can fly there together?"

In answer, Ifyrus swooped down, deposited his passenger, and in one swift motion, returned to human form. He instantly grabbed his friend's arm and concentrated all of his limited healing power on him. Fortunately, luck was on their side, and it worked like a charm. Both men cheered briefly and changed in the blink of an eye.

"Wait!" Amy said. "I have to let my troops know where I'm going!"

"Be quick about it," Ellera said. "We're running out of time!"

Amy turned to the closest guardsman and said, "Tommo, I have to go save the kids. Do you think you can take charge while I'm gone?"

"Don't worry, Your Highness," Tommo said, "we've got it."

"Thank you," she replied, jumping on Brax's back and taking to the skies.

The fearsome foursome flew fast and furious towards their tyrannical target, taking out enemies that got in the way until they reached their intended prey.

What they saw stopped all of them in their tracks: Cyndol, her blonde braids frayed and floating, flying high above the evil king. She was sporting a massive pair of lavender dragon wings and breathing fire.

"What the hell is she doing?!" Amy screamed, neatly jumping off of Brax's back as he got close enough to the ground.

Brax landed and shifted as quickly as he could, chasing after his wife.

"Cyndol!" Amy ran as fast as she could towards the partially shifted child.

Cyndol turned her gaze to meet them, looking as confused and terrified as one might expect. Ruskin had been rolling around on the ground, trying to put out the fire that had caught on his impressive fur coat. As soon as it was out, he darted for the bag on the side of his horse's saddle and pulled out a chain netting. He hurled it at the girl and caught her like an overgrown butterfly.

"*NOOOOO!*" Amy boomed, nearly flying now herself in her efforts to free the girl.

"Stand back!" Ruskin said, yanking her with a strength Brax didn't know he possessed. His sidekick jumped in to help reel her in at lightning speed, and before anyone could do anything about it, they had her.

Brax's heart stopped as he took in the scene: Ethan, fighting against his cage. Kiara, unconscious on the ground. Colt, struggling to get to his feet. Cyndol, caught in a net, being hoisted into Ruskin's arms, claws at her throat. Ellera, on Ifyrus, trying to find a way to strike without hurting any of the children, and Amy, sobbing, pleading with the wretched ruler.

"Please!" she begged. "Not her! Take me instead! That's what you wanted anyway, right? Me? You can have me! Just, please, let her go!"

"You had your chance, Amaryah, and you chose that beast instead," he said, pointing one of those claws at the Dragon King. "Besides, *she's* all I need now. My goodness, the *power* she has!" He laughed in awe of it. "Why would I let her go?"

Amy paused, desperate, and then, "Because she's my daughter, and you owe me a life for taking mine."

Brax wasn't sure how many times his heart could take a punch, but this one hit him square on. "I'm sorry, what?"

Amy faced him, terror making her eyes glow their brightest purple yet. "That's what I wanted to tell you. Cyndol... She's our daughter."

"But how?"

"I can explain later, just trust me. I promise it will all make sense. I *remember*. All of it." She turned to face Ruskin again, shaking. "*All* of it." Her fear turned to anger. "You. Owe. Me."

Ruskin seemed to mull over her words, weighing what she said with his own motives. "I can have you instead of her?"

Amy nodded, breaking Brax even further. "Let her go and you can have me."

Ruskin shook his head. "No, you come here, and we can do the exchange right here."

"I don't trust you!" Amy said, clenching her fists until her hands turned white.

"Well, I don't trust *you*!" he replied. "If you want her back, you have to come here! Or I can just kill her now." He sliced a small segment of Cyndol's neck, and a drop of blood popped up, causing Cyndol and Amy to scream.

"No! No, no! I'm coming! Don't hurt her!"

Ruskin simpered and clutched the squirming child to his chest, waiting to claim his lost lady love.

Brax couldn't wait to kill him.

Amy stepped forward, one foot after the other, gaining ground and reaching out for the child. The moment she got close enough, Brax knew this would not end well. His heart broke yet again.

CHAPTER TWENTY-SEVEN: AMY GETS TAKEN

I'm going to kill him. I just have to find the right moment. I'm going to kill him, not just for myself, but for hurting my daughter and everyone else this bastard has wronged throughout his overlong reign of terror!

"If you were going any slower, I'd think you didn't *want* to save her," Ruskin said.

"Sorry, *Your Royal Eminence*, I've been traveling and fighting all day. Seems I should have stretched more first."

"It's all jokes with you sorry lot!" He grasped Cyndol tighter and earned a squeak for his efforts. "Nobody shows me the respect I deserve, and I am tired of all of the unwarranted humor!"

"Maybe if you stopped maiming and killing everyone, you'd have more friends in your life," I said.

Ruskin glared daggers at me as I took my time approaching. I was hoping someone would find an in and take advantage to rescue us. Sadly, he was holding her too tightly to try, and his talons were just itching to rip into somebody. Everybody stayed put, waiting for a miracle. None came.

I sighed and took the last few steps toward the monster on horseback.

"I'm here. Let go of her."

"Just a little bit closer."

"Amaryah..." Brax warned.

"It's okay, I've got this," I told him, not sure I wasn't lying. Then, to Ruskin, "Please, let her go. I'm here, I'm not fighting you." Then to Cyndol, "I'm so sorry, sweetheart. I hope I'll get the chance to explain everything. It's almost over."

I saw the moment that became false. There was a rotten gleam in Ruskin's eye as the corner of his mouth drew up. He flung the chained netting as hard as he could at Viego, and shouted, *"Now!"*

In one smooth motion, the Mind Traveler caught Cyndol's netting in one hand and hurled a portable Crannie with the other, landing it in between the cart and his master.

Before I could react, Ruskin's claws sank deep into my shoulders and I cried out in agony, dropping any will to fight from my arms, while trying my best to squirm away from him. It was no use; he had me completely pinned.

Ear-shattering roars were heard from behind and above me. I felt flames sizzle past as Brax and Ifyrus gave up all intent to save the forest or the people from their fire.

It didn't matter. Ruskin and his lackey had planned this, I could see it. It was way too organized. They knew they'd use a Crannie to portal out of here if they had the chance, and they were certainly taking it, now that Ruskin had everything he wanted: Me, the necklace, my daughter, the boy who started it all. Things were looking grim.

And, with that, we were pulled through the portal, sounds of keening dragons fading behind us.

CHAPTER TWENTY-EIGHT: DARRIAN TAKES HIS CHANCE

Darrian had been trying to avoid actually killing anyone unless he absolutely had to. He often settled for just knocking someone out to get them out of the way, but occasionally he did have to give a light maiming here and there to keep himself in the Land of the Living. He hoped the ends justified the means.

Being lost in the crowd of this battle was his hardest task yet. Harder still was trying to find Cyndol and Ethan. They could literally be anywhere in this accursed war.

Something caught his eye across the village, and he looked up to see Cyndol alight in the air, dragon wings sprouting from her back. King Ruskin threw some kind of net around her, the bastard! He'd absolutely be killing him for that!

Darrian shoved a charging Mer out of his way as he hastily made a run toward his daughter. He spotted his son locked in a cage when he got a bit closer, and his adrenaline kicked into high gear. *Move faster*!

He was almost there when he saw an incredible sight: Not just one, but two full dragons descended upon the fray, one changing back to human and the other with a woman on its back, hovering above the scuffle and looking for opportunity. Darrian never thought he would get to see a dragon in his life, so he stopped in his tracks, both terrified and awe-struck.

Get your children out of there! His brain was screaming at him now, urging him to move past his fears and rescue his kids.

Just as he reached the cage Ethan was in, Ruskin's rotten right-hand man produced a Crannie out of thin air and portaled his kids away.

Darrian ran as fast as he could and, just as the Crannie was almost done closing, he hurled himself through it, barely making it through before it shut around him.

CHAPTER TWENTY-NINE: KIARA VERSUS IKAH

Kiara awoke to the sounds of "RETREAT!" and "RETURN TO THE CASTLE!". She sat up, very confused. She rubbed her head while trying to figure out what was going on.

"Kiara!" Ellera said. "You're alive! Guys, Kiara's alive!" She ran over to a small crowd of people and Kiara thought she could make out the figures of Evony, Bella, Brax and Ifyrus.

"What happened?" she asked the group.

"We lost," Evony said in a soft tone. "I'm so sorry about—" She choked up and had to pause for a moment. "I'm so sorry about your grandparents. We all loved them— very much."

The memory came crashing back to her and grief punched her in the chest. Kiara gasped while her friends gathered around to assist her to her feet. She looked around at the fleeing foes and bodies on the ground, trying to find Ruskin and the children.

"Where did they go? What happened to Ruskin? Where is Cyndol?!"

Evony laid a hand on her shoulder. "They are gone, Highness. Portaled to Ruskin's castle, I'm sure. He took Amy, Cyndol, and Ethan with him."

"No," she exhaled, refusing to believe it had all gone so wrong. "What— excuse me, sorry. Evony, please help me."

Evony moved her hand from Kiara's shoulder and set it snugly around her waist instead, finding that her princess was losing her balance. She looked her over more thoroughly and found there was quite a big wound on the back of her head, blood amassing in her beautiful battle braids.

"Are you alright, Your Highness?"

Kiara blinked, swayed, then seemed to regain a bit of herself. "Quite alright, thank you. What are the next steps?"

"Well, Highness," Evony said, "I hate to bring it up so soon, but we need to make arrangements for the service... for your— for the king and queen."

Kiara nodded numbly. "Of course."

"And you will need to have a coronation."

Kiara's eyes widened as she asked, "So soon?"

"As soon as possible, I'm afraid. We don't want Ruskin, or any other ruling power for that matter, believing there is an open seat here."

Kiara nodded again, standing up straighter and taking on a look of sheer determination. "I see. Then, once the battlefield is seen to and everyone has had a bit of rest, go ahead and start the preparations."

Evony gave her a searching glance, trying to gauge how her new queen was taking it all. Seeing nothing but her training kicking in, she nodded and passed along the orders to a few approaching Gallanorians.

"Are you alright to walk on your own, Highness?" she asked Kiara.

Kiara took a breath to reply, but something caught the corner of her eye a bit farther down the road in the tree line.

"That *monster*!" she screamed, and took off running, grabbing a fallen short sword in her path.

The bewildered group followed after her, worried about her mental and physical state, and tried to figure out what had spurred the princess into action so fast.

"Kiara!" one of them shouted, but she could not be pulled away from this.

Kiara would recognize that snaky woman anywhere. She would *not* be leaving here alive!

"Ikah!" she shouted. "Come back here and fight me, you viper!"

Ikah, seeing that she'd been spotted and that her master had left her behind, stopped in her tracks and turned to face the advancing young lady. She got herself in a readied stance, waiting for round two with the enraged teen.

"I see no trap doors *here*, Highness. Let's see how you do in a fair fight!"

"Gladly!" she replied, gritting her teeth and wrapping her hands tighter along the short sword in her grip. Her head began to ache, but she pushed the pain down to deal with later.

Nearly on top of each other now, Ikah lashed out with her twin snake arms. The snapping heads took turns trying to bite Kiara anywhere they could catch a chunk of flesh. Kiara batted them away with ease, but that was more instinct than her power kicking in to assist.

Kiara frowned a moment as she realized her power wasn't responding as it normally did. Usually, she would get at least a three second glimpse into the future to prevent any attacks on her, but her mind showed only fragments of those images now. She blinked hard and tried to shake the visions back into place, but it just made her head hurt worse. It began to pound as if in response to her acknowledgment.

Ikah cackled. "What's wrong, Princess? Did that mean old man hurt you? What a pity."

She flung a snapping snakehead at her and Kiara ducked, barely getting out of the way. Kiara swung her sword and nicked the underside of Ikah's right snake. The vile woman screeched, and Kiara almost covered her ears to protect them from the sound.

Ikah pulled her arms back and made an attempt to swing them both at the same time to catch Kiara off balance. It worked, and her left snake sank its fangs into the wound on Kiara's head, latching on and downing the princess.

"Kiara!" came Ellera's voice. "Hang on! I'm coming!"

It felt like an eternity but, finally, Kiara could feel the fangs retract and leave her skull the sodden aching mess it had become. She crumpled to the ground ungracefully and could only lay there and watch the horror going on before her eyes.

Ellera's eyes had taken on a stormy silver sheen, her black and purple braids lifting into the air without the necessity of natural wind. Her fingers had stretched out, much like Ikah's hands and arms had, though these were thankfully lacking any venomous animals.

The two women were fighting in earnest now, each one knowing this battle would only end with one or both of them dead. Ikah swung her arms this way and that, trying to secure them to any available part of her, but Ellera's power was literally growing bigger by the second, a humongous cloud of shimmery purple rising up around her. Ellera's fingers elongated and resembled the legs of a squirming squid. She saw a window of opportunity and took it, shoving those tentacle fingers into each of Ikah's temples, shutting off her will in the blink of an eye. The evil woman's eyes and arms went slack, followed by her knees as she hit the ground hard. Her mouth twisted up into a silent scream, and the growing crowd watched as the color was drained from every part of her: Hair, eyes, skin, everything a pale, dusty white.

"I believe Her Highness told you that you wouldn't be leaving here," Ellera said.

Ikah's body was drained of all life, wasting away until it became a fragile statue of dust. Ellera removed her hands and brushed them off. Her last act was to take a deep breath and blow. The viper woman, who had been full of such hate, greed, and malice but a moment ago, was now floating away on the breeze, never to be seen again.

Kiara thought she saw the ghostly figure of her grandmother standing over her, pleased, then she passed out.

CHAPTER THIRTY: KAVEA COMES TO TERMS

"I can't *believe* you wouldn't let me out there to help her!" Kit screamed at Kavea. "I would've opened the door myself, but I don't have *thumbs*!"

Kavea sighed and tried to find the words to soothe the furious fox.

"Kit, if I'd let you out, you would have either been killed or kidnapped. You don't know how bad my father can get!"

"You don't *know* that!" He thumped his hind legs on the ground so hard you would have thought he was trying to break the floor. "Maybe I could've distracted him and Cyndol would've gotten away! Or bitten off his kneecaps! Or ripped his throat out with my *teeth*! But, *no*! You wouldn't let me! And now she's gone!"

Kavea slowly approached the hysterical creature and put her hand on his back to soothe his ruffled fur.

"Don't…" he whispered. "Just— don't."

She retracted her hand and hugged her middle instead, hating everything that just happened, hating her father all over again for the pain and misery he'd caused the world, and hoping that someone would be able to put him in his place and save the day.

Suddenly, the door burst open, and an anxious Ifyrus came barreling through.

"Kids?!" he called.

"We're here!" Kavea said, dropping her arms and rushing forward to prove it.

Colt came in hot on his heels, huffing and puffing, stamping the ground in his fury before realizing he was still alicorn, then transformed back into a human.

"He took them!" Colt said. "He took Cyndol and Ethan and Amy!"

"We know," Kavea said.

"I tried to stop him, I really did!" he continued, not hearing her. "I was fighting so hard and he just—"

"It's okay, Colt—"

"And they're... they're just *gone!*" Openly sobbing now, he deposited himself on the closest bench to cry into his folded arms.

"They're in here!" Ifyrus called to someone before turning back to check everyone for damage.

Kavea waved him off and went to comfort the crying Colt. Kit nuzzled under his arm as well, the two young boys sharing their mutual pain and anguish. Kavea couldn't help but feel partly responsible, seeing as how it was her father who was the root of all this mess.

"I'm so sorry," she said softly.

"It's not your fault!" Ellera said, appearing in the doorway. "That monster may be your father, but that does not mean you have to bear the burden of his actions! He alone is responsible for this!"

Evony came in, walking stiffly and guarded. "Princess Kiara requests your presence shortly. We will be having a meeting in fifteen minutes, and she wishes you all to be included. Unfortunately, the palace has fallen, so our temporary headquarters will be over at Madame Mason's until suitable arrangements can be made."

Ellera nodded. "Of course. We will join her there. Thank you."

"Please excuse me. I must alert the others." Evony left the grieving party to mourn together.

***

"Today has been hard on us all," Kiara began once all were in attendance, "and we have lost so many." She paused to collect herself. "As you all know by now, in addition to the personal losses we all experienced at the hand of Ruskin, we also lost our king and queen." Another pause, another deep breath. "There will be a service tonight at high moon. I hope you will all be there to honor your king and queen, and those that did not survive this fight." She let her head hang in a moment of silence. "Until then, you may go and rest, clean up, do whatever it is you need to do, and I will see you all at The Overlook."

Kiara stepped down from the table she'd been standing on and Evony took her place.

"Good people of Gallanor, and those that have joined us, we thank you for everything you did today. There are no words that can change what happened, and you have all of our sympathies. Since both of our leaders have fallen, we will need to crown another before Ruskin sees this as an opportunity to strike us while we are down. The interregnum will not be long. We will have our memorial service tonight and crown our new sovereign tomorrow morning."

"Will it be Davina or Kiara?" someone asked from the back of the room.

A chorus of "Booo!" chimed in to reply.

Evony gestured for the crowd to settle down. "That is a fair question, as it *would* have gone to Davina, had she never left home. However, Kiara has been training for this since Davina left. She is aware of her duties now, and ready to take them on. Davina has given up her right to rule, both by her actions *and* just now in her words at the House of Healing. She is being tended to and is expected to recover."

"Didn't *she* kill the king and queen?" another voice asked.

The crowd became loud once again, shouting their opinions. Again, Evony waved them silent.

"We have learned much about that. Technically, yes, it was her hand that felled them, but it was not her choice. She has been under the spell of Ruskin's Mind Traveler, Viego. This has been confirmed by his sister, Ellera, after she did a thorough scan."

The people did a collective gasp and turned to face Ellera, leaning against the wall near the door.

"Don't worry," she said. "I hate him even more than *you* do. Trust me. I'll kill him if I get the chance."

That seemed to appease the crowd, and they returned their attention to Evony. "I have been asked to stay on as Right Hand to the Queen, and I have accepted. Her Highness also has asked me to inform you that there will be a rescue mission setting out after the coronation tomorrow, and any who wish to join may do so. Until the palace is restored, this will be where you can come to address Her Highness, or myself, with any needs that come up. We will be setting up on the second floor, as Madame Mason has kindly offered her offices to us for the time being. Thank you again, and we will see you all tonight."

Evony lithely hopped down from the tabletop, her frost-white braids swinging musically about her.

Kavea leaned over to Kit, still dejected and depressed between her and Colt.

"Are you still mad at me?"

He didn't look at her, just kept his eyes forward and said, "Yes. But you can make it up to me by joining me to go save her."

Kavea squeaked. "I don't want to see my father!"

Kit faced her now, growling in a low warning tone. "You will come with us, or I will never forgive you!"

Kavea's face drained of color, but she could feel and understand his fury. After all, he *did* help her rescue her mother, so it was only fair she did the same for him. She finally nodded, and Kit dropped his raised hackles.

"Good. C'mon, Colt, let's go catch bugs."

With that, the two boys left her alone to ponder the future.

CHAPTER THIRTY-ONE: KIARA HONORS THE LOSSES

The night was clear. You could see every twinkling star and gemstone in the sky, almost as if they were mourning the loss along with them.

Everyone in the kingdom turned out for the event. If they weren't directly affected, they knew someone who was. Everyone was hurting, and the feeling in the air was palpable, like walking into a spiderweb of agony.

Princess Kiara, soon to be Queen Kiara, stood at the head of The Overlook, focusing on breathing in and out. This was it, time to say goodbye. Her heart broke all over again.

After a few moments spent collecting herself, Kiara took a look at the massive throngs of people lining both sides of the cliffs above the River of **Gallé and each living tree root bridge that spanned the gap**. They were all wearing their white linen mourning robes, saved for ceremonies such as these. The lines of people seemingly went on forever, farther than she could see the end of. It filled her with a sense of pride to see how her kingdom supported one another. Even the Mer people stood on the banks below to mourn along with them.

Those with magick had helped set up orb lights along each pathway, while others adorned the tree root railings with various types of white flowers to reflect the shining moonlight. Her grandmother would have loved that.

Kiara looked down to the river and saw that the procession was beginning. The king and queen had been laid out in their finest white clothing on a raft of tree limbs and grasses, thatched together and decorated with more orbs and flowers.

Behind the king and queen were the rest of The Fallen. These people were also being honored as they gave their lives fighting for their kingdom and would join their sovereigns in whatever came next. These rafts held ten people apiece and Kiara could still not see the end of it. So many bodies, so many lives lost.

Kiara had spent the past few hours sobbing on the shoulder of Evony at the House of Healing, being tended to by their skilled healers in between her tears and preparations for tonight and tomorrow. Her sister Davina was being treated by Druce on the opposite side of the building, per her request, so she was not tempted to go after her and finish what she started. She wasn't sure she could ever fully forgive her for what she did, even if it wasn't entirely her fault. If only she had never gone to see Ruskin after their parents were kill—

The sounding of a low horn reverberated through the kingdom and Kiara felt it seep through to her bones. She shivered and forced herself to focus.

"It's time," Evony said, gently placing the handcrafted necklace that Bella had made for Kiara over her head to rest on her chest. The necklace was made specifically for communication to help Kiara magnify not only her voice, but her authority. It was a stunning piece that held four different types of gemstones: Amazonite, blue kyanite, carnelian, and clear quartz. Shades of blue, green, white, red, and orange sang together in perfect harmony. Kiara instantly felt a wave of confidence settle over her. She could do this.

"Family and friends of Gallanor," her voice boomed over the land, "I wish to thank you for coming here tonight to honor The Fallen, and to honor your King and Queen, Matthias and Miawae. Though we did not win this battle, I know they would have appreciated everything you did today. They loved you all immensely and will remain in our hearts until our own dying days." She took a small dagger out of her belt and brandished it for them to see. "If you wish, you may join me in the Cutting of the Braid. For those unfamiliar with our traditions, this is our way of sending a piece of ourselves with the dead to accompany them on whatever comes next, so they know they are loved and won't be alone or forgotten." She reached her hands up to grasp and sever one braid from each side of her face below her chin, one for each of her grandparents. "Thank you, King Matthias and Queen Miawae for your loving leadership. Thank you for the many years of peace and harmony and thank you for defending us until your death. May you rest in peace."

"May you rest in peace," echoed the crowd.

"And to the rest of The Fallen, we thank you for your love and sacrifice, and for defending us all until *your* deaths. May you rest in peace."

"May you rest in peace," the kingdom said again.

The first of the braids began to fall. Kiara watched with wet eyes as her kingdom, one by one, knowingly and lovingly, cut their hair to share with the dead. Muffled sobs and sniffling noses were heard, even over the soft, slow flute music that had started from the shores below. It was eerily beautiful, and Kiara couldn't stand it.

She stood stiffly at her post until her grandparents reached the top of The Falls. She had a flashback to when she was standing here with them and Davina as their parents went over, and a chill wracked her petite shoulders. Her body threatened to crumble. She could do this, she could do this, she just had to wait a little bit longer and then she could return to Madame Mason's and collapse.

She stared at The Falls as her grandparents went over to join their daughter and her husband in the Great Sea.

"Goodbye, Matthias and Miawae," she whispered. "Thank you for everything. I will love you and miss you forever."

***

The next morning, Kiara felt as if she had been run over by a herd of centaurs. While the healers had done a tremendous job patching her back up after the battle, the events of both the day and the night had drained every last drop of feeling she had, both physically and emotionally. Unfortunately, she would be unable to stay in bed and drown in her grief today as she wished to, as she was about to be crowned Queen of Gallanor in an hour.

Bella had already come by to make sure she was awake and asked if she needed help getting dressed.

Kiara felt another pang of sadness, thinking that usually Avery would be the one to be assisting in preparing for today's ceremony instead of Bella, but his loss was yet another hit they took yesterday. Kiara would have to find a suitable replacement, as she knew Bella was only helping temporarily.

A knock sounded at the door and Kiara let out a deep sigh.

"Come," she said.

"Pardon the intrusion, Highness, but I was instructed to give you this today before the coronation," Evony said, looking a little worse for wear herself.

"Instructed?" Kiara asked. "By whom?"

"Your grandmother."

Kiara's breath caught and her heart began to race.

"She knew, didn't she?"

"I suspect so, yes. She admitted to me just a few days ago that she had Seen a vision of Matthias's passing, but not her own. Knowing your grandmother, she would not be far behind if he left first. They really did love each other, you know. That's not as common as one might think."

"You said you have something to give me?"

Evony reddened, something Kiara had never seen her do.

"Yes, my apologies, Highness." She handed over a neatly wrapped parchment scroll, tied off with a purple and gold plaited tassel. Exactly her grandmother's style.

"Would you like me to stay or go?"

Kiara considered it, then said, "I think I would like to read this on my own, if you don't mind?"

"Of course," she replied, dipping her head. "I shall wait for you downstairs. Bella and Madame Mason have become fast friends, by the way, and I believe they are cooking up quite the feast for your post-coronation celebration. Once we finish that, the rescue party will depart."

"Is there any chance they can leave for that any sooner?" Kiara was very worried about her friends in the hands of that monster.

"I can check with the people who are organizing that and see if they can speed it up to depart after your coronation, but before the feast. Perhaps Bella can pack up some food to take on the road."

"Thank you, Evony, for everything," Kiara said, meaning it to her core. "I don't know if I could do this without you."

Evony smiled. "Of course you could."

With that, she left Kiara to read her final message from her grandmother in peace.

Unraveling the scroll, she read to herself:

My Dearest Kiara,

I am so sorry we are no longer there with you. I wish we had gotten the chance to finish your training, but there are enough people there who can point you in the right direction, should you need help. My dear friend Sovereign Sai of the Fae Realm has also graciously offered to help in the case of our deaths, which, if you are reading this, did come to pass.

I am sorry I did not tell you the outcome of this fight. In Seeing, as you know, I must be careful what I say, lest it change the outcome for the worse. Please know that I have all the faith in the world in you, and I have Seen you become the great leader I know you to be.

Evony knows where all the pertinent information is kept to continue a smooth transition of power, and she will guide you well. She has been with me a long time and knows how we run things, though you will find in time what works best for you. Rule wisely, and with great heart.

Until we meet in the next life, your loving grandmother,
Queen Miawae of Gallanor

Kiara sat back on a stool and cried.

***

Drumbeats sounded across the ravine, echoing up and down the river for miles. You could feel it through the ground with your feet as it climbed and registered throughout your entire body.

Kiara, breathing shakily from nerves, took her seat on the single throne that had been set up on the final tree root bridge, just before the Falls that led to the sea. The gathering crowd cheered as she sat, happily welcoming their new queen. As a contrast to last night's braid-throwing for the funeral, her people were now showering her with a flurry of flowers, being tossed this way and that, lending a sense of spectacular color and whimsy to this auspicious occasion.

Evony and King Ibraxus approached her, each taking turns bowing and swearing either fealty or friendship (as in the case of Brax, being a king himself). Evony placed the crown upon her head, then gestured for the kingdom to begin their declarations of fealty themselves. Brax took this opportunity to leave and begin his rescue mission with Kiara's blessing.

There were pretty words and pretty promises, all blending together as Kiara tried to take it all in, still battle-shocked from yesterday, and grieving for her grandparents. None of this felt real and would take a while to adjust.

"Are you alright, Majesty?" Evony asked.

Queen Kiara shook her head to clear it of her dark musings and nodded.

"Just tired," she replied.

Evony nodded, understanding the situation for what it was.

"We are nearing the end. You can rest soon."

Kiara wished that were true. Unfortunately, last night, she had her first Vision. Her powers were evolving.

"When we are through here, I need to get a message to Sovereign Sai."

CHAPTER THIRTY-TWO: AMY'S NEW HOME

We made it through the short tunnel of darkness to land with a jolt in an unfamiliar land.

My aching shoulders were bleeding freely from Ruskin's claw-holes. Trying to raise my arms was proving to be a difficult task.

"That stupid piece of sh—"

"This way, Princess," said Viego.

My skin crawled as he tried to put his arm around me to direct me toward the castle. I danced out of his reach and shot him a glare hot enough to melt an iceberg. He leered mockingly at me, but wisely retracted his hand. *Good dog.*

Looking out over this new landscape, I instantly felt a shudder wrack through me. This place had a taste of evil in the air, like rust and sulfur, and I almost vomited on the cobblestone pathway. I had always loved cobblestone, but this was sadly untended to, with weeds and misshapen shrubbery that had grown up through the various cracks. Dotted along the pathway was a sparse forest of twisty blackened oak trees. It gave the impression they were reaching out for help that never came. I couldn't help but wonder how this place looked before Ruskin took over. I bet it was beautiful.

I heard a *thud* behind me, but no one else seemed to notice. A man I didn't recognize popped through the Crannie right as it closed. I glanced quizzically at the stranger, but he put his finger to his mouth in a shushing fashion and darted behind a tree. Is he on our side, then? If he didn't want Ruskin's attention, I was hoping he was an ally. I chose to keep my mouth shut.

Cyndol and Ethan were both cursing Ruskin and trying to free themselves of their respective traps, to no avail. Viego slunk up to Ethan's side and threatened him by brandishing his tentacle finger at him. Ethan whimpered, shoving his body as far away to the other side of his cage as he could get. *Note to self: Kill him, too.*

"Leave him alone!" Cyndol shouted.

Viego chuckled and gave her netting a bit of a shake, causing her to lose whatever footing she'd had and catch her right dragon wing in the netting holes.

"Ouch!" she cried.

Extra kill him, I seethed.

"Viego," Ruskin said. "Stop playing with my toys."

"As you wish, Sire," he said, dropping his head and stopping his antics.

We were coming up on the front of the castle now, a massive, looming, stone-cold villain lair that reeked of danger and despair. It fit him perfectly. The urge to puke was rising.

At least I'm with the kids, and I can do what I can to help. Perhaps The Stranger will assist me as well, or at least not get in my way. I knew my husband and my friends would come for us, I just had to keep us safe until they arrived.

Book Two: Awakening

The castle was huge. (Overcompensation, much?) It stood easily five stories tall at its highest peak, boasting several battlements and parapets that came to nasty points. (I'm sure this was done to dissuade dragonfolk from landing there, once upon a time.) Every grey stone clicked firmly into the next, giving the appearance of structural solidarity that this castle would not be taken without a fight. I wonder how it stood against angry dragon fire.

We came up to the wooden drawbridge that had been roughly hewn from the nearby oaks, something that would be considered a last resort in Gallanorian culture, killing trees like that, versus their way of occupying the space with the living forests. Instead of seeing steel bolts to keep it all together as I would have seen on Earth, this drawbridge had spikes of black and red jadeite that were equal parts beautiful and horrifying. They could do real damage if you came up against one.

It seems as though there was once a decent sized moat around the castle, but the cracked and dry ground around it showed how little the land was thought of in this area. It made me furious.

"Nice moat," I threw at Ruskin's back.

He hunched his shoulders and turned around to snarl at me.

"Perhaps if you had not tried so hard to drown me the last time you saw me, I would feel differently toward bodies of water."

I let out a bark of laughter. Ruskin was scared of water? Fantastic.

He responded by shaking the bejesus out of Cyndol's net and I instantly leapt forward to attack him.

"No, you don't!" he said, taking a vicious swipe at my already damaged right shoulder to block my strike. I felt his claws slice into tissue and bone, and I stopped completely, pain forcing me to do so.

"Do I need to cage you, too?"

All I could see were cartoonish stars of pain dancing in front of my waning field of vision and I grunted. "No."

"Next time, I will."

My *also* battered left arm came up to try to staunch the bleeding of the right, but I was shaking too badly from adrenaline and fear to manage. My arms hung limply at my sides, blood flowing freely, soaking what was left of my once white linen shirt.

"Lower the bridge and open the gates for your Emperor!" shouted Viego to the barbican above the drawbridge.

There was a great deal of sound floating down from the barbican, followed quite quickly by the rumblings of the bridge being lowered to the ground. As it descended, I could see a set of wide double doors that matched the same oak and jadeite spikes the bridge was made of behind an impossibly large diamond portcullis. Once the bridge was down, the suns caught the reflection of the diamond bars and almost blinded me. The kids shouted their own discomfort, and Ruskin only chortled. I itched to smash his smug face into the spikes.

"Shall we?" he asked, waving his hand in a fake inviting gesture.

Not having a choice, we followed.

As we entered the formidable abode, I thought, *So it's come to this: I'm in the belly of the beast.*

As far as evil villain lairs go, this place was quite impressive. It reminded me of ancient European castles I'd seen in plenty of films during my life on Earth. However, instead of having rows of things such as knights in shining armor, Ruskin's halls held the skeletons of his vanquished foes. (At least, I assume they were foes, the way they were displayed so proudly, like bucks on a wall.)

After leaving the front foyer and subsequent halls of horror, we were led into another lobby of sorts, with a gray and black marbled double staircase that winded up into darkness so thick, I couldn't see the top. I had no idea how the stairs stayed up, appearing to float up to the top of the castle of their own accord. Candelabras burned brightly up both sides every thirty feet or so, and it would not have felt out of place if a few stray bats had flown by to creepy organ music. I couldn't help my shudder.

"Not up to your precious standards?" Ruskin asked.

"No. I find this place quite distasteful," I said.

"Well, I suggest you start finding things to like, or I'm afraid you will be quite miserable here," he said with a side smile. God, I hated him! How could my father have ever brought him into our lives?

We swerved to the right of the stairs (thankfully, as I did not want to see what was up there) and entered another hallway. This one, to my utter relief, did not hold any skeletons.

"This is where you will be staying," Viego said, gesturing at an open doorway.

I cautiously peered in and saw the sparsest of furnishings: A dilapidated wingback chair that was barely holding its cushions, a fireplace that was barren of any warmth, and a cot that likely had blankets from the previous tenant.

"No," I said. "That is completely unacceptable."

"Tough," Ruskin snarled, pushing me with such force that I went sprawling onto the floor and could not lift myself back up.

Face married to the rough wooden floorboards, I cursed him and spat red onto the space in front of me. He just laughed and shoved both children in after me, releasing them from their captivity. Thank God for small favors.

Slamming the door shut, his parting words were, "Supper will be brought to you… eventually."

Like I'd trust anything he'd give me. I'd have better luck eating the rotted sheets.

From my prone spot on the floor, I saw Cyndol and Ethan embrace each other and check themselves over for any damage. Luckily, there was nothing too serious. They would be fine.

"Oh! Amy!" Cyndol said, suddenly remembering I was still stuck on the floor, unable to use my useless arms to get back up. "Let us help you!"

"Tankyou," I mumbled into the slats.

The kids each gingerly grabbed an arm and did their best to lift me up to the chair. It creaked under my weight and puffed out an absurd amount of dust but was otherwise good enough for my current needs. The children sat on the bed with much the same outcome.

"Are you guys okay?" I asked, shifting uncomfortably so I could see them better.

Ethan didn't say much, but I thought I heard a soft "Yeah". Cyndol nodded but hugged her knees to her chest as she did so. I might have done the same if I was able. This situation we found ourselves in was terrifying.

"I know this is scary but, on the bright side, I know for a fact our friends in Gallanor won't leave us here. They will come after us and save us."

Ethan scoffed, his faith in people dwindling rapidly. Cyndol hmphed noncommittally, watching me intently, and I knew she was waiting for the answers I promised her in Gallanor.

"Whenever you're ready," she said.

I sighed, knowing this was going to be a tough conversation. I took a deep breath and started from the beginning.

CHAPTER THIRTY-THREE: IBRAXUS LEADS THE WAY

Faster! Faster!

Brax's brain was going into hyper speed. He was already furious at having to wait as long as he did to go after his wife and child, and the army that was left that he took with him was moving much slower than he would have if he had been able to go with just himself and Ifyrus. Sadly, he knew that he would stand no chance against Ruskin and his army by himself. He relished the thought of blowing such fire at him and his home that it barbecued the whole lot of them.

Take my family, will you?! I won't leave you anything! Castle, army, power, GONE!

Brax continued to rage to himself as Ifyrus pulled up alongside him.

"You hanging in there, mate?"

"What do you think?"

Ifyrus took no offense, knowing his king was not upset with him. So, he kept his eyes forward and plugged along.

"I'm sorry," Brax said a moment later. "I just need to get to them as fast as I can."

"I know, and we will, I promise you that. We will get them back, no matter what it takes. I would give my life for you to be reunited with your family."

Brax was surprised to hear him say that, but he shouldn't be. He knew Ifyrus was loyal to his very core. He deserved so much better than this. Brax would make sure, once all was said and done, that Ifyrus was given everything he ever wished for.

"Let's hope it doesn't come to that."

CHAPTER THIRTY-FOUR: DARRIAN MAKES A DISCOVERY

When Darrian jumped through the Crannie after his kids, he had no idea where he would land. Seeing it was Ruskin's castle made sense, of course, and now he had to act fast to make sure he wasn't spotted.

His gaze quickly fell on a twisted tree, and he leapt behind it as fast as he could. Peeking out from behind it, he searched the cobblestone road in front of him until he saw his children next to Ruskin. Fury ablaze, he renewed his inner promise to get his kids back at any cost.

He had to do a double take, as he thought he saw his wife's sister, Amaryah, with them. He'd never met her, but he'd heard many stories in his lifetime and Enid had even drawn a few pictures.

How he missed his wife. He wished that she was here with him to see this woman who looked so much like her kin.

Darrian was chomping at the bit for a chance at the man who took everything from him. He aimed to get back everything he could.

Fortunately, Darrian was able to snag a few more trophies from the battlefield that lent him a convincing disguise to blend in better with Ruskin's men. He put on everything he had that showcased Ruskin's colors, black and red, and made sure to cockishly brandish his stolen swords at his waist, as he'd seen others in this army do.

In his early years, Darrian had been drafted into Ruskin's service but found it such deplorable work that when he met a beautiful mermaid princess named Enid in Seaport, it didn't take much convincing to get him to leave his post at the castle and follow her wherever she would go. He had no idea how much his life would change, nor that it would ever bring him back here.

He watched the company before him cross the bridge and enter the castle. He cursed under his breath, knowing he couldn't directly follow. However, he did recall that there was a secret bolt hole that could be useful getting inside, *if* he remembered where it was.

***

Seventeen minutes later, and after much squelching around in the only muck left in the moat, Darrian found what he was looking for: A small segment of damaged rock that soldiers used to sneak out, usually when Ruskin's rants got too terrifying, and they couldn't handle it anymore. It was hidden by a spell that gave the illusion of a continuous wall, so unless you knew where to look, you wouldn't be able to see the damage.

Darrian thanked whatever luck was with him and went about stepping into the spell and breaching the hole. He had to remove his swords to squeeze through but pulled them in after himself before anyone could notice.

The moment he made it through, he heard the rasp of drawing swords and saw a few soldiers turn surprised faces his way.

"Oi!" the biggest one shouted. "Why you covered in mud?"

Darrian, thinking quickly, said, "Security check. I was told to check everything. Ruskin's orders. Everything looks good."

The guard sneered at him and said, "Ruskin told you that, did he?"

Darrian nodded. "Just following orders."

The men murmured to each other at this. Finally, the big man said, "Ruskin don't know about that hole, though, do he? So how could he have asked *you* to check it?"

Beads of sweat formed on Darrian's brow. He could feel his heart thundering in his chest. *Please don't make me kill you, please don't make me kill you...*

"Well, I—"

"Get him!" they shouted, all lunging at the intruder.

Darrian flung himself backward to avoid the swipe of weaponry aimed at his middle.

Another guard threw himself into the mix, and Darrian had to move faster than he ever had before! His eyes lit with remembered violence and muscle memory kicked in.

Three men were at him now, and Darrian lost his sword in a parry. He quickly shot his hands at the oncoming guard's midsection and grabbed the man's second sword from its scabbard. In one deft motion, Darrian yanked the hilt from the belt and swung it as hard as he could in a figure eight motion, taking out the man on the left's throat, then legs, followed rapidly by the same motion from the man he'd stolen from. Darrian dropped to his knees and plunged it into the stomach of the third approaching guard behind him and the fight was over.

After taking out the men, Darrian wiped his sword on the cape of one of the dead men and slipped it into his belt sheath.

Standing back up to dust himself off and look presentable enough to blend in, he stole the clean shoes off of another dead man and stepped out into the passageway to the rest of the castle.

As soon as he set foot in it, however, he quite literally crashed into a woman who was holding a tray, and both people and platter went down.

"Why don't you watch where you're—"

"I'm sorry, I didn't see you—"

They paused and really looked at each other for a quick moment before…

"Enid?"

"Darrian? Oh! Darrian!" The woman flung her arms around him in a tight embrace, trapping him in his shock. How was his wife here?

"Enid! What hap—?"

"Shh!" she said. "Not here. And call me 'Ida'. Follow me!"

Enid pulled him by the arm to a closet a few steps away, closing them inside before anyone saw them. Enid gestured for him to be quiet a moment while they waited to see if there were any more cries from guards. Luck was on their side and no shout was heard. She peeked out of the closet to make doubly sure there was no one there before closing back up and confronting her husband.

"What are you doing here?" she asked, equal parts thrilled and terrified to see him. What if Ruskin found out who he was?

"I was going to ask you the same thing!" he replied, still in shock. "I feared you were dead!"

"As did I! In fact, I almost was, but I was captured instead! I was taken here to the castle. When they asked me my name, I told them it was Ida. Nobody knew who I was, so I remained as safe as I could. I was given duty to assist Mage Davina, and I've been trying to glean what I could about the kids. I'd heard Davina mention partial visions that made me think this disaster would happen. I stayed here in case the worst happened, that Ruskin won and brought them back, which he did, the wretch. Your turn."

Darrian smiled at his wife, a happy tear in his eye that she lived and was here.

"I was nearly killed as well, but when we got separated that day, I was loaded onto a cart for the dead, though I was merely unconscious. Blow to the head, I suspect. When I came to under a few more bodies, I waited for a moment when the guards' backs were turned and I quietly slipped out of there, making my way to Seaport. Fortunately, I was able to slip in with Ruskin's army and find out where the kids were."

"You saw the kids?" Enid asked.

"At the battle in Gallanor. I'm sure you heard of the plans to invade, yes?"

"Yes, and I've been afraid ever since! My poor babies!"

"On the bright side, he brought them here, and we're both here, and I promise you, we are going to get them out!"

She took a breath to respond, but a voice shouted for her in the hallway.

"Ida?" he bellowed. "Ida!"

Enid made a shushing motion and held up her hand to stay her husband. She quickly slipped out the closet and closed it firmly behind her. Darrian could still hear them talking.

"Ida! There you are," the man said. "Here. Take this slop to the prisoners. I don't have time to do your chores all day."

She humphed as he unloaded a heavy tray into her arms.

"Uh," she said, "I will be happy to deliver this, I just have one more thing in that closet that is going to the same room. I'll just grab it really quickly and be right there!"

"Whatever. Just make sure it gets done."

"Absolutely, sir. Will do, sir."

The man left and Darrian waited until he no longer heard his footfalls to crack the door open.

"Is it safe?" he whispered.

"Yes," Enid replied just as quietly. "Just don't tip off the guards when we get to their door. Now, follow me, and act like you're helping. In fact," she gestured with her chin, "grab those linens behind you."

Darrian did as his wife bid, and the two of them made it down the lengthy winding hallways until they came to the prisoners' room.

Are you ready? she asked Darrian with her eyes.

Darrian nodded. They opened the door.

CHAPTER THIRTY-FIVE: AMY REUNITED

"Amaryah?" my youngest sister said, dropping a full tray on the floor. The blonde hair that so perfectly matched Ethan and Cyndol's was tucked neatly under a maid's cap, two purposeful curls popping out on either side of her astonished face. "Is it really you?"

"Mother! Father!" the kids said.

"Shh!" the man with my sister commanded.

One of the guards poked his head in. "Everything alright?"

Enid, thinking quickly, said, "Oh! Sorry. Dear me, I was just startled coming in for a moment. The poor children thought I looked like their mother and, well, clearly, they were mistaken. But I did drop the food, so I'll have to go fetch some more after I change these linens."

The guard gave the room a once-over, checking to see if anything fishy was going on. Seeing nothing out of place, he gave a half shrug and went back outside to guard the door with his cohort.

Once the door was shut, and Enid was sure they were safe behind it, the kids rushed to their parents, all hugging each other with tears flowing freely.

I stood there, stunned, happy memories of my precocious younger sister flooding my mind, and I joined them in their happy cry.

Enid freed one arm from her kids and held it out to me to join them.

"I'd love to, but I'm a bit beaten up at the moment," I said, looking down at Ruskin's claw holes in my arms.

"Oh my word!" she said, abandoning the hug to check me over. "You're a mess! What happened to you?"

"How much time you got?" I half-laughed. "Short answer? Ruskin got his claws in me. He's done a number on the kids as well, I'm afraid."

"Tell us everything," she said.

I proceeded to catch them up on the events as best I could, Cyndol piping in where she was able, and Ethan mumbling a few vague sentences here and there. I found out from Enid that the strange man I saw following us through the Crannie was, in fact, my brother-in-law, Darrian. It warmed my heart to see them all so happy together.

I missed so very much. My ire at Ruskin deepened and I felt my eyes burn.

"You have Ethan's purple eyes!" Cyndol said.

"So do you, dear," Enid said, waving her hand over Cyndol's face, revealing that they were also the same shade of violet our whole family possessed.

"We had to spell you children when you were born so as not to attract attention. This was exactly what we've feared this whole time."

Cyndol blinked a few times, pinpricks of tears forming as she processed the new color.

"Why didn't you ever tell us?" Ethan asked from the bed, head hanging low.

Enid sighed heavily, gently sitting down next to him. She lifted his hair out of his eyes and pulled his chin up to meet her face.

"My poor boy," she said, checking out his head scar, still not fully healed and looking angrier than I'd seen it for a while.

"What would we have said?" Darrian asked him, laying his hand on his son's shoulder. "You come from a magickal family, and the evil king may come after you if he finds you?"

Ethan laughed gruffly. "Might have been nice to know, yes. Perhaps I could have prepared myself for what was coming. Perhaps I could've done—" He stopped himself before he told his parents all the gruesome details he was trying to spare them. I'm not sure if I even knew all the specifics, and what I *did* know broke my heart. I could see why he was reluctant to share, and why he was angry about his ignorance. I didn't envy the position it put my sister in. "It would have been nice to know."

Nobody spoke for a moment. We were trying to process the collective traumas we'd all been through.

Suddenly, Cyndol's stomach growled, and Enid snapped out of her reverie.

"Oh, you poor thing! I completely forgot about the food I brought. And of course I dropped it all over the floor. I'm so sorry! I will go see if I can find some more. I should get back to my position anyway, lest they come looking for me and I blow my cover." She kissed her kids goodbye and grabbed Darrian's arm, pulling him toward the door as she collected the spilled and forgotten food things. "I will come back with food and supplies to fix those shoulder wounds for you, Amaryah."

With that, they took their leave of us and the kids, and I sat in wait.

CHAPTER THIRTY-SIX: RUSKIN THE WINNER

Ruskin gloated atop his throne, admiring his latest treasure: The now completed suns necklace he had been waiting for… but wait… What was that?

He bolted upright from his languid position, pulling the necklace closer to his face to try to figure out what the spot in the middle was. At first glance, it appeared as if there was meant to be a hole in the center, as jewelry was wont to do. However, upon further inspection, he saw there was a groove inside the inner circle that looked as if something was meant to go there.

"No. NO!" he shouted, his violent screams reverberating off the vaulted stone walls. The guards at the door wisely did nothing. "DAVINA!" he shouted, forgetting she was no longer there to be of assistance.

Ruskin drew his arm back and flung the necklace in frustration, realizing too late his mistake as it shattered upon the stone wall.

"Noooo!" he screamed again. How could he have been so *stupid*? He didn't make mistakes like this! He rushed to the shrapnel to see if it could be saved and found, to his chagrin, he could do nothing. However, if he could find a jeweler, perhaps it could still be salvaged? Did he even have any of those in his kingdom? He must, mustn't he?

"Silas!" he yelled to his head of guard.

"Yes, Sire?" he replied, rushing to his sovereign's feet.

"I have a task for you. I need you to find me a jeweler, someone you can trust to fix this as soon as possible."

Silas looked carefully at the broken trinket in his king's clawed hand and chose his next words carefully. "Well, Sire, we did have one, yes. However, you banished him last year when he failed to make Princess Davina a ring that you deemed worthy. And, might I add, that was very excellent foresight on your part to spare his life like that."

Ruskin let out a long breath. "And where might I find him now?"

"I can check for you, Sire. I will send my best men to track him down."

"See that you do. Oh! And one more thing. Make sure my army is at the ready. I don't doubt those heathens will come sniffing around to try to steal back what is mine."

"Of course, Majesty. It will be done."

"Dismissed!"

With that, Silas exited to find the missing jeweler and ready the army once more.

Ruskin sat back on his throne, contemplating the calamity in his cupped claws.

***

It took a few days, but Silas managed to find the banished jeweler and get him to repair the broken pendant. It took some encouragement (and some hefty threats to his life), but the task was managed, and the pendant was now back in Ruskin's hands. Ruskin decided to spare the man's life once more, just in case any harm should befall this fragile thing again.

Another bit of information the jeweler managed to help with was what the missing piece could be. He theorized that it had to be a gem of some sort, one of high quality and power to be able to make the whole pendant come to life, so to speak.

Ruskin hated how much time this was taking and worried that it would put a damper on his plans. No matter. He would find a way to make this work in his favor, no matter the cost.

Back on his throne once more, he contemplated what gemstone could fit here to complete it. He'd already tried fitting in any loose gemstone he had on hand, but no luck.

Suddenly, it dawned on him. *Amaryah! She must know about this necklace! Time to pick her brain about it.*

Mind made up, he flung himself out the door and made his way to the prisoners, intent on confronting her to see what she knew about the missing piece.

Shoving aside his posted guards, he grabbed the door's handle and yanked it with such ferocity it nearly succeeded in ripping the entire thing off its hinges.

The three occupants shrieked in fear (his favorite sound) and hurled themselves together on the bed. Amaryah roughly threw her arms out in a protective gesture. He was perturbed to see that someone had tended to her wounds. He contemplated what damage to inflict on her next.

"Amaryah," he said. "I have a question for you."

"And I have an answer for *you*," she replied, lifting her middle finger in a gesture he didn't recognize, but caught the gist of.

"How utterly ladylike of you."

She winked and said, "Nothing but the best for you, Wolfie."

Ruskin gritted his teeth and kept his growl in check, for now. He slunk up to the bed as the kids cowered further into Amaryah's back, lifted the necklace up to her face, and asked, "What do you see here?"

"An asshole in a fur coat?"

His hackles began to rise, a growl escaping before he could control it. The children trembled in fear, and the little one let out a chirp that was music to his ears. He couldn't wait to take a crack at her powers. But, for now, this came first.

"Always the jester. Some things never change, I see. Really, *truly* look now, unless you prefer I start my session with the girl first? Her brother can attest to my *methods*."

"Don't you touch her!" she shrieked, putting her entire body in front of the child, her brother throwing his arms around his sister as well, though his eyes were shut tightly in fear. Ruskin delighted in the response.

"Very well. Now, what is missing from this necklace?"

Amaryah sighed and focused her attention on the jewelry, knowing the answer full well. "It's an amethyst piece."

"I should have known," he replied. "Go on. Can I use any old amethyst? Or is it something specific?"

She grimaced and said, "It's quite specific, I'm afraid."

Ruskin growled again. "Well? Where can I find this amethyst piece?"

She kept her mouth shut, clearly not wanting to give him any information.

Ruskin flung his right hand out, razor-sharp claws extending. He raised it high above her head, about to slash down on her, when a guard came thundering through the doorway.

"Sire!" he said. "We are under attack!"

CHAPTER THIRTY-SEVEN: CHAOS

"Break it down!" King Brax shouted at the army hammering Ruskin's door before shifting into dragon form and taking to the sky. He let out a burst of flame onto the battlements, frying the oncoming soldiers in their tracks. Their screams were so loud Brax *hoped* Ruskin could hear them from wherever he was in the castle. *Let* him *feel fear for once*! Brax thought gleefully.

Ellera rode up on a horse a short distance from the castle behind a shifting Ifyrus, Kit poised on her lap, ready to strike at a moment's notice. He had on his lovely parting gift from Sovereign Sai: A small, mirrored locket that was affixed to a comfy collar around his neck, ready to release Kit Two whenever he was needed.

Ifyrus let out a billowing flame, catching a few soldiers that Brax had missed. The smell of charred flesh was starting to reach the oncoming fighters, and they used it to spur the bloodlust.

The contingent attacking the castle was made up of many different factions of Ruskin-opposers: The people of Gallanor, the soldiers of Mer Realm, a few surviving people from Cavar that managed to find them on the road there, and the odd creatures of surrounding kingdoms that were tired of living in fear of the Wolf King.

Nobody had heard from the Fae. Ellera was becoming increasingly worried about their silence and feared they had been attacked after they left. She had sent word via jackrabbit on their way out of Gallanor that they were attacking Ruskin's castle and asked for assistance. So far, nothing.

As if he could read her thoughts, Kit looked up at her and said, "Don't worry, they'll be here. Sovereign Sai wouldn't let us down."

She chuckled and gave his head a scratch. "I hope you're right, Little One."

Just then, an arrow came whizzing past her face and nearly took off her ear, nicking it on its flight. She clutched her right hand to it, putting pressure on the wound and bringing it back to her face to see that it had, in fact, drawn blood.

Ellera renewed her focus and pulled an arrow from the quiver on her back, but before she could nock it to the bow gripped in her hand, Ifyrus found the man who fired it and ate him in one massive *CHOMP*! Ellera smiled vindictively and aimed her weapon at a different man instead.

From above, they heard Brax's cry of, "Break it down!"

A flurry of folk was attempting to break through the diamond portcullis. What was left of Ruskin's fighting force continued to fire off arrows and hurl various boulders with the help of a catapult. They succeeded in taking out the approaching band of Mer people, sadly squashing them in their tracks.

Fury deepened, Ifyrus let out another blast. This time, they were prepared and threw up sapphire and ruby shields to protect themselves from the flames. Ifyrus bellowed his dismay and let loose more fire. Again, he was blocked.

"The gates are opening!" cried a voice from somewhere near the front of the fray.

All eyes turned to see what the warning was about. Ruskin's army poured out from the opening gates and portcullis, one by one, no room for anyone else to squeak by. They charged the dragon's army and began mowing them down. It was as if they were men possessed, and they attacked with a strength they had not shown until now.

After the line of men stopped, a giant hulking beast burst forth and clobbered the dragon's army out of the way with its club as easily as swatting flies from your face. It was twelve feet of furry fury, its blazing red eyes struck terror in the hearts of all. Another one followed behind it, and Brax's army took a collective step backward. Even King Brax himself looked worried, flying high above with Ifyrus, trying to find the best firing point without singeing their comrades in the process.

Once the creatures cleared the bridge, the gates began to close and stop any forward momentum. Ellera spotted the doors and rushed her horse forward faster, doing her best to avoid the swinging swords, whizzing arrows, and whatever else might be hurtling her way. She just knew they had to make it to the door before it closed on them.

"We're not going to make it!" Kit squeaked.

"Shut up! Yes, we are!" Ellera said.

Flames licked fire trails above their heads as the two dragons took turns blasting the furry giants. Ellera rode as hard as she could.

"We're not gonna make it, we're not gonna make it, we're not gonna make it—" Kit blathered.

Ellera knew he was right. Just before she admitted defeat, she had an idea.

"Kit," she said, "how do you feel about rolling?"

"What?"

She grabbed him by the scruff of his neck, bunching orange fluff and mirrored collar in her fist, and she bowled him, tail-over-face towards the swiftly closing door.

Kit yelped. He hit a divot in the bridge and stopped just shy of the gate, knowing he wouldn't be able to catch it in time. The locket on his neck began to buzz and it gave him the idea he needed. He wrestled his jaw underneath the collar and bit down *hard*, snapping and freeing it from his neck. He used his teeth to chuck it with all his mini might and got it in the doorway right as it was closing. "Help us, Kit Two!"

All Kit could see was an orange fog, then the door shut. Not knowing if he succeeded, he scampered out of the way of the war going on around him before he was crushed underfoot.

The guard on the other side of the gate was lowering the bar to lock it firmly in place when a tiny rust colored fox poked up from between his legs.

"Hey, little fella," the man said. "How'd *you* get in here?"

Kit Two beamed an adorable smile up at him before clamping his razor-sharp teeth on the man's most tender parts.

The guardsman screamed and tried to fight him off, forgetting he hadn't set the bar fully in place yet. Ellera came bursting through, Kit back by her side and a steady stream of Brax's army behind her.

"Find Amy!" Ellera shouted. "Find the kids!"

***

From somewhere deep in the castle, Ruskin gnashed his teeth in frustration. He wasn't fully surprised that Brax had come back for his bride. *My bride*, he thought angrily. Seeing her again brought back all the old feelings and resentments, and Ruskin wanted to thrash them again for what they'd put him through.

He'd left Amaryah and the children locked in their room so he could go and fetch Viego. He would need him in order to Crannie himself back to The Island. So what if his castle was being attacked? He had everything he needed to realize his dreams (though he was still working on that amethyst). And if everything went according to plan, they could have his castle. For now, anyway. Retribution would be swift and mighty for those that dare oppose him.

"Viego!" he shouted at the castle. "Where are you?"

A shuffling sound came from around the corner, then the disgusting half-faced man made an appearance.

"I am here, Majesty," he said. "How can I be of service?"

Ruskin focused on him and shuddered. If he didn't have need of his skill, he'd just as soon rip off the rest of his face and be done with him.

"I need to get to The Island. Quickly. We are being attacked."

"Of course, Sire. However, as you know, I can only do that outdoors. The castle walls and inlaid magick interfere with transportation and, well, keeping ourselves intact."

Ruskin gritted his jaw again but gave a curt nod.

"Were you aware there was a piece missing from the necklace? I discovered the grooves on the inner lining. Amaryah confirmed it just a few moments ago."

Viego worried his hands near his midsection but shook his head.

"I was not aware, Sire."

A crackling moment sizzled between them. Ruskin suspected his toady was keeping secrets, and his Mage did his best to maintain a neutral gaze.

"Viego, do you know what the missing piece is?"

Viego let out a breath, hoping he wasn't about to be throttled.

"To my knowledge, Majesty, the only thing it might possibly be, that could be strong enough to contain the magick you are looking for, is an amethyst of the highest line."

Ruskin rolled his exasperated eyes and asked, "How do I get my hands on that?"

"I could tell you that, My King, but I'm afraid I must ask for a specific kind of payment for that information."

Ruskin's claws slid from his fingertips and clicked a staccato beat against the sword that lay strapped to his belt.

Seeing that he had the king's attention, Viego licked his cracked lips and said, "I wish to be promoted, Sire. I wish to not be treated as a thing that could be thrown away but seen more like an equal. When you are the highest ruler in the land, when you officially become Emperor of all of Callembria, I should like to have rule of my own, under your reign, of course, but power just the same."

"And why should I grant you that request?"

"Because!" Viego shouted, greed bringing him close to his master's face. "I have done *everything* for you! I have won you *wars*! I have brought you *riches*! I have wrangled power for you year after year, and yet you only ever kick me aside! Why would I *not* want to be the one in charge?!"

The two men stared fire at each other for a moment before Ruskin smiled slowly. "Very well, Viego. I shall grant you ruling power of your own small kingdom, once my goals are realized."

Viego's disastrous countenance pulled up into his version of shock and hope.

"You will?"

"Yes," Ruskin lied smoothly. "Now, tell me what I need to know."

Viego's tongue snaked out of his mouth to wet his lips again. "Power that large does not come without sacrifice. I saw a glimpse of it in the boy's head. The power you seek lies within the eyes of the Mer Realm, specifically the eyes of the royal line. You happen to hold three of them captive as we speak."

The werewolf king began a sinister smirk. "In their eyes, you say? Marvelous."

***

Outside the castle, Brax blew another tremendous rain of fire on the seemingly endless supply of Ruskin's men to mixed results. Some went down as easily as he'd hoped, while others seemed to have fire-proof shields in varying mixes of ruby and sapphire. His own men seemed to be falling faster than he thought, and he was terrified they would be overcome. Monsters joined men on the battlefield, and Brax could no longer keep count of how many there were.

His desperate hope was that Ellera was able to find Amy and the kids and bring them unharmed from the castle, while he kept the army at bay with Ifyrus.

Arrows large and small sailed all around them, as well as boulders from the catapult, doing their best to knock them from the sky. Brax saw another load being started and took a chance diving through the air to collide full steam into the contraption. He knocked it over and pinned three men beneath it. He stopped their cries with a massive snap of his jaws, then took to the sky once more.

Ifyrus roared his approval and sent another flame to the surviving soldiers.

Just then, a horn sounded from somewhere near the front of the castle, and a tall man in death-black robes strode forth, a gnarled staff in his right hand. He shouted something Brax could not decipher.

A hush fell on the battlefield, chilling the dragon king to his core and making every hair stand on end.

In one swift motion, the bodies of the dead began to rise, pick up whatever weaponry they could, and swing it at the bodies of the living.

The Necromancer laughed in twisted glee as he guided his wooden staff through the air, directing this nightmare as if he were merely a child playing with his favorite toys. When his face turned Brax's way and he caught sight of the Dark Mage, his heart stopped. *Bannon.* But… how? How could that be? He thought he was dead! Ruskin had killed him himself! How was he here now?! But he was, he *was* here now, conducting a hideous display of monsters like a merry little band. Many of Brax's people were overcome, and he feared for the first time that they would lose this fight.

Suddenly, and almost unnoticeably, a small sphere rolled onto the battlefield amongst the melee. Brax watched it curiously from his spot in the sky, hoping against hope that it was not some fresh terror to contend with. But, after an endless moment, tiny flickers of light erupted from the top of the sphere, and those lights popped Fae soldiers into existence. The Fae had come! The Fae had answered their call! Hundreds of Fae jumped eagerly onto the battlefield, decimating the oncoming werewolf king's soldiers. Sovereign Sai themself led the charge.

Sai took one hard look at Bannon, still directing his corpse army with vigor, and closed their eyes, taking a deep breath. Brax watched in fascination and renewed hope as Bannon stopped, eyes bulging and tongue sticking out as he clawed helplessly at his throat. He dropped to his knees and became stock-still. In the next moment, he fell face-first onto the unforgiving ground before him and the army of the dead were stilled.

For the first time that day, Brax smiled.

CHAPTER THIRTY-EIGHT: AMY AND THE CHAIR

We sat huddled together on the dingy bed, hearing sounds of war outside the walls. Ruskin had left us here as soon as it started, but I had no idea how much time had passed since then. All I knew was that my husband had come for us, and we had to be ready.

"Okay, kiddos," I said, jumping up from my spot on the bed. "I don't know about you, but I'd sure love to be ready to flee the moment that door opens, how about you?"

The kids both gave me faces in varying degrees of fright.

"Look, I know you're scared, I know you're tired. So am I. But you know what else I know? Those sounds out there, those awful, terrifying, loud as hell noises are the sounds of our impending rescue by King Ibraxus, and he *will* be coming to bring us home and far, far away from this place. So, get yourselves ready. We are leaving to join them."

Ethan and Cyndol exchanged glances, something I'm sure they did a thousand times before when their parents said something they knew was crap.

"How do you know it's him?" Cyndol asked.

I chuckled. "Who else do you know that can roar like that?"

A wide grin spread across her face as she realized I was right.

"Get up! Look for anything in this room that might help to crack a door open!"

Cyndol immediately popped up to search, but Ethan just gave a half-hearted glance around the room.

Admittedly, not much was in the room at all, but my eyes landed on the chair at the same time Cyndol's did. We met each other's gaze, sharing the same thought: *This chair was going to die.*

"On the count of three, pick it up and swing it at the door as hard as you can, okay?"

Cyndol nodded and Ethan sighed, but he grabbed an open spot on the chair next to his sister, with me on the other end. My shoulders, though doing better after some magick and meds, still gave me some hell when I tightened my grip. This was going to be unpleasant.

"One... two... *three*!" I said.

We lifted the heavier-than-I-thought-it-was-going-to-be chair and swung it at the locked door. No damage.

"Try again," I said. "One... two... *three*!"

Again, not a scratch. My shoulders were screaming.

"Again?" Cyndol panted.

I nodded. "One... Two... Three."

BOOM!

A single scrape on the door showed. Hope.

"Again," I breathed.

BOOM!

"Again!"

BOOM!

The door splintered just a little... but so did the chair.

"Amy?" Cyndol asked.

I met her shining eyes. "Again."

BOOM!

"Again!"

BOOM!

"AGAIN!"

BOOM!

The door earned a hole!

The chair shattered in our hands.

"No," Cyndol cried, "no! No, that can't be it! No!"

She threw herself at the door and began hammering at the hole with her fists. She even sprouted her newly formed dragon wings and tried to take a swipe at it to widen the hole. It broke my heart to see her fighting so furiously, knowing the outcome would not be what we wanted.

"Cyndol," Ethan said. "Cyndol!"

"What?!" she screamed back at him. "What? You want me to stop? Hmm? You want me to give up like you did? Huh?" She shoved his shoulders when he went to reach for her. "I've been trying this *whole time*! I'm sorry things are so terrible right now! Things have been awful for *all* of us! But we *need* you, brother! Stop acting like I'm insane for trying to get us out of here and *help me*!"

He looked stunned for a moment, even slightly embarrassed, watching his kid sister show more strength than he was.

"You're right. I'm sorry. What can I do?"

She sighed, some of her fury ebbing. "Well, what about your purple eye trick thing? Can you blast through the rest of this hole like you did back in Gallanor?"

He looked hesitant. "I can try."

Ethan took a step away from the door and motioned for us to scoot back even more. I grabbed Cyndol's hand and led her back behind the bed to protect us, just in case any shrapnel came our way. Seeing we were as safe as we could be, he took a deep breath, closed his eyes, and seemed to go into himself to collect whatever magick was hiding within. One more deep breath and, on the exhale, he opened his eyes, his very violet eyes.

The door blew completely off its hinges!

"Aaaaaaaahhhhhhh!" came a feminine shriek of surprise.

"Mother?" Ethan called. "Are you alright?"

Enid stepped over the unconscious guards at her feet, then popped her head in the still smoking doorway with a half-laugh. "I'm fine, but your father is missing a chunk of hair! We were just coming to get you. Time to go!"

CHAPTER THIRTY-NINE: RUSKIN MAKES HIS MOVE

"Mother, you say? I thought she looked familiar," Ruskin said, appearing from around the corner of his prisoners' room.

The terrified family shrieked and the man with them came at him with his sword. Ruskin laughed and gave Viego a nod.

"Darrian! Watch out!" shouted Not-Ida. Enid, then, he surmised. She went rushing forth to block the oncoming spell. She was too late, however, his talented sidekick was much too quick. Darrian fell backwards after getting hit by a grief spell. He landed flat on his back and struggled to move. Enid fell to her knees beside him and tried to check him for damage, all the while his screams were becoming louder and louder. Viego had cursed him to see his worst fears on a loop, torturing him from the inside out.

Ruskin belly laughed, a true guttural amusement at this man's cursed fate.

"You *monster*!" Cyndol cried, dragon wings protruding from her back once again, majestic in their young glory. She charged at him, determined to kill him for what he did to her father.

"Cyndol, no!" Amaryah said. She leapt forward to catch her by her wing. "He'll kill you!"

The two ladies fought each other now, much to the king's delight.

"Grab the boy," he instructed Viego.

As Viego moved to do so, Ethan beamed his purple peepers at him and managed to singe his damaged cheek.

"You will never touch me again!" the boy said. "Never again!" He sent another blast his way, catching him on the other side.

Ruskin was quite done with this scuffle and wished to be on his way. With one swipe of his massive claws across Ethan's face, he downed the boy and made a move to lift him up. However, as his hand was about to grip his tattered shirt, a crowd of people burst through to their location, and he was charged by Ibraxus and his army.

Dropping his plan of taking the unconscious boy, Ruskin turned to Viego and said, "Out the side door, *now*! Hurry! And grab the women!"

The two of them grabbed hold of Cyndol and Amaryah, not knowing which of them would be needed. The ladies fought tooth, nail, and wing, but Viego unleashed a spell that rendered them stock-still and easy to transport.

"*Ruskin!*" screamed the sky worm behind them. "Come back here and fight me, you coward!"

Ruskin laughed again, knowing he was about to leave his foes and worries behind him. He had everything he needed.

"No, *no!*" Brax cried. "Amy! Cyndol! Leave them alone!" He turned to the woman beside him. "Ellera, help them!"

The woman, Ellera, ran towards them, arms out, eyes alighting and bringing a powerful storm around herself. Viego stopped in his tracks, suddenly terrified of this woman.

"Viego! Move! What are you doing?" Ruskin asked.

"That's—" he said, "my—my sister… but, how? I killed you."

Ellera's black and purple braids lifted into the air and static crackled all around her. "Yes," she replied. "You did try that."

She let go a massive wave of electricity that knocked him askew, but he managed to keep hold of the child. Another wave hit and his grip grew weaker. Ruskin was afraid he would be overcome, so he rushed toward the hidden side door and flung it open. Amaryah started to break through the immobilization spell and tried to kick herself free. Ruskin gave her a shake and dug his claws in deeper.

"Viego!" he cried. "Move, you fool! Now!"

One more blast from the stormy sister and Viego fell on his backside into a rolling tumble, caught up in himself and the dragon-child. They were propelled out of the castle before coming to an unceremonious stop in the dried-out moat.

"The Crannie! Now!" Ruskin barked at his Mage. "Hurry!"

The opposing army was pouring out the door after them, and Viego threw the temporary portal up against the air, ripping a hole through the fabric of their dimension. The Wolf King could see The Island before them in all its glory.

Ruskin was taking his first greedy step toward the Crannie when he heard a stern voice behind him.

"Father."

He stopped himself in his tracks as he recognized the voice of his only daughter.

"Kavea," he said. "What brings you here? Have you come to visit dear old dad?"

"Stop," she commanded. "Stop this madness. You can end this, right here, right now. Stop what you are doing, set those people free, and come home."

Viego was poised nervously next to the wavering portal, Ibraxus and his army paused directly behind the teen, waiting to see if avoiding any more bloodshed was possible. Ruskin exhaled, knowing his next move could make or break his plans. He did care for his daughter, as much as one could as an absentee father intent on world domination, but was she worth the whole of magick when he was this close to ultimate rule?

"I'm sorry, Kavea." Ruskin turned his back on her and knocked Amaryah into the portal and Viego dragged Cyndol behind him.

In a burst of courage, Kavea dove into the Crannie after them, trying to save her friends from the evil that was her father. The Crannie began to warble, its temporary power ebbing quickly now. Ibraxus, Ellera, and the fox tried to follow suit, but it was too late: The way was shut.

CHAPTER FORTY: THE ISLAND

The last thing Cyndol saw as the Crannie closed was Colt, appearing out of nowhere. He was attempting to keep it open by shoving his horn into the swiftly closing hole. Brax, Ellera, and Kit were also trying to squeeze through the hole before it shut completely.

Too late. They were all too late.

The Mage called Viego dragged her roughly behind him by her braided hair in their new location. Cyndol could feel wisps of hair breaking free as he did so, putting extra strain on her neck. Continuing along, he let her body roll over a rock or two in the path. She was still unable to move, but she could absolutely feel all the pain. She seethed even harder and tried to summon her bubble. She felt it flicker but was unable to produce it. Patience, then.

Ruskin had not moved much, other than to face Kavea with Amy clutched haphazardly to his side.

"Do not trifle with me, daughter," he said. "You are interrupting my mission, and I must ask you to remove yourself before you get hurt."

Kavea looked crestfallen. "Why would I get hurt, Father? Are you planning to hurt me? Your own child?"

"Of course not!" he said. "How could you dare ask me such a thing?" Ruskin dropped Amy roughly on the ground to free his hands and took a deep breath before he struck her down for insubordination. "Of course not," he said softer. "But you need to leave, *right* now. I do *not* have time to deal with you. I will come back to visit with you once all of this is over. Now, *go home!*"

Ruskin turned his back on his only child and gathered up the heap of his former love. He didn't see the glint that caught the reflection of the suns.

The jab of the dagger below his right shoulder was... unexpected. He couldn't fathom how his little girl could be so *ruthless*! Dropping Amy once more, he faced Kavea with a look of half bewilderment, half pride. He yanked it free without much effort.

"Daughter—?"

She didn't let him finish, just pulled a second dagger from the back hem of her trousers. She swung it upwards to strike once more, but Ruskin's instincts took over. In one smooth motion, he pulled her hand with the dagger in an arcing fashion and used her own momentum to shove it into her chest instead.

The spell holding Cyndol wavered just enough to allow a guttural, "*Nooo!*"

Amy's face echoed matching pain as Kavea's small frame sank to the sandy floor, her beautiful scarlet curls standing out against the stark whiteness of her face.

Ruskin, shaking with anger and adrenaline, realized too late what he had done. He fell to his knees beside her.

"Kavea?"

Her eyes became glassy, her breath stilted. "Father? B-b-b-but— I—" A trickle of blood appeared at the corners of her heart-shaped mouth.

"I'm so sorry, darling! I didn't mean to— You just— And then the dagger, and—" The king who never cried shed a tear for his child. "I am... so sorry." He cradled her face in his clawed hand.

A tear that mirrored his own slid down her pale cheek. With her last choking breath, she looked him square in the eye and said, "I will... *never*... forgive you."

The whole world became quiet. The only sounds were that of water burbling nearby and a light breeze in the air. Cyndol could hear her heart break in her chest, and she thought she would surely die from it. *This wasn't happening, this wasn't happening.*

"You *MURDERER!*" Amy screamed as she shook off the last vestiges of spell work that held her captive. Her eyes blazed a violent violet as she launched herself forcefully into Ruskin. The two of them went scrambling head over feet until they landed against a tree whose type Cyndol had not seen since leaving Cavar. A few of the hanging fruits dropped and pelted Viego, startling him enough that he let go of the grip he had on her. It was enough.

Cyndol's bubble burst into place and Viego was launched into nearby shrubbery. Her arms came back to her first, so she used them to crawl over to Amy to ensconce her within the bubble.

Amy kicked Ruskin hard in the face twice in a row. She scuttled sideways as fast as she could into the girl's protection. It was enough to avoid the furious swipe of the king's claws. Cyndol's translucent barrier had just wrapped around her when those claws connected. The bubble, Cyndol could feel, recoiled in horror from the sting, but held firm. *Good. Keep the king out!*

"RUSKIN!" boomed a voice that was music to Amy's ears. *Tripp*! "Get. Off. My. Island!" With every syllable he threw a ball of electric energy the king's way, causing small patches of skin and hair to burn.

Ruskin yelped in pain and snarled his fury right back at him. "Caspaar! How good of you to join us! You'll have a front row seat to my inevitable victory!"

"Oh yeah, hot shot? An' just what is it yer itchin' to get a win on, huh? What's yer plan? 'Cause, from where *I'm* standin', you ain't got doodly-squat!"

The king smiled viciously and said, "No, I don't. But *she* does." He motioned his claw directly at Amy and she blanched in fresh fear. "I know about your eyes."

The blood drained from Amy's face as she registered the truth of his words. He knew. Somehow, he *knew*.

"The eyes are the prize," he said, "and I plan to have them."

"You're gonna take her eyes?!" thundered Tripp. "Why in all o' creation would you do *that*?"

But Amy knew why. Tripp could see it on her face.

She spoke in an eerie tone. "They are the key to uniting the energies of all three cores with the suns. They unlock the magick he needs to become all-powerful."

"On the nosey!" Ruskin applauded as if she was his star pupil. "Although I only need just one, so, if you would kindly pop one out for me, it would save us all any trouble going forward. Thanks to you and your rag-tag band of miscreants, I've lost my only daughter, so it's the least you can do."

"No."

"What if I said 'Please'?" he asked with dangerous excitement.

"You can't do this, Ruskin," Tripp said.

"And why not, oh great and powerful one? Why can't I just reach out and pluck it from her pretty little head?"

Tripp huffed out a breath, furious that Ruskin was putting them in this situation. "Because, you dimwit! It ain't just about suckin' up some magick you want, you greedy sonofabitch! That there," he thrust his finger at the second sun, "that's not just any ol' ball o' energy! You start reunitin' the energies like that and you're gonna open a messy portal that leads straight back to the planet we first came from!"

The king scoffed. "What are you on about, old man?"

Tripp stomped up to the monarch and got right in his face. "How do you not know about *that*, but you know about every other damn thing? Whatta you think this island even is?"

Ruskin's lips twitched, a brief moment of hesitation. "It does not matter. I will have what I came for."

"Over my dead body!" Tripp promised.

"As you wish," Ruskin said.

Amy and Cyndol used this moment to sneak backward out of Ruskin's reach, forgetting that Viego was in the shrubbery somewhere behind them. The evil sorcerer pounced from the bushes like a crazed jackrabbit and landed on top of Cyndol's bubble. He popped it with his magickal tendril finger as he landed on top of her, breaking her wing and pinning her down in the process.

Amy launched herself at Viego, scrabbling with his whirling body, doing her best to keep his finger away from Cyndol's shrieking agony. Tripp tried to run toward them to help, but Ruskin caught him across the face with open claws, slashing the bearded flesh of his cheeks. Tripp roared in pain and turned his defense to the crazy king, doing his best to fight him off and get to the ladies before any more damage could be done.

A mighty dragon roar was heard far off in the distance. It was the most beautiful sound Cyndol had ever heard. From the look on Amy's face, it seemed she agreed. Too bad it would still be a few minutes until they made contact with The Island.

Ruskin shifted his focus to the sound in the sky, giving Tripp the opportunity to pelt him with a spell that knocked him off his feet. Ruskin went rolling into a nearby tree, and Tripp made haste to reach the ladies, flinging Viego away just as easily.

"Cyndol!" Tripp said. "Are you alright?"

Cyndol winced in pain, her shattered wing hanging limply from its socket. A dark bruise was already forming around it, the area swelling to protect the damaged appendage. Tripp swore, spat at the ground, and thrust his hand through the top of his disheveled white shirt, pulling out a bag on a string containing the assistance he sought.

"Sai thought this might come in handy. Guess this is what they meant." He fumbled with a small vial containing an effervescent cloud of dancing aqua fire. Pinpricks of white and teal light bounced off the inside of the glass, striving to get out and work their magick. It was nothing like Cyndol had ever seen. "I was told to use it wisely. It only works once."

He held the open vial to Cyndol's lips, and the icy blue flame swirled merrily from its encasement, happy to be of service. It sped down her throat, burning with a coldness Cyndol had never felt. She thought it might burn her alive.

Through agony that felt like a lifetime, Cyndol could feel the sinewy strands of her muscles start to stitch back together. The bone that had been so carelessly snapped like a dry carrot clicked back into place, fusing tissue and ligaments where they belonged. When the swelling eased and the magickal burn faded, Cyndol gave a cursory half shrug of her right shoulder, testing the fresh flesh and bone to see that all was in order. Her eyes widened in surprise, and more than a little awe.

Tripp barked at her. "Yeah. Great. Listen first, marvel later!"

She nodded, bringing her attention back to his face. Tripp lodged another set of energy balls at the two men trying to attack him on either side. He nailed them both and sent them tumbling once more.

"Now, listen up quick! I only got time to tell you this once!"

He explained to her that there was a secret Crannie in a bathtub at the top of the walkway that wrapped the inner perimeter of this section of island. He pointed at the high doorway, the entrance to Amy's house. He told her how to access the backyard where the tub was and stressed that it was the green jade handle that activated the Crannie leading to the Dragon Moon throne room. After that, she would need to find the ghost of Queen Helena. Helena would be more than happy to help her great granddaughter, so Tripp imagined.

With one hand, he held the bloodied remains of his slashed cheek and said, "Ruskin is gonna try to steal the power from the Little Sun. We can't let that happen, Darlin', you understand? If he gets that power stream started and opens the portal to another world, there'll be no stoppin' him. And there's no tellin' what to expect from any lurkers on the other side."

Cyndol's heart took a nose-dive as she let the weight of her task settle on her like a mantle.

Amy grabbed a handful of green fronds from the nearby water's edge and slapped it on the worst of Tripp's facial cuts. He waved her off. "I'm fine! Keep your focus! They're comin' back!"

Sure enough, Ruskin and Viego came lumbering up on either side of them, doing their best to block them in.

Tripp darted his gaze to Cyndol and said, "Go!"

Without a moment's hesitation, Cyndol's wings took a mighty flap and shot her into the sky toward Amy's front door. She was almost there when she felt a searing sensation rip through her right wing, decimating it once again. With agony, Cyndol struggled to keep her trajectory and fell a few dozen feet, hitting the path just past the halfway point to Amy's house. Viego's triumphant cackle rose up from below, echoing off the rocky walls around her.

Cyndol crashed into a shrub, landing on her left wing and shoulder, damaging that as well, though not as badly as her right. Knowing flight would be impossible to keep up, she swallowed the bile rising in the back of her throat and forced herself into a sprint up the winding pathway. She had to get there, she just had to!

Sounds of battle assaulted her ears, spurring her faster. She heard Amy screeching as if in a death wail, but she couldn't stop. This was too important! Tripp would have to help her, and she trusted that he would. As she could also hear sounds of electric zapping, she knew he was still in the game. She pushed herself even faster. She couldn't help but remember the last time she ran uphill: Her last day in Cavar. Memories of that fateful day rang loud in her head, and she used that rage to light the fire underneath her. She ran faster than she ever had before!

Finally, out of breath and struggling, she rounded the bend to the front door and burst through without a hint of grace. She let her eyes adjust to the dimmer lighting for a moment as she got her bearings, then scanned the small home until she saw the panel Tripp had described. She leapt forward to open it, then sprang through the doorway onto the terrace with the most exquisite tub Cyndol had ever seen.

"*Marvel later*," Tripp's words floated through her head. She darted to the tub, jumped in, and swiftly pulled the green jade lever. Her stomach lurched to her throat as the floor of it fell beneath her and she felt herself swirl into darkness.

***

I watched as Cyndol disappeared into my former home, hoping with all my might that Tripp's side mission would keep her out of this fight. *And if I was able to accomplish my task and keep Ruskin from winning? All the better! Besides, Brax and gang would be here any minute. The roars I've been hearing have been getting louder and louder!*

I darted away from Viego's extended finger (which he'd flung at me like the crack of a whip) and rolled into a somersault with a grunt. I tried to stand up but was slammed to the ground after getting hit in the chest by a blowback from Tripp's electric bolts. Ruskin had pulled Viego in front of him to take the shot, but Viego reacted quick enough to throw up a magickal shield.

"Amy!' Tripp shouted, bounding to my side to check on me.

I wheezed, breath completely knocked out of me, my body whizzing with volts of deadly currents. Tripp placed his hands above my chest, and I saw a soft glow begin to form. After a few seconds of terror and being unable to suck in air, I felt wind rushing through my lungs with a powerful punch. I gasped, breathing deeply, just in time to shriek, "Watch out!"

Ruskin tackled him with ferocity and the two went barreling into the sand at the water's edge. Ruskin let out a howl and backed away from the shore. Viego's finger lurched like a spear into Tripp's back and caught him like a fish, reeling him in.

"No!" I screamed.

Ruskin's arms were around Tripp's throat faster than I could blink. He snapped it like kindling, then dropped him to the ground without a modicum of remorse.

I took a breath to scream again, but Viego's hand muffled me before I could so much as squeak. Ruskin grabbed me roughly by the throat, Viego's hands moving swiftly to my arms to pin me in place.

"Now," Ruskin growled, "about that eye."

With one hairy paw he held my hair tightly at the base of my neck, forcing my head front and center. Try as I might, I couldn't get much give to shake free. I was trapped.

One more roar sounded high above, and I could see my friends begin their descent.

Ruskin paid them no heed. Without further ado, he jammed his right hand into my left eye socket and plucked out the amethyst orb. The squelching sound, more than the pain, will haunt me for the rest of my days. I'm sure you can understand, I passed out.

***

Ibraxus let out a roar so loud, it shook the trees that dotted the island. He just saw his worst fear come to fruition— his worst enemy maiming the love of his life!

He watched from above, helpless to protect her, helpless to get to the mad king in time. Ruskin ran full speed toward the Mushroom Statue in the tree grove.

Brax dove to the ground as fast as dragonly possible and felt Ethan cling to him with all his might.

"Hang on!" Ellera shouted from the back of Ifyrus. Kit was tucked neatly into a pack strapped to Colt, and she could see his teeth clenching tightly to it.

All three flying creatures went straight for Amy. When Brax got there, he shrugged Ethan off like a second thought and transformed faster than he ever had before.

"Amaryah!" he shouted. She was bleeding from her left eye socket and unconscious in the sand. He dropped down and cradled her head gently in his large rough hands, checking her over for further damage.

"Get back!" Ellera demanded as she pushed him aside. "I've got this!"

"Now, wait one—"

"There's no time!" she said. "I see someone's feet on the ground over there by the water's edge. Go see if they need help!"

Grinding teeth and holding his hammering heart in check, Brax shakily stumbled over to the feet and saw the body of his dear friend Tripp, motionless in the sand, his neck bent at an odd angle.

"No," he said, feelings of defeat washing over him like a raging storm. His rage swelled anew, and it burst from his throat with vengeance. "*RUSKIN*!"

As Brax took a step forward, Amy made a sound from the ground. His attention darted back to his wife, and he knelt at her side, ignoring Ellera's protestations.

"Ruskin— he— he—" she stammered, shock wracking her damaged body. She trembled along with her chattering teeth.

"Don't try to talk, Amy, let me try to heal you!" Ellera said.

Amy slapped her hands away and tried harder. "Ruskin has— my eye!"

"We can see that, dear, now let me try to fix it—"

"No!" She grabbed her hands with real strength this time, and all could see the wild look in the eye she had left. "He's going to use it to open the portal! You can't let him do that!"

"Portal?" Ifyrus asked. "What portal?"

Amy turned her terrified face to Ellera and said, "Use your mind magick! Do it!"

With zero hesitation, Ellera's eyes clouded over as she put her hands to Amy's temples. Ellera's head whipped upward as she took in the information Amy was trying so desperately to convey.

She saw the whole story play out in her mind: Ruskin found out that Amy's amethyst eye was the key to uniting the three Callembrian Cores: Dragon Moon, The Island, and the Sea Core. All three sources of magick, when in line with the Gemstone Belt and the Little Sun, would make the bearer of the amethyst immortal, all-powerful, and capable of such destruction the world had never seen. But there was one thing Ruskin did *not* know. Connecting these cores would also open an ancient portal to the sister planet they all once came from: Earth, where Amy had spent lifetimes before returning to them. There's no telling what might happen if that portal opened and Earth and Callembria were joined once again.

Ellera repeated what she had seen in Amy's mind to the rest of the group as fast as she could.

"Stop... him..." Amy said before passing out.

"Ah, hell," Colt said. He took off down the pathway they'd seen Ruskin dart down when they arrived. Kit's head popped out of the side bag with bared fangs, ready to fight.

Brax ran in human form, unable to shift through the trees. He passed the children in his haste to reach his enemy first.

Ifyrus leaned over to Ellera and, with a gentle touch to her shoulder, said, "You know, Love, if Ruskin's here, that means Viego is with him."

Ellera clenched her jaw and set Amy to rest comfortably against a smooth boulder. "I'm counting on it." She stood up, swiped the sand off of her skirts and turned to Ethan. "Ethan, I need you to watch over Amy as I go find my brother. Can you do that?"

Ethan's jaw jutted out in defiance. "No."

"No?"

"I will not let him win! I'm coming with you!"

Ifyrus interrupted and said, "I'll go fetch Colt and Kit to look after her. The boy should go with you."

Ethan nodded at the dragon as he bolted down the path to catch the kids.

Amy sat up with a start. "Kavea!"

"We'll look for her, too," Ellera said, getting ready to chase after Viego.

Amy shook her head, tears falling from her right eye and mixing with the blood and sand on her cheeks. "No, she's gone! Ruskin killed her! She's... somewhere..."

Ethan ran over to the spot Amy had vaguely pointed to and found Kavea's body lying still, a dagger in her heart. Horror rose fresh in his chest, and he promptly threw up in the bushes. He pulled himself together and dragged her to where Tripp lay by the water. When Ellera's eyebrow quirked, he said, "We should keep our dead together, not scattered about like garbage."

She nodded once and saw that Ifyrus was coming back with Colt and Kit, looking furious at being pulled from the fray. She also saw a massive beam of light erupt into the darkening sky like a volcano of energy firing straight at Dragon Moon.

"It has begun," she said. "We must go!"

Without waiting for the boys to get to Amy's side, Ellera grabbed Ethan by the hand and fled in the direction of the chaos, looking wildly around for her brother.

***

Cyndol went tumbling through the beautiful throne Crannie with no elegance whatsoever. To borrow a phrase from Amy, she said, "What the hell was *that*?!" She rubbed her head where she'd bonked it upon arrival and looked around wildly for a ghost. Not something she ever thought she'd be doing, but this was important. She needed to push her fear to the side and accomplish her task. Her first ghost, her great grandmother, if the latest information was true. She was having trouble wrapping her head around it. It was all happening so fast.

"And just *who* are *you*, child?" came a voice from above.

"No time to chat, grandmother, so I have to keep this short—"

"Grandmother? I beg your pardon—!"

"Shh! I'm sorry, Your Majesty, but there's not much time! My name is Cyndol of Cavar and I'm the daughter of Enid and Darrian— err, Amaryah and Ibraxus, if Amy's telling the truth—"

"What are you going on about, child?"

"Just shut up a second and I will tell you!" Cyndol replied.

Queen Helena flew down to Cyndol's face, looking ready to plow through her, when Cyndol thrust her damaged dragon wings to the sides and her eyes blazed violet.

"Oh!" Helena breathed (which was odd for a ghost) and halted her momentum. Her cantankerous face turned quizzical in the blink of an eye, which Cyndol took to mean she could continue.

"Now," she went on, rubbing her injured shoulder and gently putting her wings away, "as I said, my name is Cyndol and, as you can see, I'm definitely part dragon and of your bloodline, as evidenced by my wings. I'm also part mermaid, as I'm sure you can tell from the color of my eyes. Daughter of King Ibraxus and Princess Amaryah. Good? Great. Now, Tripp sent me to Dragon Moon to seek your help in accessing the Dragon Core so Ruskin can't get to it first!"

"Ruskin is after the core?" Helena shouted, fury giving rise to her short curls as if the very air around her were stirring them about. "That scoundrel!"

"Yes!" Cyndol said. "Right now, he is on The Island, trying to access the Mushroom Statue and, last I saw, Amy was trying to fight both him and Viego!"

"Who is Viego?"

"A powerful Dark Mage that I will see dead by nightfall, if I have any say in the matter! He's the one who damaged my wings and almost killed my brother, and he will suffer greatly for it!"

Helena looked shocked at the violence shining so clearly upon the young girl's face.

"Well, then," she said, "let me show you to the core."

The two ladies flew down the halls to the room where the core was kept. Helena was surprised to see that it was lively and spitting sparks of flame as they entered, as if something had made it angry. One of the sparks landed on some wadded-up paper. Cyndol could make out the name "Orelle" on it as it caught fire before her eyes.

"Quick!" Helena shouted. "Stamp it out before it sets the room ablaze!"

Cyndol quickly jumped upon the smoking embers as they began to spread, catching it before it hit the thick curtains.

"Now what do I do?" Cyndol cried.

Helena blanched, an impressive feat for an already pale ghost, as she realized what must be done next.

"I'm so sorry, child," she began.

"For what?" Cyndol asked.

"If Ruskin is doing what I think he's doing, you will need to be the counterbalance."

"Counterbalance? What does that mean?"

"Whoever is in control of the cores' magick gets it from one of the three cores. It does not matter which one they access. But as Ruskin is at the Island Core right now, and I assume nobody is trying to access the Mer Realm's Core, that leaves you to access this one. You will have to fight Ruskin for control of it."

"How am I supposed to do that?"

Helena situated herself in front of Cyndol, making sure she was understood. "There is a common misconception that the Eye of The Amethyst is what will control the world, but that's not entirely true. While yes, the amethyst eyes of the royal Mer bloodline will access the power of the Cores, contrary to popular belief, it does not require one's actual eye, just the power held within it. Also, it packs a bigger punch than just making him powerful." To herself a bit, she said, "I don't think he knows the full scope of things to come. I hope I am wrong, thinking Ruskin might try to wrench that poor girl's eyeball from her head," then, realizing she was losing Cyndol, she continued, "but you do not need to go to that extreme! Simply line your eye up to the concave spot in that statue over there, over the suns' carving, and *will* your soul's magick into it! Then you'll be able to take back control!"

"Wait, what?"

Helena pointed to a spot over Cyndol's shoulder that she had not noticed before. She turned and saw something in the heart of the fire-spitting core: A stone statue that looked like a moon. It had a double sun shaped indentation that Cyndol could see at the front of it, appearing to shine in anticipation.

Cyndol looked at Helena, terror-stricken. "I'll burn!"

Helena shook her head. "No, you will not. You are my grandchild, in whatever fashion that came to be, but I can see the truth of it when I look at you. You have my wings, dear, and dragons do not burn."

Queen Helena unfurled a pair of beautiful deep blue dragon wings, showing what was once a glory that Cyndol bet made thousands quaver. She was stunning in her half-turned form, all grace and power, with shimmering scales that covered her body like diamonds.

"Now, do as I do and transform! Your scales will protect you!" She motioned for Cyndol to try.

Cyndol gulped audibly, but knew there was no time to waste. She shook her wings free and did her best to will the scales. Helena made it look so easy, but Cyndol had yet to get that part of her anatomy to show. So far, it was just the wings, and if she didn't get her scales, there was no way she could walk into that hissing fireball!

"You can do it, child! You have to believe you can!"

"Not… helping…" Cyndol grunted, trying to pop her scales out of sheer determination.

Just then, a burst of energy rocked through the core and sent them both flying backwards, Helena through the wall and Cyndol into a thick bookshelf. Ruskin had begun.

***

Ruskin panted like the cur he was, loping down the path as he neared his destination. His eyes were wild with fervor and his cuts were bleeding freely, but all he could see was his prize! The infamous Mushroom Statue, looking as promising as the legends led him to believe, beckoned him like a temptress, urging him on with each step closer!

Sounds behind him threatened to steal his attention, but he couldn't let it. Not when he was this close! He pulled the suns necklace from his pocket, ready to assemble the key in a matter of seconds.

Arriving at his target, he slid on his knees the last few steps, putting his face directly in line with the keyhole: A double circle etched expertly into the rock intended to represent the suns. Ruskin readied the necklace in front of himself, inserting Amy's perfectly round amethyst eyeball into the center of the jewelry as easily as if it had been waiting for him.

"A perfect fit," he said. Without further ado, he shoved the key into the front panel and gave it a twist. The lock moved as easily as running one's hand through water. Ruskin shuddered in anticipation as the statue began to light up. Teeth chattering in excitement, he turned his face toward the sky as the statue's light coalesced into a small white beam, growing brighter and bigger by the second. It collected so much power, it literally burst through the sky, right through Dragon Moon and continued through the Gemstone Belts and into the Little Sun.

The Gemstone Belts gave the beam a stunning rainbow effect, and Ruskin marveled at its beauty.

A new glow on the front panel of the mushroom statue caught his attention and he put his hand to it. Instantly, he was imbued with such awesome power that it affixed him to the stone, screaming internally, though no sound came out. He could feel it coursing painfully through his veins, forging new paths in his body that would fill him with all-powerful magick, his dream come true.

Little by little, Ruskin's body grew and grew, until something sharp pierced him from behind. He looked down and saw a handful of dragon claws digging at his right kidney. At first, he was petrified! But he noticed something strange— he was healing. He laughed in delight and turned his head to come face to face with a furious foe.

"Why... won't... you... just... die?!" Ibraxus panted, thrusting his claws viciously into Ruskin's sides with every word, attempting to disembowel him.

Ruskin laughed harder. "Is it a tickle fight you're after, *Your Majesty*? You'll have to do better than that *now*."

A sudden wave came bursting forth from the waterfall next to them and covered Ruskin from head to toe in chilly wet terror. In his fear, Ruskin's hand disconnected from the stone. Trying to catch his breath, he saw Amaryah emerging from the water, her tail reforming into legs before his shaken gaze.

"Not a fan of water, huh?" she spat.

Ruskin snarled, eyes blazing. "Not since you last tried to drown me."

"Pity I didn't succeed."

He snarled again and they dropped into battle positions.

***

"VIEGO!" Ellera shouted with all her might. "Show yourself! We just want to talk!"

A sound that might have been laughter hissed through the air behind her. She ducked with the familiarity one would have through years of practice. Something clicked by her ear and she could see her sibling retract his finger like the recoil of a whip.

"You'll have to do better than *that*, foul brother! Or do you not recall how I treated you last we met?"

Viego slithered into view, showcasing his maimed face for her.

"How could I forget such art?" he mocked, smiling hideously. "But, if *I* recall correctly, it was *you* who lost the fight."

"I may have lost that fight, brother, but I will not lose this one."

"My baby sister. So calm. So perfect. So righteous. No wonder you were Father's favorite. Look at you," he sneered. "I can't believe he ever let you leave. He kept me trapped in that nomadic nightmare until I couldn't breathe. Anywhere in the world we wanted to go, but never home to the castle and lands we ruled over. He let it all fall into dust and decay. And then we just volleyed from place to place, ever moving on, but never on my own, and always, *always* with him. Always him."

"He was trying to protect you from falling into the wrong hands! With power like yours, he was afraid someone with evil intentions would get his claws into you, and *look*! You did *exactly* that! You chose poorly, Viego! You chose poorly the moment you killed Father."

"Well, with Father gone, little sis, are you going to try to save me, too?"

"I'm not here to save you, brother. I'm here to kill you."

Viego faced the sky and belly laughed. It was at that point that Ethan, who had been holding a rock in his fist behind his back, fired it as hard as he could and connected with Viego's throat.

Viego made a choking noise and dropped to his knees, clutching frantically at his esophagus. He tried his best to mutter an incantation but struggled through loss of breath. Ellera took advantage of his predicament and summoned her own psychic powers. She clutched his head with both of her hands and deep dove into his mind.

It was wild, erratic. Everything was shrouded in darkness, but she could still make out glimpses of horrific things he had done either on behalf of Ruskin or himself. Ellera repressed a shudder and kept diving, searching, looking for any weakness she could exploit to end the reign of terror he'd inflicted upon the world.

Viego was starting to get his breath back and was fighting with every ounce of his being, lashing out with hands, feet, teeth, anything that could move. Ellera clung on as their very lives depended on it. He connected with Ellera's flesh a few times, but she held firm.

Ethan, adrenaline coursing through his body, felt his eyes take on the same eerie glow they had in the Sky Prison and Gallanor. This time, though, he felt the confidence to go along with it. He focused his gaze at the same spot he'd hit Viego with the rock and aimed his anger in all its glory.

Viego gurgle screamed. Blood came pouring out of the opening and, in a last-ditch effort to get Ellera off of him, he flung his monstrous finger at her. She was ready for it, though, and grabbed it with her left hand, redirecting it with all her strength into the hole and shoved it up into his brain. With her own psychic abilities combined with his, she was able to show him every awful thing he'd done in his horrid little life, mimic every ounce of pain he'd caused to another living soul, and fire off all of her resentment and hatred for his treatment of her in their youth. It short-circuited him entirely and he collapsed into a heap of smoking flesh.

Ethan ran over to blast him a few more times, sending bits of bone and offal in every direction, pelting Ellera's skirts and painting the trees in violent technicolor. The last blast he got off before Ellera threw her arms around him to restrain him bathed his face in crimson. His purple eyes shone through the blood like stars poking through a rainy night sky. Ellera repressed yet another shudder and held him tighter, trying to calm the terrified boy as best she could in this horror.

"Ethan!" she cried, "Ethan, it's okay! It's okay! He's gone, Ethan, Viego is gone! He can't hurt us anymore, he's gone! You're okay! We did it, Ethan! Can you hear me? Ethan!"

Ethan took several deep breaths, trying to calm himself. His eyes were unfocused and wide with terror. He blinked a few more times before turning his gaze to her, the purple still bright, but no longer a threat. Ellera could see the Mer in him clear as day now.

"Ethan?" she said quietly. "Are you okay?"

He nodded, though she was only half convinced.

"Can you walk? We need to get to the rest of the gang."

He nodded again, took another deep breath, and wiped the blood off with his dirty sleeve. His face took on a sharp focus she had not seen before, and he said, "Let's go."

With that, Ellera and Ethan went off to find the others and continue the fight.

***

I couldn't believe what I was seeing right now! Not only was my worst nightmare coming true, but it was happening with such speed that I was having trouble processing what I was watching.

After waking, I'd run from the boys, straight to the Mushroom Statue, despite their protests. I found Ruskin attached to the stone as if he had always been there, with Brax doing his best to rip the flesh from his bones. It seemed as if Ruskin was healing faster than Brax could inflict damage.

Knowing that I couldn't do much to help if a dragon wasn't able to take him down, I decided to do the next best thing: Scare the crap out of him!

With his back to me, I dove into the water beside him and swam up the waterfall a bit, bringing out my tail and heaving as much water as I could at him. He yelped and disconnected himself from the statue as I climbed out of the pool and got my land legs back.

"Not a fan of water, huh?" I spat, my wet hair clinging to my neck.

Ruskin snarled, eyes blazing. "Not since you last tried to drown me."

"Pity I didn't succeed."

I readied myself for the attack I knew was coming, but as Ruskin launched himself at me, Brax jumped in front of me and took a swipe at Ruskin's middle. Out of instinct, Ruskin jumped back, but he quickly remembered that he had just imbibed a serious amount of power and laughed it off, attacking again.

At that moment, Colt came charging out of the bushes in full alicorn mode, his horn gleaming and pointing straight at the wolf king's heart. Unfortunately, Ruskin's new magick was still allowing him to grow, so by the time Colt connected to skin, he had missed Ruskin's heart by a couple inches. It still managed to pierce his stomach, and the king roared in pain. *I guess the magick of an alicorn is stronger than the might of my dragon?*

Ruskin pulled away from the horn and backhanded Colt, his newly upgraded strength sending the boy tumbling into the water.

Kit emerged from another bush, teeth bared and ready to sink into any available ankle space. I tried to shout at him to stop before Ruskin killed him, but then I saw Ifyrus running up from behind him. Perhaps this was meant to be a distraction?

With eyes focused on the fox, Ruskin pulled his foot back, readying a kick that would decimate the animal, but Ifyrus grabbed it from behind him and yanked as hard as he could. This pulled Ruskin lightning-fast and face-first into the ground, sounding like smashing a pumpkin on Halloween, but with teeth snapping. I almost threw up.

Brax jumped on top of the downed king and started to transform, but Ruskin reached as far as he could and managed to touch the statue once more. The connecting light blazed and sounds of electric zapping echoed all around me. Brax looked as if he had been tased and fell off of him, landing hard in the dirt, halting his transformation.

Ruskin let go of the stone again and focused his attention on Brax, claws out and ripping at his back. "You took my *love!*" S*wipe*. "You took my *wife!*" S*wipe*. I charged at him, trying to gain purchase of his arm to stop his attack. He continued screaming, "You screwed up my life and, worst of all, you turned my own daughter against me! I will kill *all* of you for her death!"

Ifyrus and I both grabbed at Ruskin's clawed hands, his entire body growing wolfier by the second. His face began to elongate and showcase an impressive maw of razor-sharp teeth. *All the better to eat us with.*

Ruskin flung us around like ragdolls, hurling us to the ground like pests and swinging on Brax again, who was only just now getting up. It didn't look good for us.

I saw Kit and Colt approaching as if they intended to join in the fight. Ellera and Ethan were coming around the bend behind them. It gave me an idea.

"Ellera!" I shouted, reaching for claws again, bleeding from where he'd already connected with my shoulders and cheek. "Get my eye out of the stone! Take the kids!"

Ellera looked to where I was desperately trying to point and noticed the glowing purple orb inside the suns necklace, currently attached to the Mushroom Statue. I could see the moment she understood.

I breathed a sigh of relief, even as I narrowly avoided Ruskin's jaws taking a *chomp* at me. I punched him in the face as hard as I could and continued to cling to his right arm. Ifyrus and I were doing our best to keep him distracted so Brax could get back to his feet and transform.

Meanwhile, Ellera led the boys over to the statue and began to attempt to pry the necklace out. It would not budge. *Dammit. I didn't know how much longer we could keep this monster at bay!* He took another bite at me, just catching some of my hair and ripping it from my scalp. It was painful enough that I slipped off of him and he got his arm free. He took a swipe at Brax and sliced his left shoulder open. Brax roared and took a few steps back, trying to clear enough distance to bring forth the dragon. Ruskin leapt forward to stop him.

Just then, however, the beam of light from the statue to the Little Sun started to waver... It was nearly imperceptible at first, but then I noticed it flickered. I wondered what was going on up there?

***

Cyndol awoke with a start, the ghost of her long-dead grandmother shouting above her to get up.

"There's not much time! He has begun! You've got to move, girl, *now!*"

Cyndol's hammering heart seemed to pull her to her feet faster than she herself could, but she shook off the pain and pressed on.

"Come on, scales, come on, scales," she muttered, screaming at herself when it didn't happen. "AH! I can't do it!"

"Yes, you can, dear! You can do this! I promise you! Now, try again!"

Cyndol let a tear slip down her cheek. "I'm trying! I'm just so tired..."

"Hang in there, girl! You are a dragon! You can do anything! If you're truly my kin, and I believe you are, then you can do this!"

Cyndol took a few deep breaths, closed her eyes, and pictured her father. She hadn't known him long, but he seemed so strong, so sure of his abilities. Ibraxus could do anything. And if she was truly the daughter of a dragon, she could *do* this, she *could*! She took one more deep breath and tried again. This time, she felt something cold and smooth slither over her body.

"That's it!" Queen Helena cried. "Marvelous! Keep going!"

Cyndol, sweating and panting like she'd run a marathon, slowly sprouted shining sets of lavender scales so bright they were nearly blinding to look at.

"Good job, girl!" Helena said, proud grandmother that she was. She watched triumphantly as Cyndol's wiry frame was covered head to toe in self-protection, thinking nothing could hurt her now. "Quickly," she continued. "You'll have to wrench that beam of control back from Ruskin before you can seal the statue with your eyes. I don't think he's aware of the enormity of his actions. This isn't just a grab for power, this will open a portal to Earth!"

"Earth? That fantastical planet Kavea was always going on about?"

"It's not fantastical. It is our sister planet, but it is a terrible place. One without magick or dragons, among other atrocities.

We mustn't open a portal there. It could spell the end of life as we know it! This cannot happen. Do you understand?"

Cyndol nodded, more terrified than ever before.

"Good. Step into the fire."

Cyndol turned to face the crimson circle and did as she bade, one foot in front of the other, confident in her purpose for the first time since getting thrown into this crazy new life. She crossed through the hissing flames around the statue. The flames weren't an evil in this moment, they were *inviting. Come in,* they said, *we won't hurt you...* Cyndol could feel the fire flicking around her, but it didn't feel intrusive, it felt like a welcome.

She could see the white light beam from outside bursting through a fresh-looking hole in the floor. It streamed through the bottom of the statue and went as far up as Cyndol could see through the ceiling and into the sky. It appeared to be pulling power through the statue. Cyndol could see the flames around her start to dim, and the light of the new white power beam brightened. She surmised this was Ruskin's handiwork. She wished that he'd let go long enough for her to stand a chance at taking back control of it!

With one last grounding breath, Cyndol shot her arms forward and grasped the sizzling hot beam as tightly as she could. The electric heat she felt race through her body was enough to jolt her off of it for a moment. She let go and checked her hands for damage. She was surprised to see there wasn't any.

"What are you doing?" Helena shouted. "Take control back from Ruskin before he finishes opening that portal!"

Cyndol shook herself back into focus with more confidence now, and she grasped the beam and slammed her eyes shut, pulling on every ounce of strength she had left to wrench control of this thing. She felt it shudder, as if she'd hit it with her fists. Was this a living thing? She could have almost sworn she heard a man scream… Ruskin? Did she hurt him?

"Grandmother?" she called out through gritted teeth. "Can I connect to Ruskin from here?"

"I don't know, child. I suppose it would stand to reason, if you were both connected to the statues at the same time."

Cyndol heard a definitive snarling and knew she was right. Just to test her theory (and also make him mad if she was correct), she held on tighter and began laughing. Laughing the hardest she's ever laughed in her life. For every snarl of fury, a laugh. She could feel his seething anger, revealed in it, in fact. She used that anger and pulled it deep into herself, unleashing her own fury at losing her home, her friends, tearing her family apart, and now, possibly, her entire planet! Her life was based on a lie, and it was all his fault! She screamed and pulled on the beam as hard as she could!

With a mighty rush, she could feel the power enter her body, filling her fuller and fuller until she had to let go, lest she be overcome. She fell backwards onto her rump.

"No!" Helena said. "Get up, girl! Get back to that beam! You must not let him win!"

"I... can't... hold it..." she gasped. "It's... too much." Her scales began to retreat on her face.

"You cannot let him win, do you hear me? All will be lost! No one will survive! Get back up and finish this fight!"

Tears cleaning streaks down her dirty cheeks, Cyndol sniffled and wiped them hastily away. In her mind's eye, she could picture Amy and Ibraxus fighting Ruskin below. If Ruskin was as powerful as she had been led to believe, then Helena was right. She needed to get up and get back in this fight.

She steeled her resolve and pushed off from the floor, right back up to the statue and grabbed hold of the beam once more.

"*AAAAHHHHHHH*!" was ripped from her vocal cords. She could once again feel Ruskin get knocked off the beam below. She hoped it was enough to keep him gone and gain control of this thing for good!

No such luck. He was back a moment later, just as she thought she was winning. The back and forth continued.

***

Ruskin felt a snap from the beam as that harpy continued to laugh her way through stealing his power. He let go with a snarl and flung another clawed hand toward the oncoming dragon king. *Why won't these nuisances cease so he could finish his royal transformation?!*

On and on this went, he and the child fighting for control of the power, as Amaryah, Ibraxus, and their gang of incompetent fools fought him. *How could he get anything done with them hammering away at him like that?*

With one last human snarl, he let himself go full werewolf mode. He could feel his face elongate, his serrated teeth descend, and his body contort to allow for a bigger and more dangerous mass. With one meaty paw, he palmed the beam and pulled with every ounce of strength he had.

A Crannie began to open next to the water. No, not a Crannie. This was something different. *What the blazes could that be?*

He heard the collective gasps and cries of terror from the others and smiled to himself. *If this was something they feared, perhaps it was something he could enjoy? What was that place his daughter was always going on about? Earth, or some such rot? Could the stories be true?* His smile became a sneer as he remembered the death of his daughter and his fury doubled.

More back and forth with him and the girl above. He kept one eye on the gang and the other on the portal. When he could feel the girl taking the lead, the portal would fade. When he pulled control back, it got brighter, much like the power beam itself.

Once, Ibraxus was able to get a hand to the stone but was immediately shocked so badly that it sent him flying. Ruskin guffawed at his opponent's failure.

Now that the power struggle had gone back and forth so much, he could see that the portal was becoming unstable. It wasn't able to hold its place, and it tilted back and forth, back and forth, sucking whatever was closest to it through the hole. Everyone backed up a few steps and alerted the others of this new danger. Ruskin hoped it pulled them *all* through and left him in peace to assume his role of the Callembrian Ruler!

***

The portal slowly picked up steam and sucked in a few flowers. *POOF*! Gone. Ellera knew they had to get this done *fast*! Since Ruskin would not leave the statue for long, she couldn't risk the kids getting hurt just to get the necklace and Amy's eye back. She knew what she had to do, and she hated it.

With an eerie shudder, she called upon not only her usual powers, but also the power she shared with her now deceased brother. She could feel the extension of that hideous tentacle finger and she hurled it at Ruskin's furry head. It connected with a sickening squish and buried itself in his temple. Ellera repressed the desire to be sick and focused her attention into the mind of this monster.

She dove deep. She could feel him screaming in pain as she rooted around, but she couldn't stop now. All of their lives depended on this! She dove past the offenses of his elongated past, one that should have ended centuries ago, but due to dark magick from her brother and the ones that came before him, they kept this filth alive far beyond his expiration date.

"Colt…" she ground out through clenched teeth, "get… the necklace…"

Colt needed no further urging, and he leapt toward the stone statue again, now that Ruskin was wobbling away from it. He jammed his horn into the bottom of the necklace and tried to pry it out, much like one would remove a biter bug from your flesh along the wooded trails. It wouldn't budge.

Ellera continued to distract Ruskin, along with Brax and Amy, now both up and fighting him. Ifyrus made sure to block the statue with his body any time Ruskin would make a move to get back to it and punched him in the throat when he got too close.

"It's not working!" Colt said.

Ethan was pulling at it with his hands now, grasping at anything that would give him an ounce of purchase. He even tried blasting it with his laser eyes.

Kit looked up at Colt and said, "Wait. Don't alicorns have magick in their horns?"

"We do?" he asked, a ray of hope gleaming in his eyes.

Kit nodded. "Yes, Colt! Use your magick! Alicorn magick is said to be some of the most powerful magick on Callembria!"

Colt took a step back from the statue and centered all of his determination into lighting his horn. After an eternal moment, a golden glow emanated from the tip. With one smooth motion, he inserted his horn once again under the suns necklace and snapped it free.

The necklace dropped into Ethan's outstretched hands, and he held it tightly, cursing it for all the trouble it had brought him. He wished he'd never picked it up in the first place. Colt flicked his head at Ethan, indicating he should mount him. After he did so, the two boys took off as fast as they could to get away from the wolf!

Ellera could feel Ruskin fighting back, could sense that she was hitting a sleeper curse that her brother had left behind, and yelled for Ifyrus to get the kids out of the way. He did so just in time! Ruskin slashed around and connected with the finger still attached to his temple. She could feel the severance of it ricochet through her whole body and she dropped like a rock to the dirt, cupping her mutilated hand.

Ruskin immediately went after the necklace, knowing without it he would lose everything he'd worked so hard for.

Ellera lifted her head and saw the portal was getting closer to the bodies of Tripp and Kavea, growing bigger with every moment. She worried that they would be sucked inside it, and they'd never get the chance to lay their bodies to rest.

The chaotic nature of the wavering magick beam was causing the reflection of the Gemstone Belt to shower them in rainbows. She had never seen anything like this in her entire life and, though it was somehow beautiful, she wished for a speedy ending to this nightmare.

***

There was a noticeable change in the magick beam. Cyndol felt like something was missing. Could it be that they were winning down below? Her own strength was rapidly waning, and she didn't know how much longer she could keep this up.

"I'm so tired, Grandmother."

"Just keep holding on!" she said.

Cyndol knew she wouldn't be able to. She was struggling to stand now, let alone hold on to this much power for so long. Her footing slipped and she landed hard on her right knee, grimacing in pain and almost let go.

"No!" Helena yelped. "You must hang on! We are so close now! I can see the beam getting brighter up here!"

"I… I can't…" She stumbled again, her left knee joining her right on the floor now.

Helena knew at that moment they would fail. If Cyndol couldn't wrench full control from Ruskin, Ruskin would take it all. She would not stand by and watch that monster wreak any more havoc on the people of this world! She made her decision and flew quickly into the core to join her granddaughter. Cyndol's scales were retreating, and Helena could see more of her pale skin pop back through. Such a beautiful child, she could see now, despite the dirty cheeks, the unkempt hair, and the defiant look on her face. Yes, she could see herself there, once upon a time.

She gave a specter's sigh and clasped her intangible fingers around Cyndol's, willing the last of her life's essence into her.

Cyndol gasped and shed a tear as her ghostly grandmother disappeared, absorbed by the light. She felt a zap of extra strength and used that for one last pull.

The magick came back so hard and fast that it blasted Cyndol out of the nearby window. It happened so quickly that she didn't have time to process that she was falling... falling... still falling... faster now, back toward the island below, toward her friends and toward death if she couldn't find her wings in time! She tried desperately to will them back. She could feel the familiar poke of them protruding from her shoulder blades, but they were still badly damaged, and she was so tired.

***

My heart stopped. I could see Cyndol's body falling from above, but there was nothing I could do to stop it. Her wings weren't working properly, and I didn't have my own to get her.

"Brax!" I screamed at the top of my lungs. "Cyndol!" I pointed at her small frame descending at a rapid rate.

Ruskin chose that moment to reappear from his pursuit of Ethan and charge us. Brax looked torn between helping me and helping Cyndol.

"Get Cyndol! I'll be fine!" I lied.

He shifted where he stood and took out a nearby tree. Ruskin smirked at me with his big, wolfie teeth and launched himself backward onto Brax's wing. Both men went hurtling through the air, zig-zagging this way and that, fighting with literal tooth and nail. All the while, I was left to watch helplessly as my daughter fell from the sky.

"Ifyrus!" I cried. "Can you get her? Colt! Where's Colt?"

Ifyrus looked up from Ellera. He was cradling her in his arms, trying to help her with her damaged hand, blood flowing freely and staining everything around them.

"He and Kit took off with Ethan to protect him!" Then, to Ellera, he said, "I'll be right back, Love."

He placed her gently on the ground and shifted mid-run, not caring what he hit in his path. He took to the sky as fast as he could, but Cyndol was falling too fast.

Brax and Ruskin were still locked in mid-air battle. Ifyrus was doing his best to get to her, but I didn't think he was going to make it.

Just before she was about to collide with the earth, Ifyrus snatched her with his talons and rolled with her to the ground, encasing her in his wings to protect her. When they stopped, I could feel my heartbeat nearly through my chest. I was frozen in fear, unable to move in that moment. Every fiber of my being wanted to be there, to see if my daughter was alright, but my feet were firmly planted in the dirt.

I saw him get up, unwrap her gently, and lay her in the grass to check her over.

"Cyndol?" came his soothing timbre. "Cyndol, love, are you okay? Are you alright? Cyndol?" He prodded her gently at first, then harder when she wouldn't respond.

Ifyrus lifted his gaze to meet mine and time stopped. He let out the breath he'd been holding and slowly shook his head. I felt the weight of my body collapse and I knew she was gone.

Ifyrus gulped and wiped a tear from his eye. He scooped Cyndol's body up as respectfully as he could and walked sadly over to me, laying her down at my feet so I could see her. She looked so peaceful, not a scratch on her, just layers of dirt and a faint glimmer of lavender scales.

Ifyrus took a breath and said, "It must've been too much for her. I'm so sorry."

Bile and fury rose within me in equal measure and my lips curled back in a snarl.

"*RUSKIN*!" I bellowed. "You will *die*! *Right* now!" I whipped my mangled face around to Ifyrus and ordered, "Bring him to me."

Being a smart dragon, he did as I commanded. He took to the skies again and bumped Ruskin off of Brax's wing. The wolf king landed with a *BOOM* that shook the surrounding shrubbery, and he popped up immediately, ready for an attack.

The dragons set to sending plumes of fire to rain down upon Ruskin, catching his fur and making him howl. He was shrinking to normal size again, not being connected to the statue's power anymore. My darling daughter had seen to that, as had the wonderful children in our small, but mighty, army.

The portal was gaining speed now, continuing its wobble back and forth, sucking up shrubbery, trees, and anything in its path. When it got to Tripp and Kavea's bodies, it pulled them in as well, and I could hear a brief scream from Ruskin. Whether he saw her body disappear, or was taking a hit from the boys, I couldn't be sure. Either way, he was getting closer to me again, and in my rage, I couldn't help but launch myself at him.

I landed punch after punch while trees caught fire around me. I didn't care. I wanted this man to die.

Ifyrus called down to Ellera, "Love! Can you stop the fire before it takes this whole island?"

She stood on shaky legs and mustered what strength she had left. I saw not only her eyes cloud over, but the skies as well. Rain came pouring down upon us. Brax and Ifyrus continued to set fire to Ruskin's ever dwindling fur, and Ellera's targeted rain put out the stray embers threatening to destroy our home.

The portal wavered on, making its way across the water and closing in on Cyndol's body, currently left abandoned, unprotected.

Kit scurried through the trees at that moment and saw what was going on. He took in the dragons in the air that were lighting the wolf king aflame, me doing my best Rocky Balboa and knocking the hell out of him, and the erratic path of the hungry portal. When his eyes landed on Cyndol, I heard a foxy cry that will linger in the depths of my soul for as long as I live.

"Cyndol! Noooo!" He bolted for her in a fit of furry fury, tears streaming from his golden eyes to join in with Ellera's rain. "Kit Two! I call on you! HELP ME!"

A flurry of foxes exploded into being, all copies of Kit, just as Kit Two had been, but there were an uncountable lot now, popping up all over our battle ground from each rain and tear drop that hit the land. Ruskin tripped over one in his haste to escape another firebolt and landed hard on his elbow, cracking it into two pieces. He howled in pain. Score for the Kits!

The portal was almost at Cyndol now, and so was Kit. I watched in horror as the portal pulled my daughter's body into it and Kit leapt through of his own free will, managing one last *HOMPK!* onto Cyndol's shoe before they both disappeared from my sight.

Brax's roar was deafening. Seeing our daughter slip into the void was more than either of us could bear. Ruskin took one furious swipe at Brax, but Brax's giant maw came chomping down on his clawed fist so hard and fast that Ruskin pulled it back missing.

"*AAAAHHHHH!*" he gurgled, clutching his bloodied stump. For the first time, Ruskin looked scared. *Good.*

Ifyrus came up from behind and took a bite of his leg. Another scream. They took turns biting and swiping at him, connecting more often than not, as Ruskin was forced toward the water. I beat them there, waiting for my chance to pull him under. Ruskin was about to die.

With one mighty exhale, Brax blew a fire so fierce it lit Ruskin from head to toe. Knowing he had no choice, he ran to the water and threw himself in to put it out. We let him thrash around for a moment, believing he still had a chance. I was getting ready to yank him to the depths when a familiar glimmer caught my eye under the water: The scales of Orelle.

She was resplendent, a full-scale goddess of the sea. There were no signs now of the mouse she had become under the reign of Ruskin. No signs of doubt lingering in those determined violet eyes. No fear. I had never loved her more.

"Orelle! My darling!" Ruskin cried upon spotting her. "Please! Help me! They've killed our daughter and now they're trying to kill me!"

He continued to splash around with his missing hand and broken elbow, sucking down gulps of water with every other breath.

I paused, waiting to see what she would do. We all did but remained ready.

Orelle surprised me. She smiled. Paying no attention to the rest of us, she beckoned Ruskin with one finger. Desperate, he did his best to swim to her, bloodying these sacred waters as he went. When they connected, she smiled bigger, eerily, and then kissed him deeply. It was not a nice kiss. In fact, I could see him struggle harder now. What was left of his face was freshly bleeding, but Orelle did not relent. She pulled him under with her, farther, farther, and farther down. The only things we could see now were tendrils of blood and bubbles.

We never saw him again.

***

Ellera saw the portal was increasing in its erratic movements and cast her voice over the increasing ruckus from it.

"Amy! The portal!"

Amy snapped her head up from the shoreline and focused in on what Ellera was pointing at. The portal seemed to be growing in strength and agitation the longer it was attached to the beam's presence, consuming tree, rock, and shrub as it went along, aiming for no one and nowhere in particular. It will pull this whole damn island, hell, the whole damn world into it, if it could! She knew she had to get that beam shut off, *now*!

Just then, Amy spotted Ethan making his way carefully towards the Mushroom Statue, her purple eye clenched in his fist. She could see the lavender facets glinting from in between the gaps of his fingers.

"What is he doing?" she threw over her shoulder at Brax.

Helpless to answer, he only shrugged.

"Ethan!" she yelled. "Hang on! I'll be right there to help!"

Ethan turned furious eyes at her and shook his head *no*.

"Ethan, please! I'm coming right now!"

"No!" he screamed. "This is all your fault! If you had never come here, Cyndol would still be alive!"

Amy looked as if she'd been slapped and stopped in her tracks. "Ethan, I—"

"She *would* be! And you *know* it!" Tears flowed freely down his cheeks in anger, and everyone could see the resolve on his face. "If it weren't for you, this would never have happened." He inserted the eyeball back into the necklace socket and gave it a quick turn with one hand while grabbing the beam with the other. Everyone gasped as his body jerked in reaction to the power source, but then his voice came warbling through his clenched teeth, "Take... me... home."

A blinding light and ear-splitting *BOOM* forced all to close their eyes and cover their ears. As the flash faded, they opened their eyes again to see what damage was done. Miraculously, the portal was gone. But so was Ethan.

Colt chose that moment to burst through the bushes and say, "Wait, was that Ethan?"

Amy nodded, stunned.

He let out a deep sigh and said, "Where the hell did all these foxes come from?"

CHAPTER FORTY-ONE: AFTERMATH

Viego arrived via beam portal to his childhood home in Viñyan, the home he knew as a child, but one his father had uprooted him from "to protect him". There it stood in all its former glory. Static shocks danced along his body, making his hair stand on end. He ran his fingers down his arms, collecting the electric particles until they formed a neat ball in his hands. He played with it nonchalantly as he kicked open an old wooden door and roamed the halls of the once vibrant fortress now covered in vines, cobwebs and dust.

Walking along the stone walls, he let a tendril of electricity trail down his finger and clash against the stone, sending sparks off behind him, as if welcoming him home. He paused in front of a tarnished old mirror in the hall and stopped to take in his new frame.

He was taller than he'd been last time. Younger, too. Putting away the energy ball by absorbing it into his palms for later, he examined the face he'd be wearing from now on.

Dirty blond locks tickled past his ears, but didn't go past his strong, young jawline, barely a hint of matching stubble to speak of. There were claw marks left by his former master, but they would heal in time. Perhaps even be covered by facial hair as the boy aged. His eyes claimed hazel, but he could see the purple peeking through. Good. He was going to need that.

He preened for a moment more, flexing and moving this way and that, getting used to this new body. He stopped and smiled at his reflection.

"This is going to be so much fun!" he said.

And Ethan's head began to itch…

EPILOGUE

I could hear the familiar comfort of lapping waves and laughing voices. I was sitting in sand under a tree, that much I could tell. For a moment, I thought I was home in Cavar. An aggressive ray of sunshine hit my eyes and made me squint harshly. I raised a hand to shield them from the light and check out my surroundings. As my battered eyes adjusted to the brightness, a colorful ball landed at my feet with a soft *plop*.

"Hey!" called an unfamiliar voice. "Little help, please?"

I looked up at the voice and saw a very tan boy, a few years older than me, in strange clothing, holding his hands out, waiting for me to give him back his ball.

"No, it's fine. Take your time," he teased.

I threw it back to him awkwardly and it fell sadly short of his reach. He laughed, as did the friends I saw standing behind him. They must have been the laughing voices I'd heard a moment ago.

"Mahalo!" he said, retrieving it and rejoining his friends before heading back to their spot on the beach, picking their way over debris scattered in the sand.

"Cyndol?" Kavea asked behind me.

I turned around and saw the confused expression that mirrored my own. Her glorious red curls were in disarray, and she had a smudge of dirt stuck to her cheek. She was *also* wearing clothing I'd never seen before, oddly tailored and covered in flowers that reminded me of Callamays. Startled, I looked down and saw that so was I.

"Oh, good!" I heard Kit say from behind me. "You're awake! Finally! I hope you like the clothes I stole. You were both naked as the day you were born when we got here. Even more so for me, if you can believe it!"

I looked down to see what he was talking about, but there was no fox to be found.

"Kit?" I cried. "Kit! Where are you? I— I can't see you!"

Panic set in, but the new boy walking towards me laughed in the same Kit chuckle I'd grown accustomed to. My gaze shot to his face.

"Wait— what— *Kit*?"

"It can't be..." said Kavea.

"In the flesh!" he said. "Get it? Instead of fur?"

In front of us stood a tall, gangly teenager, with spiky red-blond hair and amber eyes. He had familiar pointed features and a wry smile. If I looked really hard, I could still see the fox underneath.

"But— but we..." I said.

"Died?" he finished. "Oh, yeah. *Big* time!" He made a gesture of crossing his eyes and sticking out his tongue.

"What?" yelled Kavea a bit too loudly. A few people on the beach turned and gave us quizzical looks.

Kit held his hands up (*he has hands now?*) and tried to calm us down.

"Look," he said, "I'm sorry to sound unfeeling, but, yes, you died. Both of you, in fact, and I jumped in the portal after you to try to save you and, well, we all ended up *here*."

"What?" I shouted.

"*Portal?*" Kavea asked.

Kit sighed heavily. "Oh, boy. We've got a *lot* to discuss, haven't we?"

THE END

See you soon for The Callembria Chronicles
Book Three: Legacy

www.ingramcontent.com/pod-product-compliance
Lightning Source LLC
LaVergne TN
LVHW091626070526
838199LV00044B/950